The Essence of Perfection

Also by Nita Brooks

Redesigning Happiness

Published by Kensington Publishing Corp.

The Essence of Perfection

NITA BROOKS

KENSINGTON PUBLISHING CORP.
www.kensingtonbooks.com

DAFINA BOOKS are published by

Kensington Publishing Corp.
119 West 40th Street
New York, NY 10018

All Kensington titles, imprints, and distributed lines are available at special quantity discounts for bulk purchases for sales promotion, premiums, fund-raising, and educational or institutional use.

Special book excerpts or customized printings can also be created to fit specific needs. For details, write or phone the office of the Kensington Sales Manager: Kensington Publishing Corp., 119 West 40th Street, New York, NY 10018. Attn. Sales Department. Phone: 1-800-221-2647.

ISBN-13: 978-1-4967-2194-5
ISBN-10: 1-4967-2194-2
First Kensington Trade Paperback Printing: April 2020

ISBN-13: 978-1-4967-2195-2 (ebook)
ISBN-10: 1-4967-2195-0 (ebook)
First Kensington Electronic Edition: April 2020

10 9 8 7 6 5 4 3 2 1

Printed in the United States of America

To everyone who's ever thought they didn't belong.

Acknowledgments

Thank you to Yasmin and Jamie for taking the time to read the story and provide feedback. To my husband, who pushed me to keep writing when I thought I couldn't finish this book, I appreciate your belief in me. Thank you to my agent Tricia for working with me as I brainstormed this idea. A big thanks to Selena James and the awesome staff at Kensington. You've been amazing and I appreciate your support. Finally, to my readers. Thank you for giving me a chance.

The Essence of Perfection

Chapter 1

Strong hands, skillfully gliding across a delicate surface, bringing something beautiful to life. That was the way to a woman's heart. At least that had to be the way to Nicola's heart. Because, right now, as she watched a video of Damien Hawkins, owner of Hawkeye Pottery, use his magnificent hands to create a vase, she was seriously reevaluating her previous dating choices.

She'd always avoided artists just as she would walking in a bad neighborhood alone at night. Her past boyfriends could be spit out from an executive CEO cookie-cutter machine. Suit, tie, expensive smartphone. If she'd had the guts, she'd go for a guy like Damien.

She didn't have the guts. Still, Nicola bit her lip, tilted her head to the side, and clicked the replay button on her phone. Watching for the fifth time a video of him turning a lump of clay into a beautiful vase on his pottery wheel.

She should sign up for his pottery class. Not to get the guy's hands on her. She was a chemist and perfumer, but she also had an appreciation for the arts. This would be a way to explore her creative side.

Nicola tossed her phone on her desk. "Dammit," she muttered. She had too much stuff to do. Now was not the time to indulge in fantasies she'd never follow up on. Taking a pottery class was about as practical as her going on vacation in the spring when most of the new perfumes debuted. She didn't have time to take a pottery class.

There was a quick knock on the door to her lab. "Congratulations, superstar!"

Nicola glanced up as her sister entered her domain. Quinn held up a bottle of champagne in one hand and brought a party horn to her mouth with the other. The high-pitched sound of the horn echoed across the various vials of essential oils, alcohols, and other compounds used to make perfume. Quinn's bright smile brought out one from Nicola. Her high heels clicked on the smooth floor as she drew closer to Nicola's desk.

Eighteen months younger than Nicola, Quinn smelled like honeysuckle, vanilla, and lemon. Bright and rich. Her honey-highlighted, shoulder-length hair hung in a wavy curtain to her shoulders and complemented Quinn's golden-brown skin. Per usual, Quinn was effortlessly beautiful in her off the shoulder black top and distressed jeans.

"What is the champagne for?" Nicola slipped off the glasses she wore when working and stood. Making a mental note to add *Sign up for pottery class* the latest entry into her *Things I Will Do One Day* list, she took the champagne bottle Quinn shoved in her direction.

"Who's got the juice? You do! I just found out you landed the Desiree account," Quinn said with emphasis. "You are officially one of the top perfumers on the East Coast. No wait, make that the entire world."

Nicola clutched the champagne to her chest. Her juice, as it was called in the cutthroat world of perfume making, had made the final cut for Desiree. The R&B superstar had launched a makeup line the year before and was now entering the world of fragrance.

"I'm not the top fragrance chemist in the world," Nicola said. "She only sent briefs to two perfume houses."

Briefs, which could be anything, from a list of the scents the client wanted, to a vision board covered with inspirational pictures, were sent out to guide perfumers when a new scent was under development. Nicola had expected someone like Desiree to send her brief out to all the big names in perfume making, most of which were in New York or Paris. The fact that she'd chosen her mom's once fledgling but now popular cosmetics company, Queen Couture, based out of Atlanta, was a shock that still reverberated through the industry.

"But we all know she wants to work with you," Quinn, ever optimistic, countered. "She said she wanted to work with someone more down to earth, and she wants to support minority creators. She sent it to the International Fragrance House because she had to, but she chose Mom's company because our perfumes are consistently the best of the season. So, once again, you're the best in the world."

IFH was *the* name in perfume making. Some of the most successful and long-lasting fragrances came out of that company. Perfumers longed to work there. Nicola was pretty sure if they instituted a cage match for the chance to fill one of their infrequent openings, people all over the world would enter. The fact that her juice samples were the ones Desiree picked over theirs was a nice golden feather in her cap.

"Not the best in the world, yet." She winked at her sister.

Quinn grinned and snapped her manicured fingers. "Yes, girl, yes. Own it. I am so proud of you, Nicola. When Desiree debuted her makeup line people bought it in bulk and refer to themselves by their foundation color number. This perfume is going to be huge. Soon, the fragrance you create will be on every woman between the ages of nineteen and ninety." She reached into her bag and pulled out two crystal flutes. "This is worth a celebration."

Nicola had no argument for that, and peeled the foil from the top of the bottle of Moët. She'd been nervous, but her instincts hadn't failed her when she'd put together the ideas for Desiree's perfume. Her instincts failed her most of the time in her day to day life. If there was one thing she'd taught herself, it was to be confident in her ability to develop scents. Her good sense of smell and knowledge of biochemistry had helped her excel when she'd taken perfumer courses instead of going to graduate school.

"Well, who am I to turn down champagne at..." She glanced at the fitness tracker on her wrist. "Two in the afternoon."

Quinn rolled her shoulder gracefully. "Oh, live a little. Lord knows it won't hurt you to take a break from being the serious one and have a little fun."

The frequently tossed taunt didn't bother Nicola as much today, yet she couldn't stop her automatic retort, "I'm not the serious one."

Quinn's big coffee eyes turned to the ceiling before she held up the glasses in her hand. "Are you opening that or not?"

"Give me a second." She took several seconds to finish with the foil and carefully twisted the cork out of the bottle to avoid champagne spraying everywhere.

"Oh, wait, we have two things to celebrate," Nicola said.

"What else? Are you making perfume for Meghan Markle next?" Quinn's offhand comment carried a hint of mockery. That was the way with them. They loved each other and would always be there for the other, but they were different.

Quinn was the spontaneous, beautiful life of the party. Nicola was the serious, book smart, quiet one. Everyone loved Quinn just for being Quinn. Everyone loved Nicola after she'd made the perfume that saved the company. Triumph was their signature scent, and six years later, remained one of the top three best-selling perfumes.

Nicola's success with Triumph had stolen some of Quinn's do-no-wrong, everybody-loves-me thunder. Their parents now viewed Quinn as less focused. More of a screw up. Her antics no longer cute and funny. With each passing year, Nicola got more praise, Quinn more criticism. After years of being the ignored child, Nicola appreciated the attention. She just wished it didn't come at the expense of her sister.

Ignoring the hint of shade in her sister's comment, Nicola poured champagne into their glasses. "No, Mom told me you and Omar are trying to have a baby."

Quinn coughed. She placed a hand on her chest and shook her head. "Wait, what?" She said between wheezing breaths.

"Yeah, she told me yesterday after the call from Desiree's people. She said the day was full of great news. We were going to be the most influential perfume house and you were about to give her grandchildren."

"Oh no, that's some crap Omar is spouting to her. He wants to talk about babies." Quinn ran a hand down her flat stomach. "I am not about to ruin my figure having a baby."

"First of all, tons of women bounce back after having a kid. You won't ruin your figure. I thought you wanted kids."

Nicola wasn't sure if she wanted kids. She didn't deal with them often, had no clue how to talk to them, and had never actually held a baby. If Quinn had kids, she'd have to learn more about babies. A scary thought, but the idea of being a great auntie held some appeal.

"I wanted kids when I was in high school and thought the idea of a family was cute," Quinn said. "Today, I'm very happy with my life as a trophy wife."

Nicola cringed. She hated when Quinn used that phrase. "You are more than a trophy wife. Stop saying that."

"You stop saying trophy wife as if it were a bad thing." Quinn sipped her champagne then continued. "My looks are all I've got. Everyone knows you're the brains, and I'm the beauty."

"You're more than a pretty face."

Quinn had gotten a degree in cosmetic science. Everyone, including Nicola, had expected Quinn to take over things at their mom's company. After Nicola created Triumph, her sister decided to use her minor in communications and focus on branding the company rather than making the products. When she'd met and married a rich and influential man, she spent even less time working for Queen Couture and built her own brand as a social media influencer. A title Nicola still didn't quite understand.

"I'm also a good time girl," Quinn said winking and shaking her hips. She picked up the champagne bottle and poured more liquid in her flute.

"Quinn." Nicola's voice was thick with disapproval.

Quinn put the bottle back with a thud. "Nicola, please, let's not go there. I am happy being the beautiful wife to a handsome successful hedge fund manager. I keep up with his schedule to make sure we never miss an important event. I'm also on the board of dozens of charities and throw the best parties for potential investors. My life is a privileged one."

"You're smart."

"And doing everything I listed before does not reduce my intelligence," was Quinn's succinct reply. "I've chosen to use all of my talents, including my looks."

Nicola shook her head and sipped her barely-touched champagne. Quinn may have always been the pretty one, but up until the company's success she'd never seemed to care that she was the pretty one. She'd never relied on her looks to get her through life. That was one of the reasons she'd been so popular. Quinn could make anyone smile and feel better. Now, she only cared about her waist circumference, if there were new lines on her face, and the best hair for her extensions.

Nicola decided to just let the conversation drop. She had more important things to focus on than convincing her sister to do something other than post about the latest bra she was wearing on Instagram, complete with picture of her in the bra. For the next several weeks her focus was going to be on making Desiree's perfume. IFH was not completely out of the running. Their juice samples were good. Desiree was partial to Queen Couture, but if Nicola screwed up the final blend, the star could just as easily go back to the larger corporation. Being favored by Desiree and later dropped would have people question the viability of their company.

"I'm not going there with you today," Nicola said. "Though, it would be nice to have a niece or nephew."

Quinn waved her hand. "Mom can adopt grandbabies if that's what she wants." Quinn didn't even allude to Nicola one day having kids. Truth be told, Nicola's prospects of getting pregnant were zero to negative two thousand. She needed to at least date to have the possibility for sex, which in turn resulted in pregnancy. Nicola's dating life had dried up faster than a grape in the Mojave Desert since her last relationship ended two years ago.

"Oh, did you like my latest picture on Instagram?" Quinn said, excitement back in her voice. "I'm wearing this new lipstick, and I promised the company I'd get at least five thousand likes."

She picked up Nicola's phone and punched in the code. Nicola also knew the code to Quinn's phone. Nicola didn't worry about her sister going through her phone. Not like she had much to hide anyway. Quinn went into Nicola's phone more than she went into her sister's. Mostly when Quinn needed likes or retweets on something she knew Nicola would forget to signal boost later.

Damien's feed, in all its strong hand, muscular arm goodness, filled the screen. Quinn's eyes widened. "You're still cyberstalking Damien Hawkins?"

Nicola put down her glass and snatched the phone away from her sister. She navigated away from Damien's screen. "I'm not cyberstalking."

"Will you sign up for his class already? Then you can at least get a close-up of the man instead of watching him online."

"His class is super exclusive to get into."

Damien Hawkins pottery was in high demand. Celebrities, politicians, and wealthy clients all boasted about having one of his pieces. To make him even more likable, he also made a line of pottery that was reasonably priced, so average Americans could purchase. His short videos posted on various social networks received thousands of hits. Not only was the man talented, he was hotter than hell on a Sunday. Many of the comments on his posts referred to his work and his sex appeal.

"Plus, working on Desiree's perfume is my main concern." She pulled up her sister's page and liked Quinn's latest post. A picture of her sister, lounging in the sun, wearing what looked like nothing but a loosely tied silk robe, a bright red lipstick on her full lips. "There, your picture is liked."

Quinn clapped her hands and beamed. "Thank you." She pulled out her own phone and checked her page. "You know you make time for the things you really want to do. You want to take one of Damien's classes. Stop waiting for life to happen to you and live it."

"I am living life. I'm a world-renowned maker of fine perfumes and scents. I attend several parties a year, and I'm happy." *Most of the time.*

Quinn rolled her eyes. "All you do is make perfume and attend parties that are tied to your work. For instance, the Johnson and Johnson party tonight."

"Which is always fun."

Attendance was part brand promotion and part networking with the various people in the industry who worked with them. She wouldn't tell Quinn that she'd considered skipping this year so she could do more research on Desiree as she worked on the perfume. Not unless she wanted another speech about getting out and having fun.

Quinn's side-eye said she knew just how much Nicola didn't want to attend the party. "You know what I mean. Actually, get to the stuff on that list of yours."

Heat prickled Nicola's neck and cheeks. Quinn would bring up her list. "My *list* is for me. One day soon I'll get to everything on it, but for now I'm working on one of the biggest projects we've ever had. You can't fault me for that."

Quinn waved her hand dismissively. "Fine, but remember one big project is often followed by another. If you don't make time for what you want to do now, you'll be old with bad knees and unable to have fun."

Nicola laughed. "I've got bad knees now. Don't worry. Desiree's project is the last one, and then I'll be ready to cross off items on my list."

Quinn gave her a *yeah right* eye roll before looking at her phone. While Quinn was engrossed with her phone, Nicola scrolled back to Damien's page. She sighed before locking the screen and sliding it in the pocket of the lab coat she wore when working. Make love to an artist. She'd add that to her list, too.

Chapter 2

The club for the Johnson & Johnson party was nearly packed to capacity. Singers, actors, and athletes who had any sort of sponsorship with the company, along with their entourages and the behind the scenes people like Nicola, filled the place. After six years making fragrances for soaps, candles, and cleaners along with perfume and colognes, Nicola wasn't typically star struck when she attended these events.

They were more of a chore than anything. Something she had to do to keep Queen Couture in everyone's mind. Her mom typically attended these parties, too. She was better at socializing and small talk than Nicola, but Adele King was out of town. Their parents' anniversary was that week and her dad surprised her mom with a romantic vacation in Paris. Leaving the Johnson & Johnson schmoozing to Nicola and Quinn. Her sister's internet fame included wearing some of the products connected to Queen Couture and helped their brand on more than one occasion.

An arm slipped through hers and she was pulled in close

to her best friend's side. "I am going home with one of these guys tonight."

Shonda fluffed the side of the halo of curls framing her face, straightened her shoulders and puffed out her chest. She smelled of coconut and spice. A bright smile showcased a row of bright white teeth. Her skin-tight red dress fit in perfectly with the various sexy outfits worn by women in the club. Nicola had opted for a white, one-shoulder top and rose gold, high-waisted skirt that gave off a more cocktail party vibe. Shonda looked ready to party. Only her clammy hand on Nicola's wrist and the tightness around her eyes gave away her nervousness.

Nicola patted her friend's hand. "You don't have to go home with anyone, you know. You can just get a few numbers. Smile and talk. Have a guy buy you a drink."

Shonda shook her head. "No. It's been eighteen months since I kicked Bryan's ass to the curb. I've devoted myself to making the split as easy for the kids as possible. Now it's time for Mommy to get back out there."

Nicola kept her mouth shut. Shonda's divorce had not been pretty. That tended to be the case when cheating was involved. Bryan was the last person Nicola would have suspected to be out there sleeping around. If someone had asked her for an example of a happily married man who completely adored his wife, Nicola would have immediately pointed to her best friend's husband. She'd helped him pick out the engagement ring. Saw the tears in his eyes when Shonda came down the aisle. Witnessed the roses he would surprise her with every Valentine's Day, birthday, and anniversary. Unfortunately, the man Nicola frequently compared her own boyfriends to had not only been sleeping around, but he'd gotten Shonda's administrative assistant pregnant. Talk about some bull.

"Get back out there slowly," Nicola warned. "Don't do something stupid just because you want to make Bryan jealous."

"This has nothing to do with Bryan and everything to do with me. Oh, look, isn't that Quinn?"

Nicola looked in the direction her friend pointed and spotted her sister at the end of the large bar. Quinn hadn't noticed them. She was deep in conversation with a tall, handsome man who wasn't her husband. Nothing surprising there. Quinn was beautiful, men were attracted, but her sister never strayed.

Why mess up the good thing I got for a few minutes of mediocre sex? Quinn's favorite reason for why she wouldn't ever step out on her husband. Never because she loved him. Nicola never brought that up.

"Let's go see who she's talking to," Nicola said.

Shonda leaned her head to the side and raised a brow. An appreciative gleam brightened her eye. "Yes, let's do that, because from here his ass is fantastic. And since your sister can't do anything with him, I'm more than happy to start my quest to reintroduce my body to sex sooner rather than later."

Nicola shook her head and laughed as they headed over to her sister. "Quinn, hey," Nicola said when they reached her sister.

Quinn faced them. Irritation flashed in her sister's eyes before the sentiment was hidden behind a bright smile. "Nicola, you finally made it." She leaned in and hugged her.

"I got caught up at work," Nicola said. "I would have been here sooner, but I started working on—"

"I know. It's always work." Quinn waved her hand. "Shonda, girl, what's up? I didn't know you were coming," she said after hugging Shonda.

"I'm getting back out there," Shonda said. Her eyes focused on the guy hovering behind Quinn. A calculating gleam entered their brown depths. "Speaking of getting back out there, please introduce us to this handsome fellow."

Quinn grinned and slid an arm around the man in question, pulling him into their conversation. "Ladies, let me introduce you to Joseph Martin. His company produces most of the commercials for Johnson and Johnson."

Joseph held out his hand and shook theirs. "Ladies, it's a pleasure to meet you."

Shonda's perusal intensified after Joseph spoke in a smooth baritone voice. Nicola wasn't completely immune. Tall, dark, and handsome, with a voice made for late-night pillow talk. But then her analytical mind kicked in. His handshake was too hard, and he smelled like baby powder. She hated that scent on a man.

He also didn't separate himself from Quinn during the introductions. Her sister's hands lingered on Joseph's arm as he gave them a thirty-thousand-foot overview of what goes into making a commercial. Joseph's eyes frequently lingered on her sister's cleavage. Quinn's all white pantsuit seemed stitched together to show off breasts and butt.

Nicola fought not to check her watch to see what time it was. She'd much rather be at home, drinking wine, and brainstorming smell combinations than getting a headache listening to Joseph talk while breathing in the thick mixture of perfume, sweat, and pheromones in the club.

Joseph's cell phone rang. He pulled it from his back pocket and frowned at the screen. "Excuse me ladies. Quinn, I'll give you a call."

Quinn's grin was flirtatious. "I look forward to hearing from you."

As soon as he walked away Nicola leaned into her sister. "What was that about?"

"What was what?" Quinn moved back to the bar. Nicola and Shonda settled in on either side of her.

Nicola ordered a club soda from the bartender. She didn't like drinking at these events. Shonda got a vodka and cranberry.

Shonda raised an arched brow. "You were doing a lot more than flirting with that man."

Quinn chuckled and slid long fingers through her honey-colored hair. "Whatever. He said I'd be great for a campaign they're working on. I told him I was a model."

"Instagram model count?" Nicola shot back.

Quinn cut her eyes at Nicola before shaking her head and laughing in her *you're just jealous* way. She turned to Shonda. "A model is a model. That's the great thing about the world today. You no longer have to depend on some agency to land big jobs. I have thousands of followers, and I'm an influencer. That's all that counts."

Nicola opened her mouth to argue, but Shonda caught her eye and shook her head. Nicola sucked the straw in her club soda instead. Tonight was about networking and mingling. Not arguing with Quinn, again, about her life choices.

"That's really cool, Quinn," Shonda said. "Let me know how it turns out. Then, maybe you can introduce me to a male model who is only interested in no strings attached orgasms."

Nicola laughed, sending soda down her windpipe. She cleared her throat and grinned at Shonda. "I'm going to have to put a caution sign on you."

"Nope, Shonda, don't listen to my sister," Quinn said. "She just got the deal of the century. She's at the top of her game and should be out here living her best life. Instead, she is working late and not paying attention to that very sexy man at the end of the bar trying to get her eye."

Shonda stood up on tiptoe. "What guy?"

"The one in the tan suit," Nicola said, having noticed the guy a few minutes earlier.

He reminded her of her last boyfriend. Not in looks, but in the vibe he gave off. Rich, confident, CEO type. She wasn't about to go down to Hawkins Studios and sign up for a pottery class just to meet the guy she drooled over, but she also wasn't in the mood to go down the same road as she had before. Hence the reason for her current dating drought.

"I don't have time for foolishness." Nicola finished her drink.

Quinn shook her head and gave Nicola an annoyed glance. "Who says that man is foolishness?"

"You know what I mean," Nicola said.

Shonda waved at the guy and grinned. "No, I don't."

"See what I mean," Quinn said pointed at Nicola. "Refusing to live."

"I'm not refusing to live. I am living my best life," Nicola argued. "I am very excited about the Desiree deal. I'm working in a field I love. I'm very happy."

Shonda and Quinn exchanged a look. Shonda gave Quinn the same *don't-go-there* head shake she'd given Nicola a few minutes before. Shonda was good like that. She always knew when one sister was about to step over a line and could pull them back before they did something dumb.

"You know what, you're right." Quinn turned and waved down the bartender. "Can we get three shots of Patrón over here."

"What are the shots for?" Nicola asked. "You know I don't drink at these things."

"Again, celebratory drinks." She handed a shot to Shonda and the other to Nicola. "To living our lives like they're golden. And don't you dare slide that to the side, Nicola. You will take this one shot and loosen up."

Shonda bounced on her toes. "Come on, Nicola. One shot to celebrate the Desiree deal."

Nicola rolled her eyes and sighed. "Fine."

Shonda and Quinn both clapped like they'd won something. The three held up their hands, clinked the glasses before tapping them on the bar and bringing them to their lips. Her sister and friend downed the shot in one try. Nicola sipped. It burned going down and her eyes watered. Yep, not doing that again tonight.

"Ugh!" Quinn said, glaring over Nicola's shoulder. "Omar is here. I specifically asked him not to come tonight. The one night I don't want to be his arm candy." She slid her empty shot glass across the bar. "Let me see if I can get rid of him." Quinn shot off to intercept Omar before he made it to the bar.

"What's that about?" Shonda asked.

Nicola shrugged and frowned after her sister. The annoyance on her face was gone by the time she slid up to her husband. "I have no clue."

Quinn didn't typically get upset if Omar showed up at a party she was at. Despite the image of marital bliss Quinn curated as part of her online persona, she and her husband led separate social lives, showing up together only for family events or occasions when they needed to be a power couple. Nicola watched as Quinn slid her arm through Omar's and tried to lead him back the way he came.

Shonda tapped Nicola's shoulder. "Look, are you really not interested in that guy at the end of the bar?"

Nicola glanced at the guy. He still watched them, but maybe he'd felt her disdain, because his attention veered toward Shonda.

"Be my guest," she said. "I'm going to find the executives and the party planner. Thank them for the invite. Tell them it was great and make my way home."

Shonda gave Nicola a disappointed look. "You know I don't always agree with Quinn, but she's right."

"About what?"

"About your refusal to take your life into your own hands. Live in the now instead of putting things on that list of yours in the hopes of getting back to it one day."

Nicola drummed her nails on the bar and sighed. "Not you too? Quinn just got onto me about that."

"I know. We talked about it last night."

Nicola held up a hand. "You and Quinn are talking about me behind my back now?" Nicola didn't like the thought of that. Were they sitting around discussing all the ways she didn't live up to the role of being one of the star employees for a popular cosmetics company? Did they laugh about her boring social life?

Shonda must have seen the hurt in Nicola's expression because she rubbed her forearm. "Don't get like that. Quinn called me about something else and we got to talking. You know anything we said on the phone we'd say to your face, which is why I'm telling you this now. You're at the top of your career, your family's company is finally stable, you don't have to keep putting things on a list. Start doing what you want now."

Nicola relaxed. Shonda and Quinn would be more than happy to tell her straight up what they thought. She still didn't like the idea of her sister calling up her best friend. Quinn had a way of snatching up Nicola's friends and making them her own.

Shonda's attention shifted. Nicola followed her gaze. The man at the end of the bar motioned for Shonda to join him.

Shonda gave Nicola a pleading look. "Unless doing what you want means changing your mind about him."

Nicola motioned with her hand for Shonda to head toward the guy. "Go for it."

Shonda squeezed Nicola's hand. "Thanks. Now go find another guy to talk to. Or at least dance. You never dance."

Shonda patted Nicola's knee before she strolled to the end of the bar and sat next to the guy Nicola had chosen to ignore. Nicola watched as the two immediately leaned into each other and started flirtatiously laughing. She wasn't interested, but that didn't stop envy from twining around her heart. One day she'd be bold enough to approach a guy at a bar. With a sigh, she got up and searched the crowd for people she needed to speak with before leaving. Today was not the day for bold.

Chapter 3

Nicola wafted her hand over a vial of blended essential oils. Lemon, rosewood, and black pepper drifted through her senses. She cocked her head to the side, closed her eyes, and considered the blend. Tried to picture a scene in her mind based off the blend.

Summer. A cottage in the country. Roses outside. Spice in the air from something amazing in the kitchen.

She opened her eyes and met the expectant gaze of the lab coat-clad perfumer who was part of her team at Queen Couture. Tia bit the corner of her lip. Her kinky red hair was pulled back in a tight ponytail. A red flush beneath her tan skin highlighted the freckles across the bridge of her nose. The young perfumer had worked with Nicola for two years. She looked to her for guidance and thought she was a genius. Nicola still had to stop herself from looking over her shoulder when Tia pointed her way and said "ask the expert." If only she knew.

Yes. The scent Tia brought her would work as a summer blend for the specialty soap manufacturer they worked with.

Pleased with her protégé, Nicola put the vial down and grinned. "Great job."

Tia pumped her fists. "I tried distilling the rose after you mentioned it was too heavy before."

Nicola nodded as she wrote notes in her notebook. She wondered if nutmeg would work to enhance the scent or clash with the pepper. She shook her head and scratched out the word nutmeg. Nope, no second guessing. Once she liked a blend, she went with it. Otherwise she'd fret for days about ways to further perfect it.

"It really lightened things up. I like it and I think our client will, too."

Tia let out a relieved sigh. "Awesome. Now that we've got that settled, do you want me to work on the briefs we got from Pearl Cosmetics?"

Nicola closed her notebook and stood. "Please. I'm going to be tied up with blends for Desiree's perfume, so if you'll go through the briefs and put together some suggestions, that would be great. Get Scarlett and Bo to look at some of them, too. I'll go over your initial suggestions."

Scarlett and Bo were two interns they'd brought in before the spring rush. Delegating tasks to others hadn't been Nicola's strong suit, but after two years of having Tia remind her that she had help, Nicola relented.

Tia nodded and grabbed her own notebook. "I'm on it."

Nicola left the lab where Tia and the interns worked and went down the hall to her office. She passed the offices of the other chemists who created the boutique makeup and beauty products for Queen Couture. As the lead perfumer, Nicola and her team of chemists were responsible for creating the scents for every product, from face cream to lipstick. But the company's big money came from the scents Nicola created for other larger companies and celebrities.

Desiree's perfume was going to require every ounce of her creative abilities. A basic blending of various scents hadn't been what had gotten her this far in the process. The southern singer was far from basic. Desiree was from South Carolina's Lowcountry and had taken her sultry southern persona from young pop star to worldwide phenomenon. Desiree oozed sex appeal and confidence with a healthy dose of *mess with me at your own risk* bravado. The brief Desiree sent out included words like sexy, excitement, thrill, comfortable, home. She'd also included pictures saying her perfume needed to be sexy as a red thong and comfortable as flannel pajamas.

Nicola had seen briefs with similar contradictions. Each time she'd feared she wouldn't be able to make magic happen. Each time she'd managed to come out on top. She would do the same this time. She needed something bold, sensual, and unforgettable. But not too exotic as to turn people away, or too complicated that it didn't work on the millions of diverse fans the singer brought in.

She was meeting with Desiree the following week to discuss specifics of the last blend Nicola had sent over. The meeting was scheduled after the singer performed for a Scandinavian prince, who was apparently in love with her. Or, at least, that's what he'd claimed when he'd tagged her on social media requesting she perform at his thirtieth birthday celebration.

Nicola pulled out her cell phone and navigated to the Instagram page for The Tea, an account focused on celebrity gossip and trending topics in social media. At the top of the page was a picture of Desiree and the prince. According to Desiree's assistant, she'd gone days ahead of the celebration to get to know him. The fire in the prince's eyes as he looked at Desiree while they sat in a café was apparent even in the grainy photograph.

If only she could inspire that kind of passion in a prince. Scratch that. When was the last time she'd inspired any type of passion in any man? The real question was, when was the last time a man inspired passion in her? She thought of Damien Hawkins's arms, forced herself not to go to his page and get lost down that thirst trap, and slid her cell phone across the desk to combat her weak willpower.

She could never inspire that kind of passion in a man. Not really. Finding a man to have sex with wasn't that hard. Finding a man who was passionate about her was an entirely different thing. Desiree's life was filled with the kind of drive and hunger poets wrote about. A real life. An impassioned life.

She looked around her lab/office. She loved her job. Loved being the person who helped create the things that made a person feel refreshed, beautiful, comfortable, or happy. Her work touched people every day, even though they may not know she had anything to do with it. But, fun it was not. She thought of Shonda's text last night after she'd gone home with the guy at the bar. The guy Nicola had thought was handsome but convinced herself she didn't have time to get to know.

Nicola rebooted her computer and opened the file sharing program she used. She clicked on the file she loved and hated. *Things I Should Have Done.*

She never should have told her sister about this file. Her attempt to prove she wasn't a complete dud was further proven by her explanation. Quinn had told her she would die with a list of regrets a mile long, and Nicola's brilliant comeback had been *"No, I won't, because I'm keeping a list of all my regrets and I'm going to go back and do all of them one day."*

She'd regretted the words as soon as they'd come out of her mouth. Which is why she'd moved the list from her hard drive and strictly kept it in the cloud. Quinn was sure to seek it out and had asked to see it on numerous occasions. Something that would never happen. No one was seeing this list except for Nicola.

I, Nicola King, do solemnly swear to return to this list and complete every item on it. I will not do what my sister predicts and die with a list of regrets. I will live my life to the fullest.

The opening lines on a list that was now three pages long. Nicola let out a heavy sigh and hit control and end to navigate to the end of her list.

- Don't be afraid to talk to a handsome man at the bar.

Unoriginal, yes. Probably higher up on the list in another variation, most definitely. She scanned the other items on the list:

- Tell a man you love him.
- Go out clubbing and actually enjoy yourself.
- Spend more time with family doing non-work-related stuff.
- Have one-night stand with sexy guy when the chance arises.
- Say yes next time a billionaire asks you to dinner.
- Pet a tiger.
- Ask out the next guy you have a major crush on.

That last one was added right after college graduation. When she'd known she was completely in love with Bobby Bradford, a guy from her biochemistry class. She'd spent four years imagining half a dozen ways to have her way with Bobby, and her sister swore Bobby had hearts in his eyes when he looked at her, but Nicola hadn't worked up the nerve to ask him out. Relied on the *we're friends* excuse never to ask him out.

On graduation day, when she still hadn't worked up the courage to ask him on a real date, and he'd given her a hug and brief kiss on the cheek before running off to join his family, she'd realized she'd possibly let the man she would marry, have three kids and a dog with, slip through her fingers. She'd tried to be okay with the *if you really are meant for something it'll come back to you*, but thanks to the miracle that was Facebook, she'd discovered he'd met and married his soulmate a year after graduation.

She had to do better. She scanned the list. All the things she'd found a reason to back out of. Last night she'd said she was living her life like it was golden, but was she really? This was a pretty long damn list.

Her desk phone rang. A New York number, she could tell by the area code. Having clients all over the world who called from various numbers meant she didn't hesitate to answer or screen calls from unknown numbers.

She picked up the phone. "Hello, Nicola King speaking. How may I help you?"

"Nicola, hi, this is Stacie Brown one of the producers for *Your Morning Wake-Up Call*. Do you have a few minutes to talk about appearing on our show?"

Nicola sat up straight in her chair. *Your Morning Wake-Up Call* was a popular morning show. One of the most popular morning shows in the country. The co-hosts, one a long-time charming television host and the other a former soap opera star with dozens of Daytime Emmys under her belt, were recently named the most loved daytime duo on TV. What in the world did they want with her?

"Yes, of course," Nicola answered quickly. In this business, sounding unsure or thrown off balance could be the difference between getting or losing a job. She might not know why they were calling. Her mind went back to the picture of Desiree and her prince on her cell phone. Her hand tightened on the phone. Was this about working with Desiree?

"Great!" Stacie said in a cheerful tone of voice. "Next month we're starting a new segment on inspirational people behind things we all love. After Desiree's camp announced your company was working with her to make the perfume she plans to launch next year, we looked you up. Your resume is amazing. You're responsible for so many of the soaps, perfumes, and even some detergents used all over the country. You are definitely an inspiration, and someone we think our viewers would love to know more about. Would you be interested in coming to talk to us?"

Nicola was nodding before Stacie finished speaking. She loved *Your Morning Wake-Up Call.* Sometimes she even recorded shows with guests she really wanted to see so she could watch on the weekend when she caught up on television.

The world of perfume making used to be a carefully guarded secret. Only the names on the bottles were given credit for the juice within. In the past decade, perfumers were being more vocal about their art. Granted, Nicola had never done media interviews, and she didn't know how to make the chemistry of mixing fragrances exciting for television, but if they thought she was interesting enough to come on the show then they must have a way to make it sound good.

"I'm definitely interested," Nicola answered. She tried not to let her excitement bleed too much into her voice. "What would I need to do?"

"Not much on your end. We'll send over a list of topics for you to review, along with a few questions to answer. Your answers will help us guide the conversation during your interview and give you an idea of how the discussion will flow. If there's something you really want us to hit on, then point it out in your response."

"When would you like to do the interview?"

"Would you be available for taping in New York the second week of May?"

Nicola pulled up her calendar. That would be two weeks after her meeting with Desiree. Which was great because she'd have more time to come up with an idea of what to mention about the process. She would also find out if Desiree wanted her to bring up anything specific during the interview. For a second she worried Desiree might disapprove, then dismissed the concern, considering how much Desiree catered to the media. She'd run this by the singer's assistant as soon as she got off the phone just to be sure. She hoped Desiree didn't have a problem with this. If she did, Nicola could possibly direct the interview away from the specifics of Desiree's perfume and more on the process of how she approached any project.

"Yes, I should be able to be in New York at that time. I will only need to be there for a day, right?" She wasn't trying to spend too much time out of town when she still had other projects to work on.

"That's right. Give me your email address and I'll shoot over the details."

"Sounds great." She rattled off her email address. Stacie repeated it back to her and then they ended the call.

Nicola jumped up and did a quick two-step behind her desk. *Who was living her best life? This girl right here!*

Forget Shonda and Quinn and their *get out of your comfort zone* advice. Her approach to things was going perfectly.

Her cell phone rang again. Still grinning and dancing, Nicola picked up the phone. "Hey Mom," she practically sang into the receiver.

"Don't you sound happy? What's going on?" Adele's husky voice brimmed with curiosity.

"Nothing, but I just got a call from *Your Morning Wake-Up Call*. They want to interview me in three weeks for their show."

"That's great, Nicola!" Her mom said. "You can definitely mention that during your quick speech at the Foundation's luncheon today."

Nicola's hips froze mid shimmy. She checked her watch

and silently cursed. She'd completely forgotten about the fundraiser. Leave it to her mom to get back from Paris and jump right back into things the next day.

"I'm on my way. I got caught up with work." Nicola shut down her computer and scribbled *Call Desiree* on a sticky note she placed on her monitor.

"I know you did. You always do," her mom said, sounding both exasperated and accepting. "I'd fuss at you about getting out of that lab and getting a social life, but you're too successful for me to stand in your way."

Nicola left the desk and hurried to her lab table. "I'm leaving right now, Mom." She sealed the vials she'd been working with before going to check on Tia's progress.

"You're just leaving! Nicola, come on. You should be almost here." Adele's disappointment sped up Nicola's steps.

"I know. I know. I just got off the phone with the producer." Nicola hurried to put each of the vials in their designated spots. "Quinn is coming, right? Get her to do the speech."

"Hmm... Well... I'll just try to delay things until you get here." Not quite code for ain't-no-way-in-hell.

"Mom, Quinn is perfectly capable of doing the speech. It's just a simple your work here is important, and we're happy to donate to your cause."

"Quinn barely does any work for the company," her mom rationalized. "She's too busy being an internet model." Nicola didn't have to see her mom to picture her nose wrinkling up as she said the words.

"We're a family-owned company and Quinn still markets some of our products."

"And you're the star of our show. Now hurry up and get here. Having Quinn talk... well, I'll find a way to stall."

Her mom ended the call. Nicola let out a loud sigh as she rushed out the door. She had no one to blame but herself.

She'd done what had to be done to be the star of the family. Now she couldn't get frustrated when her pretenses resulted in what she'd wanted. Nicola thought of the one item she didn't dare write on her list. The one regret she refused to let anyone discover because there was no way to change it, fix it, or make it better. No, she couldn't afford to be frustrated. She stood to lose a lot more if every one of her regrets was brought to light.

Chapter 4

Nicola rushed through the doors of the downtown Marriott hotel and scanned the digital sign listing all of the various events happening in the hotel that day. The Midtown Foundation for the Arts was one of the many organizations her mom served on the board of. If she remembered correctly, today's luncheon was to raise funds for arts programs in schools. Nicola hadn't prepared a speech but decided to go with her basic talk about the importance of school programs related to the arts and sciences and how she used her background in chemistry in an artistic field.

She found the location of the room for the luncheon. The Foundation's event was in one of the salons farthest away from the entrance to the hotel. Nicola speed walked through the maze to find her way there. When she rounded the corner she abruptly came to a halt.

A man stood just outside the door to the salon she needed to enter. He stared at his phone with a frown on his face. Nicola blinked her eyes several times just to be sure her eyesight wasn't deceiving her.

No way in hell was that who she thought it was. Her fantasies were spilling over into reality and making her see things that weren't really there. He must have felt her gaze because he looked up and gave her a hesitant, I know you're staring at me smile. She sucked in a breath.

Oh god! It was him. Damien Hawkins.

He was dressed casually. Way too casually to be attending the society luncheon. Long dreadlocks, the sides pulled back, fell to the middle of his back. A white linen shirt fit loosely on his wide shoulders. The top buttons were open enough to reveal several silver chains resting against a golden-brown chest. From all the videos she'd watched of him, she knew one chain had a cross on it, another a thick ring, and the third an imprinted dog tag. The shirt was paired with jeans that were just fitted enough to enhance strong thighs and a firm behind.

His eyes were light. A cross between honey and whiskey. Right now, they were focused on her with a mixture of curiosity and humor. He quirked one of his thick brows.

"Do you need to get in here?" he pointed to the door.

Nicola let out a breath. She needed to breathe. Not gawk at him as if he were some fairy who appeared out of nowhere to grant her secret wish.

"Um . . . yes. Sorry, I didn't mean to stare. It's just I'm late and didn't expect anyone to be standing outside of the door."

A ridiculously lame excuse if she'd ever heard one.

His lips lifted in a half smile. "I'm on my way back in. The keynote speaker didn't bother to show up and someone else is filling in. I stepped out to check my emails."

Heat spread up Nicola's cheeks. She raised a finger. "That keynote speaker would be me. I got caught up at work."

"Aha, well then you better get in there." He opened the door and motioned for her to go in.

Feeling foolish, and unexpectedly hot, Nicola nodded.

She inhaled as she passed him. He smelled of clay, something citrusy like bergamot, and cedar wood. Smells that reminded her of being outdoors, the Earth, bright sunshine, and lazy afternoons. She liked it.

"Thank you," she mumbled as she entered.

"Even though I don't really do well interacting with kids I do think it's important to give them hobbies. Which is why your work is important. Keep them off the streets and out of our hair, you know." Quinn's voice poured out of the speakers into the room.

Nicola groaned and took her attention off Damien and redirected it to her sister behind the podium. Around the room wide eyes and shocked expressions accompanied the hush of whispers that followed Quinn's comment. A horrified expression covered their mom's face at the front of the room.

As if sensing the answer to her prayers in the back of the room, her mom's gaze swung to the door. Nicola could practically hear the *Thank God* in her mom's head. The horror in her face switched to a mixture of relief and *I'm going to kill you for being late*. Adele rushed up on the stage and pulled the microphone away from Quinn.

"Thank you, Quinn, for giving us that perfect segue," her mom said as she inelegantly ushered Quinn to the side. "I'd like to turn the microphone over to our keynote speaker for the afternoon. My oldest daughter, the lead perfumer of Queen Couture, the person responsible for making many of the scents we know and love, and soon to be a guest on the popular daytime television show *Your Morning Wake-Up Call*, Nicola King."

Her mom pointed toward the door. A hundred or more pairs of eyes swung toward Nicola. They clapped in response to her mother's enthusiastic applause. Nicola's face burned hotter than the sun. Sweat slickened her palms, and her stomach clenched. Public speaking never got easier.

A hand gently touched her arm. Damien's touch. Electric sparks skipped across her skin. "You're on," he said in a low voice.

Nicola trembled. Not from the momentary stage fright. She pulled away from him quickly, ignored the impulse to turn and run out the door, and made her way to the front of the room. Forcing her lips upward into her practiced, happy-to-be-here smile, Nicola nodded and waved as she strode with feigned confidence to take the mic.

Breathe in. Breathe out. One foot in front of the other. Look toward the back of the room. Not at anyone in particular. Don't make eye contact with Damien. Don't think about your secret crush being in the room. And, no matter what you do, slow down!

The familiar mantra worked, and by the time she was in front of the podium her heart beat as if she were doing a brisk walk instead of a mad dash for her life. Quinn looked just as relieved as their mom to get out of the spotlight and turn over the microphone to Nicola.

Her mom hugged her. "I'm going to kill you," she whispered in Nicola's ear.

"I made it just in time," Nicola whispered back. They separated, and Nicola took the microphone.

"Thank you, Quinn, for filling in for me. I apologize for being late, but I'd like to piggyback on Quinn's earlier sentiment. How the important work you do through your programs helps keep kids busy with something beautiful and creative. When I was a young girl, sometimes the only place I could express myself was in the lab. I excelled in a chemistry lab. I learned how to work as part of a team, how to follow instructions, and how one slight variation in a formula could change the entire process. For the good and for the bad. You can ask my mom later about the time I burned my eyebrows off." A low murmur of laughter went through the room. Nicola's shoulders relaxed. "The arts and sciences can give kids access to a place of wonder. A place where they can always ask why, how, and what if. That is one of the reasons why we've always supported this foundation. For those who don't know me, I'm Nicola King, and because of programs like the one you support today, I've gained access to a world that I never knew existed. Let me tell you how I got started."

The shocked expressions from earlier were now filled with encouragement and appreciation. Her mom nodded her approval from her seat at a table in the front of the room. She didn't want to admit it, but she knew Damien was seated three tables back and to the right of her mother. She staunchly gave the rest of her speech to the left side of the room. She got into the flow of things and forgot about being nervous. Once again, Nicola had to come in and save the day, and once again she didn't mind doing her part to keep the family's reputation clear.

After her speech, Nicola sat at the table with her mom and Quinn while the director of the association gave out awards, thanked their donors, and gave highlights of some of their projects over the year. Her mom paid close attention to the speeches. Nicola tried to focus on the talks, even though her mind kept bouncing between the various projects she had waiting in the lab and wondering why Damien was there. He must be a contributor to the foundation. He was an artist, so it only made sense. Would she get to talk to him again after the luncheon ended?

She checked her watch again. When would the luncheon end? She'd gotten here late, and they were still an hour and a half in. She had so much work to do.

Quinn didn't bother to pretend she was paying attention. Her fingers tapped quickly and silently on the screen of her phone as the texted or updated her social media accounts. When Nicola tried to ease closer to look at what her sister was doing, Quinn picked her phone up off the table and leaned away.

The moment the luncheon finally ended, Quinn stood and pressed her phone to her ear. Instead of being able to escape back to her office or search the room to see if Damien was sticking around to talk, Nicola was pulled into a conversation with one of the members by her mom. Nicola did as was expected. Smiled, nodded, answered questions, and listened. Never once checking her watch to see how much time had passed even though the need to check the time was like a hot poker in her chest.

When the board member finally walked away to talk to someone else, her mom gave her a hug. The scent of roses, undertones of vanilla, and high notes of cedar surrounded Nicola. Their signature scent. The one that saved the company and her mom wore every day.

"I'm still mad at you for being late, but thank goodness you got here when you did." Adele's husky voice was filled with gratitude. Her mom looked like the head of a cosmetics company. Reddish brown skin, soft black natural hair, and makeup always flawless. She looked more like Nicola's cousin than her mother. Nicola refused to say sister.

"Quinn could have finished her speech," Nicola said after pulling back.

Adele shook her head. "No. I don't know what road your sister was meandering down, but it was the wrong one. I love Quinn, but there's a reason she isn't the face of the company."

"You know she could just as easily be the face of the company." If things had worked out differently, she would be the face of the company.

"She had her chance to do so and she chose not to. Quinn has her strengths, but we all know she was never really interested in doing more than what she's doing now." Her mom looked over her shoulder and waved. "Oh wait, I need to talk to Roger before he leaves. Thanks again for coming."

Nicola kissed her mom's cheek and gave her another hug. "No problem at all. I'll give you a call later."

"Do that. And call your grandfather while you're at it. He's been acting weird. You've always had a good way of getting through to him."

"Weird how?"

Her only living grandfather was the epitome of crotchety old man. He yelled at the kids in the neighborhood if their shoes dared to touch his lawn. He called the police regularly if something seemed fishy at a neighbor's house. And, as the president of his homeowner's association, he frequently walked around giving out citations to neighbors without a hint of remorse. He wasn't weird, he'd just been in a bad mood for as long as Nicola could remember.

"He's grumbling about something at the clubhouse. Some kind of fundraiser he doesn't want to do, but as a member of the community center he has to participate. It's got him riled up. Just give him a call and try to calm him down, okay?"

Her mom walked away without waiting for a confirmation. Nicola pulled out her phone and opened her task list. She added *Call Grandad* to the list of things she needed to do. Even though he was unpleasant most of the time, she loved her grandfather. Partly because he viewed her as indifferently as her mom considered Quinn. In his eye, she wasn't the savior of Queen Couture. She was just another relative who didn't appreciate the sacrifices he went through for them to live the good life. It was nice to be just another unappreciative grandkid. Which is why she'd call him and get to the bottom of whatever had him riled up now.

"Good speech."

Nicola's skin pebbled. A rush went through her midsection as her attention went away from her phone and focused on Damien Hawkins's handsome face. She'd thought he was gone. She'd seen him slip out the door when her mom hooked her into the conversation with the board member. She'd been disappointed, but also resigned. What was she really going to do? Ask him out?

Nicola ran a hand over the smooth black hair of her ponytail before smiling nervously. "Thank you. I hope it was beneficial."

"It sounded rehearsed. Do you give the same speech often?"

Her spine stiffened as her defenses rose. She did give the same speech pretty much everywhere she went. She would change it up a bit every year, but she was busy. Writing a new speech every time she had to speak at one of her mom's functions wasn't practical.

She lifted her chin. "I like to focus on a few key points whenever I talk."

"I didn't mean anything by it. Just noticed that it seemed kind of practiced. The words were great, they just didn't have a lot of passion behind them."

Nicola crossed her arms over her chest. "I wasn't aware you critiqued speeches."

The corner of his mouth tilted up. He settled back on his heels and held out his hands in acquiescence. "I don't. Again, the words were great. I agree with everything you said."

"It doesn't sound like you want to admit that."

He hooked his fingers into the back pocket of his pants. His shirt stretched across his broad chest revealing the chains he wore. "I just wondered, the work that you do making perfume. Do you love it? The way you talk about it doesn't sound as if it's your calling."

Nicola jerked her gaze away from the chains resting against the base of his throat. "I love what I do. I have a great job and I get to meet lots of interesting people." Her voice came out sharper than she'd intended. At least that hid how breathless she felt.

"I'm sorry. I obviously came about this the wrong way. You did a great job. Thank you for coming out to talk to our group today."

"You're a member of the foundation?"

"I'm on the board. I think it would be great if you came and spoke to one of our youth groups. Tell them how you turned a degree in chemistry into something in the high-end fashion world. Would you be interested?"

"I don't know. I may not convey my enthusiasm for what I do," she replied.

Damien chuckled and pressed a hand to his chest. "I deserve that. I'll be the first to admit that I'm a genius when it comes to working with clay, but I'm not always the best when it comes to expressing my thoughts. You did a great job on the speech, and, if you can find it in your heart to overlook the foot I put in my mouth, give me a call and let me know if you can make it to one of our youth events."

He pulled a card out of his back pocket and held it out to her. Nicola's heart flipped in her chest. A giggle bubbled in her chest. Her actual crush was giving her his card and telling her to call him.

Yeah, so you can talk to kids. Don't forget he said you didn't convey passion.

She swallowed the giggle, took the card and slipped it into her purse. "Thank you. I'll check my schedule and get back to you. Things are kind of hectic for me right now."

"Just consider it. I hope to hear from you." He gave her one last easy but heart stopping smile then strolled away.

Quinn came back into the banquet hall as Damien left Nicola's side. A bright, calculating smile spread across her sister's face and she hurried to her.

"I wondered if you knew he was here," Quinn said. "Girl, I take back everything I said the other night. You do have some fire in you. Going after Damien when you finally have him in the vicinity."

"I'm not going after Damien. He's on the board. He wanted to tell me my speech was good and ask me to speak to one of their youth groups."

Quinn's smile deflated. "Oh."

Nicola was pretty sure the disappointment in Quinn's voice was more for Nicola failing to entice Damien to ask her out. Nicola hid her discontent with a nonchalant shrug. "Yeah, oh. Don't worry. He's nice, but I don't think he's my type or that I'm his type."

"How do you know that?" Quinn asked with a don't be ridiculous eye roll.

"I just do. No sparks." None on his side at least. "Now forget about him. I'm sorry about the way Mom pushed you off the stage."

Quinn waved a hand. "Please, I never should have been up there. I'm just glad you arrived when you did. I never know what to say at these things."

"You're really funny. You should go with that." Nicola had seen Quinn speak. When she was relaxed and comfortable with the crowd, she always did great.

"This group didn't come here to listen to me try to be a comedian," Quinn said flippantly. "They came to hear about all of the great things their money goes toward and how we're happy to continue receiving their money to do great things. In other words, they needed your inspiration."

"Yeah, well, my inspiration is ready to go." Nicola checked her watch. Man, she'd have to work until nearly eight to make up for this lost time.

"So am I, but I'll at least do one round and make nice with Mom's friends."

"You did spend most of the day on your phone. Mind telling me who you were texting?"

"Oh, I was talking to Joseph. He was serious about using me for a campaign. I'm going to have drinks with him later to talk about it more." The words flew out of Quinn's mouth easily, as if going out to drinks with someone other than her husband wasn't a big deal.

Nicola raised a brow. "Drinks? Are you sure that's smart?"

"Why wouldn't it be? You're always giving me a hard time about being social media famous. Well, this is my chance to move to a bigger level."

"Not that. What about Omar?"

Quinn sucked her teeth. "This is not a date. It's business. Omar will understand. In fact, he's already excited about being able to tell his friends his wife is a real model, not just online. Don't worry about him at all."

Nicola thought about Quinn's irritation when Omar showed up at the club. The way she'd tried to usher him out, unsuccessfully, and how Omar had strutted next to her side the remainder of the night. The way Omar loved to show her sister off like he would a new car often irritated Nicola. Maybe he would be indifferent to Quinn having drinks with a man who'd increase his wife's appeal. "If you say so."

"I know so. Oh look, Mom is waving me over. You better get out before you're sucked back in."

"I'm out." Nicola and Quinn hugged and then Nicola left.

On the way out, she thought about Quinn's drinks meeting with Joseph. Quinn was married, beautiful, and having drinks with a good-looking guy who wasn't her husband, while Nicola hadn't even worked up the nerve to try and flirt with Damien today after drooling over his social media pages for months. Another thing for her list. Grow a backbone and get her own damn life before she started to hate Quinn's.

Chapter 5

What inspired you to start your career?

Nicola stared at the question on her computer screen. The questions had come from the producer with *Your Morning Wake-Up Call* not long after she'd agreed to the interview. They weren't groundbreaking. Basic, tell me about yourself and what you do questions. She'd answered most of them easily enough. The inspiration question had her stumped, and she wasn't sure why.

She wanted a cool answer to the question. Some inspirational story about an experience which made her realize what she wanted to do with her life. If only her life had unfolded that way. She gave that speech over and over about how she'd taken a love for chemistry and a great sense of smell to ultimately land a career in the glamorous world of perfume making. Most people assumed she always wanted to work at her mom's cosmetics company. Being a part of the glitz and glamor of making perfumes for celebrities and famous brands.

Except that had been Quinn's dream. Nicola's dream had

been much different. Nicola had dreamed one day her family would find her accomplishments outside of the world of Queen Couture worthy of their praise.

This was all Damien's fault. If he hadn't pointed out that her speech was overly practiced. That she lacked a *passion* for what she did when she spoke. Well, then she wouldn't be here staring at a simple question she'd answered a hundred times before.

Minimizing the screen with the one unanswered question, Nicola logged into her cloud-based account and opened her list. Right there near the top was her former dream job. *Work on project to help victims of stroke. Find treatments for recovery.*

A lofty goal, but it was what she'd wanted to do. She'd watched her grandmother fail to recover fully after suffering a stroke when Nicola was in college. She'd died two years earlier, having never fully regained the ability to speak clearly or be fully mobile. Watching the once-vibrant matriarch of her mother's side of the family lose so much of her personality and freedom after the event, Nicola had planned to pursue a doctoral degree in biochemistry and focus her research with the hope of helping her grandmother.

She'd had the chance after presenting a project on sensorimotor retraining. Her biochemistry professor had encouraged her to continue her studies and work with him on his ongoing research into the same topic. He'd seen potential in Nicola's ideas and told her she was on the verge of something brilliant.

At the same time Nicola was finishing undergrad, her mom's company took off. Adele worked for L'Oréal as a cosmetic chemist when Nicola and Quinn were younger. Adele spent years creating formulas for makeup, skin care, and other personal care products. When she'd been passed over for a promotion, Adele left and started Queen Couture, using the money she'd saved and investments from the contacts in the industry she'd made over the years.

Twenty years in the industry and a master's degree in cosmetic science meant Adele knew how to create products, but she didn't know how to run a business. Poor moves, and an expansion into fragrances when Nicola was in college, almost bankrupted the company. Unwilling to give up, Adele brought on someone she could trust to make management decisions, took business classes so she wouldn't be completely in the dark, and focused on product development.

Then one of Adele's friends from her days at L'Oréal, supermodel Alexandria, agreed to give her mom a bone by allowing her to make a perfume with her name on it. Until then, both Nicola and Quinn worked at Queen Couture during the summer and between semesters. Nicola to help, and Quinn because she'd always fit seamlessly into their mother's world of glitz and glamour. They'd both seen Alexandria's scent brief and they'd both played around in the lab working on it, but neither expected one of their concoctions to be chosen. That was until Alexandria tried and loved the juice Nicola created. The scent became a hit, immediately taking the perfume side of the business to the forefront.

The day Triumph became the number one selling scent of the season was the first time Adele looked at Nicola with pride. Nicola walked away from her graduate studies and caved to the pressure from Adele to take cosmetic science courses. Instead of becoming a brilliant medical scientist, she'd received something else she'd always wanted instead. She was no longer the smart one. The independent one her parents didn't need to worry about because she was too sensible to cause trouble. She became the brilliant one. The star of the family who'd helped save Queen Couture.

Nicola sighed. No way was all of that going into the

otherwise simple question. *It was always my dream to work at my mother's company. This allowed me to use my love of science in a beautiful and glamorous way.*

Her cell phone rang. Shonda's number. Nicola answered, welcoming the distraction from the steps up the ladder to parental approval that led her to where she was today.

"What's up?"

"I got an email from Vacation Destination and they have round trip tickets to Cancun available for a hundred dollars," Shonda's excited voice came through the phone. "Say yes, and I'll buy the tickets right now."

Nicola grinned at her friend's enthusiasm. Sandy beaches, fruity drinks with umbrellas in them, sun, and blue skies. She could practically feel the breeze in her hair. When was the last time she'd been on a vacation?

She indulged herself for a moment. "When would we go?"

"We'd have to go within the next month. I'm thinking we make it a long weekend. Fly down Thursday, come back Monday morning. Super simple and just what we both need."

"What about your kids?"

"They've got a dad," Shonda said sounding affronted. "Besides, he owes me one for—you know—being an asshole and ruining our marriage. Come on. I want to get out of town and have a little fun."

"Didn't you have fun the other night with that sexy man at the club?" Nicola was curious—what was up with that guy? *Stop living vicariously through your friends.* She'd have to add that to the list.

"Yes, girl, yes." Shonda's voice turned warm and silky. "I had fun multiple times with that man. But this is completely different. We haven't gone out of town and had a great time in forever. Let's go."

Nicola scanned her regrets list. Her body begged her to let the yes pop out. To relax and not deal with traffic, scent briefs, collaboration meetings, and hearing that she didn't sound passionate about her work after speaking at a society function. Desiree's perfume was pretty much in the bag. She could delegate her other projects to Tia and assign the work of smaller projects to some of the other perfumers at the company. After she met with Desiree today, she'd be even closer to knowing what the singer wanted and could easily get away for a quick weekend.

But what if Desiree demanded something Nicola hadn't expected? What if her initial thoughts for the scent weren't what the singer expected? She'd have to put in extra time to work on this. Plus, how would it look to skip out of town to Mexico when she was in the middle of an important project?

Nicola turned her chair around so her back was to her computer and her list. Digital proof that she was forever a coward when it came to living her life to the fullest. "I'd love to, Shonda, but I can't. Not right now with the Desiree project."

Shonda sighed. "I figured you would say no."

"Then why did you ask?"

"So, you wouldn't get mad when I told you that I am going. Oh, and Quinn is going too."

"You asked Quinn?" Before she asked her? That stung. Like a million mutant wasps attacking sting.

"Yeah, I'm not turning down this deal," Shonda said in a sorry-not-sorry tone. "Your sister has insisted we fly first class, but that's fine. All tickets are on sale."

Which meant Shonda had called Quinn before calling her. "So, you two *are* going?" Plans made and bags packed. She'd been the afterthought. The obligatory invite.

"Yep, and because you're my best friend, I didn't want to go without at least giving you the chance to say what I already knew you were going to say."

Nicola didn't get a chance to reply to that, because

LeShawn, her assistant, knocked on her door before pushing it open. "Desiree is here to see you."

She'd have to dissect her thoughts about Shonda and Quinn becoming BFFs and find a way to make sure she didn't lose another friend to her more outgoing sister later. "Shonda, I've got to go."

"No problem. Hey, knock it out of the park with Desiree. I know you're going to do great. Once this is over, we'll plan another trip. Okay?" Nothing about Shonda's tone indicated she believed they ever would go out of town.

"Yeah, sure."

She got off the phone and tried to ignore the kernel of jealousy irritating her like popcorn stuck in her teeth. She minimized her list on the screen. No need to be reminded of all the reasons why no one expected her to do anything. By the time she stood and walked around her desk, LeShawn was escorting Desiree into her office.

Desiree was just as stunning in person as she was on television. The thirty-year-old singer entered the office with a flourish behind a large male bodyguard. She wore a thin, bright yellow t-shirt that stopped right beneath her breasts and a tight miniskirt of the same color. The shade made her chestnut-brown skin glow and brightened her dark eyes.

"Nicola, I can't wait to smell what you've come up with for my perfume," her husky voice filled the room and she walked with a sexy swagger Nicola could never emulate.

Desiree hugged her. Sunshine, saltwater, and persimmon. That's what Nicola got from their embrace. Nothing like the samples Nicola had put together for this meeting. Nicola shook away the tickle of self-doubt about what she'd created. Desiree wanted something new and fresh, otherwise she wouldn't have liked what Nicola sent over the first time. Her perfume today didn't mean anything about what she'd want to debut.

Nicola gave Desiree a confident smile. "I took the notes you sent with the last samples and tweaked the formulas. Follow me into the lab and I can go over some of the various ideas."

She led Desiree and the bodyguard she felt scanning her and the room behind his dark shades toward her lab tables. "How was your trip?"

A devilish gleam brightened the singer's eye. "I had the best time. There is nothing like being spoiled by a prince. He's about to make me give up dating men who don't have their own country." Desiree laughed. "Do you know how crazy royalty can be?"

Nicola shrugged. "Actually, I do. Last year I made a special blend for the Prince of Marobi's sister. She loved it so much he offered to let me pet his tiger."

Desiree's perfectly manicured brows rose nearly to her hairline. A new spark of interest came to her eyes. "A tiger?"

"I said no of course. I do my work to help the client, and not for privileges."

Quinn had called her crazy for not accepting the offer from the ruler of the eastern African nation. Hence the reason *pet a tiger* was on Nicola's list. The next time royalty offered her a once in a lifetime experience, if ever, she was going to accept.

"Tell everyone you know that you made perfume for a prince and you'll be the perfumer everyone goes to. If I'd known that story, I would have chosen you to make my perfume sooner." Desiree tilted her head to the side and eyed Nicola with a little more interest.

"I don't like to brag. Word of mouth combined with my end results is what brings people here. I just hope I meet their expectations."

The Marobi job had come thanks to Quinn. The princess was a fan of Quinn and her brother had reached out to see what she could recommend as a gift. Quinn had turned the blatant attempt at a hookup into a business opportunity for Queen Couture.

Nicola waved to the row of vials on one of the tables in the lab. "Shall we?"

They went through the fragrances. Each one Nicola explained how she'd tweaked the formula based on Desiree's suggestions. She'd tried to be bold and daring. To portray Desiree's sex appeal, fury, sweetness, and danger. As they talked, and Desiree made comments, Nicola realized she hadn't met Desiree's expectations. More musk here, too much vanilla there, too sweet, too bitter.

"This still isn't what I wanted." Desiree shook her head and eyed the vials with disappointment. "I was hoping you'd understand my notes. I want life, desire, excitement, and comfort. I want realness that's timeless in a bottle."

Nicola swallowed as unease tried to morph into panic. "I took your notes very seriously. I've studied the items you mentioned and made changes."

Desiree shook her head. "Something is still off. The perfumers at IFH sent me another sample that I like, but I don't want to work with them. Keep trying and we'll see what you come up with by the end of my tour, okay?"

Nicola nodded and tried to smile. "Okay." Her stomach hurt as if she'd swallowed the perfumes on the table. What if Desiree didn't like what she came up with? She'd known IHF was still in the running, but Desiree's enthusiasm to work with Queen Couture had made her overly confident they'd have the job. If she didn't come up with an answer would she lose the account?

She couldn't lose the account. She would come up with the answer.

Just like you did with the signature scent for Alexandria?

Nicola pushed that thought to the very back of her mind.

In the dark corner where her deepest regrets and memories were put to be forgotten.

"One last thing," Nicola said when Desiree looked as if she was ready to leave. "I was asked to do an interview on *Your Morning Wake-Up Call* about my work, and specifically being a perfumer working with you. I have no intention of mentioning anything we discussed here, but I do want to let you know it's happening."

Desiree pursed her full lips then flipped her wrist. "Fine, it'll be good publicity before the launch. Everyone is trying to get an idea of what I'm going to do."

Nicola's stomach settled a little. Desiree didn't sound like she was ready to walk out on Queen Couture. Nicola forced herself to breathe. Clients could be challenging. She'd gone through thirty different combinations before settling on the perfume the Prince wanted for his sister. She could make this work for Desiree.

"The show sent over a list of questions. I can go over the answers to them if you want me to."

Desiree nodded. "Sure, I'd love to read them."

"I can email them to you. I was working on that before you came." Nicola pointed to her desk.

"Oh, well I can look at them now." Desiree strolled over and plopped down in the leather chair. "Is your computer password protected?"

"Um... yeah. Just let me type it in." She hurried over. She hadn't really expected Desiree to want to go over everything now, but again, clients could be spontaneous along with challenging.

"Really, Nicola, do you think I'm going to sneak in here later and steal your secrets. Just tell me the password." Desiree laughed and wiggled her fingers back and forth in a come-on motion.

She felt foolish for hesitating. Desiree was not coming

back to steal her trade secrets. She rattled off her password. She'd change the password tomorrow.

Desiree read a few sentences, then her eyes widened. "I solemnly swear that I will—"

Nicola nearly peed her pants. "No, no, that's not what you should be reading." She rushed over to the computer.

Desiree leaned toward the screen. "Wait a second. Tell a guy I love him. Sleep with a prince the next time I have a chance. Go on spring break." Desiree's eyes jumped to Nicola's. "Do you really keep a list of regrets?"

She would never open this list away from her house again. Her cheeks burned and she wanted to disappear into thin air. "If you'll close that then we can open the actual document you need to review."

"Forget the television show. You and I need to talk about why you have so many items on this list. You rub elbows with some of the most influential people in the fashion industry. This makes no sense."

"Desiree, can we please not talk about this." Nicola hurried round the desk and hastily pressed the button to close the document.

Desiree jumped up, pushing Nicola's hand away. "This explains it."

She tried to breathe, but her lungs felt frozen. "Explains what?" she asked in a tight voice.

"Why you're having trouble making a fragrance that is the essence of what I want. The essence of a life well lived. You haven't lived."

Not from Desiree too. "I have lived. I'm very happy—"

"Not if you're keeping a list like this. You know what, spend the time I'm away thinking about those things and maybe you'll make something better than that stuff over there." She pointed with a flip of the wrist to the vials on the table. "And you are coming with me right now."

"Coming with you where?" She couldn't leave. She had work to do. She had to fix the samples to try and meet what Desiree wanted. She needed to find and eat a pint of ice cream to cool the mortification burning through her midsection.

"Go on a shopping trip with the next celebrity who invites you is on that list. I'm inviting you. We will get to the bottom of this."

Damn. Damn. Triple Damn! "I really have a lot of work to do. I've got to get those questions to the show today." Not spend the day listening to one of the most desired singers in the word lecture her on how to be more interesting. Bad enough she had to hear that from her more interesting and desirable sister.

"You have an assistant, right? Ask her to email it to the show. I trust your professional judgment. You wouldn't say anything that will piss me off, but your personal judgment. That's another thing." Desiree hurried around the desk and linked her arm through Nicola's. "Let's go now."

Desiree pulled Nicola out of the office. Now mortification burned from the roots of her hair to the tips of her toes. Nicola would need a gallon of ice cream. The most outgoing and popular celebrity she could think of had just seen all of the things that made Nicola the most uninteresting person in the world. Maybe something good would come of this. Maybe shopping with Desiree would keep her happy and possibly make sure she continued working with Nicola.

"LeShawn, please email the questions back to the producer of *Your Morning Wake-Up Call*." Nicola said as Desiree tried to pull her out the door.

LeShawn looked from Nicola to Desiree with wide eyes. "Are they saved on the network?"

"No, but it's open on my computer. Just send that over to her, please." She'd been working on the questions before pulling up the list of regrets. That what she got for getting distracted and not focusing on work. If she'd never opened her list, Desiree wouldn't have seen it, and she wouldn't be dragging Nicola out to make her perfumer less dull.

Desiree tugged on Nicola's arm. LeShawn's lips twitched as if she were holding back a laugh. She nodded. "I'll do it now."

"Thank you," Nicola called over her shoulder as she was pulled from the office.

For a second, she worried about LeShawn seeing the list. But she was sure she'd closed the document before Desiree had pushed her away. She thought so at least. She really didn't need her assistant to also discover that Nicola's *I can do anything* attitude was just a front.

Chapter 6

"Today's guest is someone whose name you probably haven't heard before, but her work may touch you daily. She's responsible for creating some of the most beloved and memorable fragrances, from celebrity perfumes to household items such as soaps, deodorants, and lotions. She is also the person international superstar Desiree sought out to help develop a new perfume. Something every one of her millions of fans is dying to get. Please welcome our latest guest in our series of spotlights on influential people, fragrance chemist and perfumer, Nicola King."

Nicola took a deep breath, smiled, and walked from the dim backstage to the brightly lit set of *Your Morning Wake-Up Call*. The live studio audience clapped on cue. The show's hosts stood and greeted Nicola with handshakes and air kisses over her cheek.

Even though she'd had a brief conversation with both of them backstage, she still couldn't believe she was sitting there on a stage set up to mimic a living room, a huge cup of coffee in a *Morning Wake-Up Call* mug on the coffee table before her. The hosts, Tom Rogers and Cassandra Duncan, both wore megawatt smiles as they sat on a sofa next to Nicola. Tom, who was in his mid-forties and had been on the show for over a decade, looked trendy in a stylish aquamarine blazer and dark blue pants. Cassandra's bright green eyes watched Nicola intently. She appeared elegant in a sleeveless white blouse and rust colored skirt that matched her red hair. Her small stature was dwarfed by Tom's, but her over-the-top personality honed by years playing in daytime soaps allowed her to more than hold her own with the veteran next to her on camera.

"Nicola, oh my God, thank you for coming onto the show," Cassandra said.

Nicola sat straight in the comfortable plush red seat next to Cassandra and Tom. She ran her hands over the navy skirt of her suit. Her nerves from being on live television preventing her from fully relaxing. "Thank you for having me."

"When I read through your list of accomplishments, I mean, I was blown away," Cassandra said placing a warm hand on Nicola's arm. "I hadn't realized I've worn or smelled something you've created almost every day for the past few years. How did you get started?"

Nicola licked her lips and shifted in the chair. She didn't look at the audience. Tried not to think about the thousands of other people seeing her live on the air. *Just focus on Cassandra and Tom.*

"I've always been interested in science, chemistry especially. My mom started out working for another cosmetics company and after twenty years there decided to step out on her own. When I realized I could use my love of science and my interest in the fashion industry, well, I jumped at the chance."

Tom rubbed his chin and studied her. "But you do a lot more than perfumes. Isn't that right?"

"I do. When we first started of course our focus was on making perfume. We were very fortunate to make our signature scent that supermodel Alexandria put her name on." There was applause and cheers from the audience. Nicola chuckled at their enthusiasm and relaxed a little. "Thank you. We were very excited about that and we made more perfumes, but then companies asked us to look into developing scents for other items. I've made fragrances for things like soaps and lotions to even a few fabric softeners and cleansers."

Cassandra clapped and nodded. "That is impressive. But, tell the truth. Making that other stuff isn't as fun as making perfume though. Am I right?"

Nicola leaned in and admitted in a conspiratorial whisper. "Not as fun." The audience laughed right along with Cassandra and Tom. Nicola relaxed, now that her attempt at humor had landed. "The other projects are just as vital, but my focus is mostly perfumes."

"Speaking of perfumes, you're close to landing the biggest partnership of the year. Working with Desiree. Tell me about that," Cassandra said, then picked up her coffee mug and took a sip.

"I'm very honored to be working with Desiree. When I heard she wanted to branch into perfumes I knew I had to at least try to be the person she worked with. I still can't believe she reached out to me."

"Any hints on what she's going to do?" Cassandra asked.

Tom placed a hand on Cassandra's shoulder. "Come on, Cassandra, you know she can't spill the woman's secrets on national television."

The audience cheered and begged for the secrets. Nicola's face burned and her heart thumped. She knew this was just for show, but that didn't stop her nerves from fluttering. "No, not here. You all will have to wait until the debut to find out.

But, I can assure you that when working with someone as outgoing, influential, and original as Desiree, she's going to insist on creating a scent people all over will love."

Once she figured out the perfect formula, that is.

Cassandra nodded and pouted as if conceding to tremendous pressure. "You're right, I guess. I mean, I am so inspired by the way you turned your mother's company around from the brink of bankruptcy with the creation of Triumph. Now Queen Couture is one of the companies everyone is going to."

Nicola's gaze shifted to the camera and back. "It wasn't just me. My mom and sister both worked hard to get us where we are." Quinn more than most people realized.

"Yes, but it was *your* creation that became the number one selling perfume multiple years in a row. From that, you've had hit after hit. You're invited to celebrity parties, I hear you're on a first name basis with the Prince of Marobi, and now you're working with Desiree. Some would say you're the embodiment of living the dream."

Nicola would've laughed at that if she didn't hate discussing how she'd supposedly saved her mom's company from the brink. At least Cassandra appreciated what she'd been telling everyone since the party. Cassandra wasn't telling her she wasn't living it up enough. She didn't need more excitement in her life. She had enough as it was. "I have been very fortunate. I couldn't be happier."

Cassandra pursed her lips and tilted her head to the side. "Couldn't you?"

A prickle of unease crawled up Nicola's spine like a phantom spider. Sweat trickled down her back. Had the heat from the cameras intensified? She glanced at Tom. He raised his brows in a go-with-it fashion. "I mean. I guess we all could find ways to be happier."

Cassandra's eyes brightened as if Nicola had just given her

the lead she'd wanted. "For instance, getting a chance to do the things a person never got around to."

The phantom spider now had friends that crawled over Nicola's arms and chest. "You could say that," Nicola said slowly.

"And that's what you're doing now, too. Going back and scratching items off your list of regrets."

Nicola froze in the middle of putting her coffee mug back on the table. Her gaze shot up to Cassandra's. "Say what now?"

If Cassandra noticed the panic coursing through Nicola she didn't let on. If anything, her eyes sharpened. Reminding Nicola of a ferret about to snatch a morsel of food. "When you sent over your list of regrets, it made us realize how courageous you must be to go back and scratch those things off. I mean, you've got a lot of things on that list."

Nicola dropped the mug on the table with a thud. "My list." Forget phantom spiders, Nicola's entire body stilled. *No. God no. Please Lord No!!*

She struggled to keep her breathing normal when sweat broke out across her forehead and upper lip. Nicola eased back into an upright position. This could not be happening to her. How did they know? This had to be a mistake. They couldn't possibly have seen her list. Her eyes darted to the exit. How bad would it be if she took off running right now?

"Yes, we have a copy right here." Cassandra, ever so helpful, miraculously pulled a sheet of paper from between her and Tom. Her green eyes eagerly scanned the paper. "Ask a guy out. I think most of us have done that. Take the trip to Cancun you missed on spring break. Pet the Prince of Marobi's tiger if asked again. Go skinny dipping with the former secretary of state."

Her hand gripped the arm of her chair. "You have my list," Nicola's voice sounded thin and scratchy. And now the audience was cheering and murmuring excitedly. Sweet mother of everything holy, how did they have the list?

"Of course," Tom said, seeming to have noticed her distress. "When you forwarded it to us, we understood you'd sent it over to show no matter how successful you may be there may be things that you regret not doing."

He was throwing her a life preserver. She could either take it, pretend as if this was intentional, and pray to every deity out there that this blew over. Or, she could demand to know how they got it and break down in a fit of embarrassment that would make internet memes for years to come. As much as the second option was what she wanted to do, her professional common sense said she had to go with the former.

"Yes . . . of course. That's exactly why I . . . I sent it." She wanted to die. Right here. In front of all these people. God could send down a lightning bolt and strike her to dust.

Cassandra leaned forward. "But what are you going to do with the items on this list? Are you going to start living with no regrets?"

The audience clapped. A few people called out "Do the list!" Nicola looked at the people there. All cheering her on. A sea of smiling, eager faces. Eating up her embarrassment as if it was free samples in the grocery store.

"Sure, in fact, it's one of the reasons I sent it over. To talk about how even though my life appears glamorous, I still miss out on the little things. I'm trying to make time for those things. In fact, I struck one thing off the other day." Thanks to the shopping trip with Desiree. "I'm making this a priority, you know."

"Well then, you will come back and let us know how things went, won't you?" Tom asked.

There was no way in—"Of course!"

* * *

How in the world had they gotten ahold of her list? The question ran through Nicola's mind like a freight train on greased tracks. Her phone was blowing up. Texts, emails, calls, and social media notifications. She ignored them all as she jumped out of her car and sprinted inside her office.

Nicola rushed through the doors and skidded to a stop in front of her administrative assistant's desk. Slapping her palms down on the surface she stared into LeShawn's wide, dark eyes.

"What did you send them?"

LeShawn jumped from her chair and held up her hands as if Nicola had her at gunpoint. "I swear only what you had opened on your laptop."

"I did not have—"

LeShawn nodded. "Yes, you did."

Nicola's hands balled into fists on the desk. She felt lightheaded and sick. "Why did you send it?"

"You said to send what was open on your computer."

"Did you read it?" As if that mattered. Everyone had heard her list this morning on the show.

"I did."

"And what made you think that was supposed to go?"

LeShawn shrugged and eased back until she stood behind her chair. "I don't know. I just followed directions. Then Desiree was talking about you striking things off your list and doing things you always wanted to do. I thought it was part of the angle you wanted to portray on the show."

Nicola covered her face with her hands. Her chest constricted. She couldn't breathe. "I can't believe this is happening."

"Don't worry about it. Your story was actually really inspirational. You make me want to go back and try out some things."

Nicola glared at LeShawn between her fingers. "I wanted this to be about the business and everything I've worked hard to achieve. Not everything I gave up just to get here."

"But you really didn't give up," LeShawn argued. "You're going after those things you let pass you by. Which I think is great. You don't get out there enough. This will be good for you." Her eyes brightened and her voice grew more confident with each word.

Nicola slowly dropped her hands. Great, so now her admin was telling her she needed to get out more. What the hell was happening with the world? This wasn't how things were supposed to go. Sure, she'd given up doing some fun things for her career, but she didn't regret the choices she made. Not really. Her list was more to celebrate all the awesome opportunities she'd had on her way to the top. Not doing them wasn't a sign that her life was lacking in some way. She was very happy.

The door to the office burst open and Quinn came in like a bolt of lightning in her all-white halter top and capri pants. She stopped and stared at Nicola. One brow raised and confusion in her dark eyes.

"You regret not going to Cancun in college? So much so you wrote it on your list?"

Nicola rolled her eyes. And now it would begin. "It's not like that. The list wasn't supposed to go to them."

LeShawn bit her lip and eased back down into her chair. Nicola turned away from her sister and escaped into the sanctuary of her office. But like any meddling relative, Quinn ignored sanctuaries.

"That doesn't matter, it got to them," Quinn said, following her. She closed the door to Nicola's office before continuing. "I knew you had a list, but I didn't think it was that big of a deal. The way you talked about it on the show made it sound like you really hate that you missed out on so much. I didn't know work was such a sacrifice for you."

"It's not. That's the way Cassandra made it sound. I think she was trying to make things sound a lot more dramatic than they actually are. I'm completely happy with my life and with everything I've had to do to get here. That list is just something fun to keep up with. Not something I do because I'm keeping a tally of major disappointments or anything like that."

Quinn's head tilted and her lips pursed. She studied Nicola for several seconds. "Are you sure? You said you were going to do the things on the list."

"I'm not doing anything on that list. LeShawn accidentally sent it. They thought it would make a good story to show the woman who has the perfect career." She made air quotes with those words. "Also goes after a perfect personal life. Instead of further embarrassing myself on camera, I agreed with what they said."

"People are going to want to know if you went through with it."

That was not a possibility she'd considered. The idea made her stomach flip even more. "No, they aren't. I was one unknown person on the show between a television actress and a best-selling novelist. No one is going to care about whether or not I do the things on that dumb list."

"Maybe you're right, but the audience seemed to really be into you. I know people. They love to see an underdog come out on top."

Nicola went to her work area and picked up the vial with the scent she'd mixed together to evoke feelings of calm. She screwed off the top and breathed in the mixture of vetiver, lavender, and ylang-ylang. The trembling in her hand did not go away. "Look, I appreciate you trying to help, but you know people on social media. Half of the time the big ruckus people are absorbed in isn't even a blip on the radar in the real world. No one is going to care."

Quinn's cringe screamed *You're being delusional.* She even

flipped her hair in a whatever motion. "For your sake, Miss I'm Going To Keep My Head In The Sand, I hope no one does care, but trust me. People in your so-called *real* world are the same people devouring stories on social media and television. If there's a few things people love, it's a scandal, a story of redemption, or someone overcoming adversity and you, my dear, are setting yourself up as the comeback kid of the year."

Chapter 7

"Nicola, hey it's Stacie Brown with *Your Morning Wake-Up Call*. I'm following up to see when we can schedule a follow up on your interview."

Nicola nearly dropped the phone into the bowl of cereal she'd been eating at her kitchen table. A week had passed since that dreaded television interview. A week since she'd tried to convince everyone from her mom to her pharmacist that she was very happy with her life, and her list had just been something fun to keep up with. She'd expected the interest to have died down by now. Quinn, damn know-it-all that she was, had continued to send her articles and blog posts that mentioned Nicola's interview.

Apparently, the video of her biggest embarrassment had over a hundred thousand likes on YouTube. People obviously had way too much time on their hands. When Quinn hadn't emailed anything yesterday or this morning, Nicola had hoped everything was finally disappearing in pop culture memory.

She just had to pick up the phone.

Nicola wiped away the milk dribbling down her chin.

"Follow up? I didn't know there was going to be a follow up."

"Oh, we have to do a follow up. The response to your interview has been overwhelming. People are still commenting on your interview on social media and contacting us to find out if you're going to come back with an update on what items you scratched off your list. In fact, we've considered having a camera come with you to record your new adventures. It'll be a good way to show the viewers what it's like to take the step out of your comfort zone."

"Recording my adventures! Wait a second. I was just going along with Cassandra and Tom up there. I really don't have any plans to cross items off my list. I only started it as something fun to keep track of."

"Then why did you send it to us?" Stacie asked, in a tone that implied Nicola was playing a game with her.

"That shouldn't have come. My administrative assistant mistakenly forwarded that to you. My intention was to only send you the answers to your questions."

"Or," Stacie said drawing out the word. "Your subconscious put out a cry for help."

How in the world would her subconscious have any influence on what LeShawn did? "It wasn't a cry for help."

"Okay, I get it, you may not have wanted the list to be a part of your interview, but your story resonated with our viewers," Stacie said, sounding every bit like a program director who made quick decisions daily. "The idea of someone actually going back and getting a second chance at the things they missed out on has a lot of people talking about what they would do differently if they could. Most people won't get the chance to do that. You can be the surrogate for America."

"That doesn't sound pleasant." Nicola pushed the bowl of soggy cereal away. She leaned her elbow on the counter and massaged her temple. This had gotten way out of control.

"Hear me out. You are at the top of your life, but you were able to be vulnerable on our show and admit that there are things you wish you could do over again. Then you told the audience you were going to do those things over. Combine that with your work with Desiree and everyone is going to be excited, about not only the fragrance, but the kickass woman behind the scenes. Let us follow you on this journey. Let our viewers see you take life by the horns and fix your past mistakes and regrets. Be the person the rest of us want to be."

Nicola stopped massaging her temples. Well, when Stacie said it that way, the idea didn't sound completely ridiculous. Could this be a good thing? A way for her to finally have the fun Quinn and Shonda said she needed to have while also creating good publicity for Queen Couture? Maybe she could turn this embarrassment into something worthwhile.

"Okay, I'll come back on the show." She agreed hesitantly. Still not sure if this was a good idea or if Stacie was gassing her.

"And what about the cameras?" Stacie asked hopefully.

The idea of cameras in her face constantly made her want to change her mind. But, if she chose some fun things on the list for them to film, nothing too personal, it could be good optics for the story. "Not for everything, but maybe a couple of items. If you really think your viewers will be interested."

"Oh, they will be," Stacie's voice buzzed with confidence. Silly her. Cameras following Nicola wouldn't lead to an interesting story. Obviously, they hadn't gotten the Nicola-is-the-boring-one memo. "Don't worry, Nicola, this is going to be one of the best received stories we've ever done."

That or Nicola's biggest regret.

Chapter 8

Nicola got up early Saturday and drove the hour and a half from Atlanta to Aiken, South Carolina. Since she'd decided to go through with striking items off her list she might as well start with the one item that was most important. Spending more time with family. More specifically her grandfather.

When her grandmother died two years ago, she'd been heartbroken. Then she'd been twisted with guilt. She was supposed to go into biomedical research. She was supposed to have helped find a cure or some solution to ease her grandmother's discomfort. Not spend her life going to parties and making perfumes. Even though her Grandma Cynthia had never once blamed her for working at Queen Couture instead of pursuing a career in biomedical research.

Her grandmother had always been a part of her life. Someone who supported and cheered for Nicola just as much as Quinn. When her parents chose to go to Quinn's pageant, which was the same night Nicola was getting an academic award, it was Grandma Cindy who'd called Nicola and asked how the banquet had gone and told her that she was proud of her. Whenever Quinn made everyone laugh and smile with her jokes and sparkling personality, it was Grandma Cindy who sat next to Nicola reading quietly in the corner and asked about the book. When people gushed over the job Quinn had gotten as a model in a local magazine, Grandma Cindy had followed up the excitement by bringing up that Nicola had once again gotten straight A's and was named valedictorian.

She'd loved her Grandma Cindy more than anyone in the world. Had cried for weeks after seeing the way her stroke had changed her so completely. She'd never imagined a life without her grandmother there. Even as she'd watched her grow weaker, slower, frailer every year. Until Nicola had stopped visiting as much because being there hurt too much.

Her death had hit hard. A heart attack in her sleep. Even though she'd been disabled by the stroke, no one had expected her to go so suddenly. Then all of Nicola's plans to visit and call more once work slowed down seemed like weak excuses.

Now, as she drove down the tree-lined street and pulled her car into the long drive of her grandparents' brick ranch home, she fought back a case of nerves. She hadn't been back here to visit her grandfather in over a year. Hadn't called like she'd promised her mom she would two weeks ago. She would do better. Had to do better. That's why she'd come today.

She strolled up the walkway to the front of the house. The quiet of the morning broken by the sound of birds chirping, the rustle of leaves on the trees, and the far-off hum of a lawn mower. The grass was higher than normal in her grandfather's yard. Her mom had mentioned he was thinking of firing his landscaping crew. Looks like he carried through with the threat. She'd try to convince him to rehire them if that was the case.

She rang the bell twice before a grumpy voice yelled from the other side. "I'm coming. I mean really. People aren't patient anymore."

The door swung open and Jeremiah Coleman frowned at her. A faded Atlanta Falcons t-shirt and ripped jeans fit snugly on his five-foot-six frame. Dark eyes similar to her mother's, the irises rimmed in blue, stared at her with only annoyance. His hair was white around the edges and nonexistent in the center of his head.

"Why are you here?"

So much for getting a welcoming smile and bear hug. "To see you."

"This about that damn list?" One bushy white brow rose.

Really? Even her grandfather knew about that. Would she never escape this? "*America's second chance. That's what we're calling you.*" Stacie's words rang through her head.

"C'mon, Grandpa, I don't need a reason to see you."

His eyes narrowed. The glare that had made her confess all her sins as a kid or lean in to kiss his cheek to make him grin when she was a teenager came to his face. Nicola was proud of herself for not fidgeting.

"Okay, it's kind of because of the list."

His head lifted and lowered. The glare was replaced with a look that said he'd known that all along. "Come on in. Might as well help me if you're gonna come around." He stepped back, froze, then gave a narrow-eyed glance over her shoulders. "No cameras."

"Grandpa, I don't have a camera."

"How am I supposed to know? Your mom said cameras would be following you." One more suspicious look over her shoulder and up and down the street.

"The cameras are only for fun stuff."

"I'm not fun?" His chin lifted.

"You're a loveable grump, but you're not fun."

Her grandad grunted but finally allowed her to enter. Nicola kissed his cheek before going further into the house. She was immediately struck by how much the house still smelled like her grandmother's perfume. No matter how successful and famous Nicola had become, her grandmother hadn't agreed to change the perfume she wore and stuck with the Imari perfume she'd purchased from her same Avon sales representative for nearly two decades. The blend of citrus and musk with hints of jasmine and vanilla had blended with her grandmother's own perfect scent. Nicola loved Grandma Cindy's loyalty to her friend who sold her the perfume, and therefore, hadn't gotten upset when her grandmother didn't want to switch.

The house smelled the same, but it didn't look the same. The furniture in the den was different from the last time she'd been here. The plush, dark purple sofa and love seat she remembered her mom saying Grandma and Grandpa had fought over purchasing was replaced with a tan leather set. A new rug covered the floor, and the curtains were gone. Only blinds kept the inside of the house shielded from prying eyes outside.

"You redecorated," Nicola said.

"Obviously. I hated that purple sofa. Your grandmother's choice," he grumbled. Nicola stopped in the den, but her grandfather kept walking. "I'm working."

"What are you doing?" When he kept going down the hall, she had no choice but to follow.

"Cleaning out the attic."

They went into the hall where the extendable ladder to the attic was down. "What are you doing that for?"

"Because it needs to be done. I need something to keep me occupied. I can't just sit around in this house listening to nothing all day." Jeremiah grabbed the ladder and put one foot on the bottom rung.

Nicola crossed her arms and raised a brow. "Is that why you fired the landscaping crew?"

Her grandfather gave her a mind your business smirk. "I fired them because they weren't cutting the grass right. I like parallel lines in the lawn. They were making them diagonal. Your grandmother's idea."

If anyone else had said that, she might not have believed them. Coming from her grandfather, who was prickly but loveable when you caught him at the right moment, it was believable. She'd argue about the landscapers after she found out what else was going on with him.

Nicola eyed the wobbly ladder. "Do you think you should be going up and down this ladder? It doesn't look secure."

"I've gone up and down this ladder a hundred times in the past few days. So, either stay down here and entertain yourself, or come on up here and help me."

He went up the ladder without a hitch to his step. Sighing, Nicola looked up into the dreary darkness of the attic. Images of spiders, dust, and the dank smell of mildew filled her mind. Good thing she'd worn a pair of jeans and an inexpensive red t-shirt today. She put her foot on the bottom rung and made her way up. This is what she was here for.

They worked in silence for over an hour. Going through old boxes and putting things into keep, donate, and throw away piles. The keep, she'd been informed, wasn't for him to keep. Those were items he thought her mom, one of her aunts and uncle, or the grandkids would like. There wasn't much in the keep pile. Her grandpa was trying to get rid of as much stuff as possible.

The junk in the attic seemed endless. Piles and piles of boxes all with dates going back fifty years. They were starting with the more recent boxes and working their way back. Her grandfather's logic. Each box contained reminders of a family reunion, holiday party, or cookout where she and her grandmother had sat together and talked or laughed. Nicola's eyes burned with tears and her throat clogged up. She couldn't empty another box that brought up fresh memories of her grandmother—filled with her grandmother's clothes and other items she'd worn in the years before her stroke. Nicola decided to tackle things differently.

Nicola pushed aside the last box of clothes she'd sorted and reached for a box from the early 1980s with her grandfather's name on it.

Jeremiah stopped going through his own box of old Easter decorations to peer at her. "What are you doing with that?"

Nicola scraped at the old tape on the box so she could pull it off. "I'm going through it."

"That doesn't follow my process."

"Well, Grandpa, the process doesn't have to be followed to the letter." She removed the last of the tape.

"Says who?"

"Says me. The girl who is supposed to be breaking rules and trying new things, remember?"

He pursed his lips and shook his head. Showing Nicola exactly where Quinn got her skeptical scowl from. "I saw that interview. They set you up."

"I'm glad you noticed. Everyone else seems to believe I sent that list on purpose."

"Who would send a list like that on purpose?" He pointed at her. "They got ahold of it and smelled a story. I don't like it."

Nicola flipped back the top on the box. "I don't either."

"So why are you going through with it?"

She sat back on her heels and sighed. Her reasons had all sounded logical when she'd had Stacie on the phone. In her grandfather's dusty attic, with his don't come at me with any bull personality, she didn't feel as confident in her decision. "It'll be good publicity and hopefully bring in more business."

He grunted. "There you go again."

"What's that supposed to mean?"

"You and your excuses for why everything has to be about work and that cosmetics company. You're always thinking of an angle. Always trying to make your mom and sister respect you."

"I am not trying to earn their respect. I'm trying to turn an embarrassing situation into something good. This will be fun for me."

Jeremiah did not look convinced. "Amazing how you've found a way to turn something that's supposed to be fun for you into something to do with work."

"If I don't turn this into something that will benefit Queen Couture, I not only put our account with Desiree in jeopardy but all of our clients. I can't have them think the fancy perfumer they trust is really a fuddy duddy. I might as well turn this embarrassment into a win."

He shook his head and went back to rifling through his box of stuff. "Or you could just try to enjoy yourself."

"I enjoy myself all the time. Thank you very much."

She looked away from what was sure to be a frustrated scowl to the box next to her. The dim light of the attic glinted off what looked like toys. Her brows drew together. Unfamiliar toys. She pulled out a black cape and top hat. Decks of cards. A microphone, sequined vest, and thin black stick.

"What is all this?"

Jeremiah shuffled over. His brows rose and then a smile creased his face. "My magic kit."

Nicola swung around. The giddy excitement in his voice was something she'd never heard from him. "Magic kit? Whoa, wait a second. You like magic?"

He lowered to the floor beside her and ran wrinkled hands over the items. "I thought she threw this stuff away." His eyes glistened and his lips trembled.

Nicola placed a hand on his shoulder. "You know grandma wouldn't throw away any of your stuff."

He shook his head and cleared his throat. "No, you don't understand. Your grandmother almost left me over this. She said either get a real job or get out."

"W-what?" Nicola sputtered. "I never knew Grandma almost left you." The idea was ludicrous. Her grandparents had always seemed perfect for each other. Grandma Cindy was able to easily soothe Grandpa Jeremiah's ruffled feathers.

His laugh was filled with nostalgia and melancholy. "Midlife crisis. That's what she called it. I'd always wanted to perform, you know. Be on stage in front of people. So I started dabbling with magic. Learned a few tricks. Added a few jokes. People hired me to do birthday parties and things like that. I got it in my head that I could be good. Do it up. So much so that I quit my job at the bank."

Nicola placed a hand over her mouth trying, unsuccessfully, to hide her smile. "You didn't seriously do that?"

"Where do you think your mom got her dramatic personality from. It definitely wasn't from your grandmother."

Her mom could be dramatic. Tending to go with wherever her impulses lead. Part of the reason she left a good job at L'Oréal to start her own cosmetics company. Her grandfather, on the other hand, always seemed to be so taciturn.

"But you were always so serious."

Jeremiah chuckled and twirled the wand between his fingers. "Which is why I wanted to do something fun. I loved your grandmother. Loved the kids. But raising a family isn't always fun or fulfilling. I wouldn't ever leave my responsibilities, but getting on that stage gave me a little bit of joy I didn't get at home when we had to worry about bills, braces, and bad bosses. Your grandmother indulged me until I quit my job. She didn't think I should follow flighty ideas. So, I quit. Got my job back at the bank and moved on. Before I could even consider getting back on stage, she had that stroke. After that, all I wanted to do was take care of her." His voice cracked on the last. He blinked several times. He may complain, but the love between her grandparents was real and had always been apparent. "I never believed she would have kept this."

"Because she was so against the idea?"

"She said one day when the kids got out if I still wanted to play magic then I could again. But I thought she was just trying to humor me."

Nicola thought about how she'd given up her original plans in order to help her family's business. She didn't regret it. She would do it all over again. There was no way she could watch her mom's company fail if she had the ability to make it succeed. Still, she knew what it was like to make a change for others and put your own dreams on hold.

"Well, maybe you should."

His curious gaze met hers. "What?"

"I'm doing the things I always wanted, maybe you should, too."

He shook his head. "I don't know."

"Just think about it. Grandma obviously realized you loved entertaining people, otherwise she wouldn't have kept your stuff. She's not here to tell you to try, but I am. So try."

A slow smile spread across his face. With a soft sigh, he placed the top hat on his head and nodded. "Maybe I will. But that means you, too."

"I am, Grandpa, everyone who saw me on that television show knows I'm going to try something new."

"Don't just focus on stuff on your list for publicity. Pick something that you really want to do and do that, too." His stomach rumbled and he checked his watch. "Time for a break. Want a sandwich?"

"Sure." As she left the dusty attic to go make a sandwich with her grandfather, Nicola thought about something she really wanted right now that wasn't on her list. Make Desiree's perfume the most successful out there topped her list. There wasn't much outside of that.

Yes there is. Just admit it.

"What are you thinking about?" Jeremiah asked while he spread mayonnaise on bread.

Nicola smiled. "About signing up for a pottery class."

Chapter 9

"Please let this be a good idea."

Nicola whispered the thought to herself for the third time as she sat with six other members of Damien Hawkins's latest pottery class. She'd barely gotten in on time. Thanks to the persuasive tactics of LeShawn—tactics that were used in earnest after accidentally sending the list to television producers—Nicola was allowed to slip into the hard to get into class.

They were spread out between two long rectangular tables in the art studio behind his gallery. Shelves filled with pottery in various stages of completion, a variety of clay, and buckets of stains lined the walls. Paint stains covered the tables, floor, and the wooden stools they sat on. A row of pottery wheels was lined up between two doors marked office and storage.

She was excited to be there, but after meeting Damien, she wondered what he'd think of her sliding her way into his class. He had to know about her embarrassment on *Your Morning Wake-Up Call*. LeShawn had used Nicola's appearance as a reason why she wanted to sign up in the first place. Maybe he'd taken pity on the woman who had no passion for what she did in her life, or he hoped to gain cross publicity based on her embarrassment. Regardless of the reason, Nicola was going to try and enjoy this. She'd convinced her grandfather to do magic on stage, the least she could do was honor her promise to do something for her, unrelated to the promise she'd made to America on national television.

A dark-haired woman who looked to be in her mid-forties and wore a pair of stained jeans and a Hawkeye Pottery t-shirt stood at the front of the room. "Hello, everyone, I'm Fran Cogdin, and I'm one of the master potters who works with Damien at Hawkeye Pottery. I'm happy to welcome you to our newest class and I hope you not only learn a little about making pottery, but also learn something about yourself. Every person puts a little piece of themselves into the things they create. You may be surprised by what you put into your work over the next six weeks."

Several people in the class nodded and grinned as if they couldn't wait to begin the journey of art and self-discovery. Nicola could barely stop herself from rolling her eyes. She didn't need yet another expectation that she find herself.

"I'm with you." The man to her left leaned in. "I'm just here because my wife went to this class a year ago and loved it. She says I need to learn to be creative."

He was older, with pale skin, kind brown eyes behind frameless glasses, a neatly trimmed grey hair and beard, and a slim build. Immediately she got the sense he was a no-nonsense kind of person like her grandfather. She immediately liked him.

"I convinced my grandfather to do something different and promised him I'd do the same," Nicola said. "Learning pottery seemed like a safe bet."

He held out his hand. "Larry Goldberg."

"Nicola King." She returned his handshake.

Fran continued her introduction. "I will be taking you

through this six-week journey of discovery and creation. Damien will check in once a week to view your progress and answer any questions you may have related to making pottery."

A woman at the next table raised her hand. "He won't be teaching himself?"

Fran shook her head. "No. He wants to introduce more people to the joys of working with clay, but as you can imagine, he doesn't have the time to commit to teaching the class."

Larry leaned toward Nicola. "He's very busy you see."

Nicola covered her grin. Yeah, she was going to enjoy sitting next to Larry. His remark had distracted her from the flame of disappointment that tried to ignite at Fran's announcement. Disappointment quickly followed by an overwhelming relief. Not having Damien You-Don't-Have-Passion-In-Your-Voice look over her shoulder for six weeks would make the class better.

Less pressure. Less distraction. Less temptation.

After a basic housekeeping message of how the class would progress, first making items by hand, then moving on to the wheel, Fran went around the room so everyone could introduce themselves and say what they hoped to learn from the class. Nicola said she hoped to learn more about the basics of pottery. No one seemed to recognize her from the television show and she preferred to keep it that way for now.

After that was done, Fran showed them where the clay and other materials were stored. The class put on aprons to protect their clothes before Fran jumped into the day's lesson on the different types of clay and working it with their hands.

Even though Fran continued talking about letting your *inner self* guide your hands and allowing your *essence* to flow, Nicola stopped herself from laughing every time Larry rolled his eyes whenever Fran told them to "become one with the clay," and followed the techniques taught between the spiritual therapy lessons.

Their assignment was to make whatever came to mind. Whatever the clay told them it needed to be. A piece of instruction that annoyed her the moment Fran said the words. Sure, her imagination helped her when she made scents, but she also had a brief to follow, and the knowledge of how various chemicals would react. Some sort of starting point. How was she supposed to know what the clay needed to be? The possibilities of what to make were endless. A lopsided bowl? A long roll she could call a snake? A circular bracelet or a dozen rings?

She'd spent her adult life making things in a lab, but not something solid she could hold in her hands. Eventually, she stopped thinking about what to make and squeezed the clay. Surprisingly, she enjoyed the feel of the stiff cool material becoming soft and pliable in her hands. Slowly, Nicola's mind cleared. Her fingers worked to turn the lump of clay into something. She wasn't sure what exactly. If Fran asked what she was making, she could say she was letting the clay do the talking and Fran would believe her.

"That's interesting. What are you making?"

The question, spoken in a smooth tenor voice with mild humor lacing through, sent a tremor across her skin. Her head snapped up and she spun around on her stool. Her foot made hard contact with the side of Damien's knee. He swore and skipped back a step.

"Oh no, I'm so sorry." She reached out a hand to grab his knee, but he'd moved forward and her fingers brushed his crotch. Her face burst into flames. She snatched her hand back. Great, she was groping the man.

He waved her off. "Not a problem," he said massaging his knee. "I didn't mean to startle you. I thought you heard me come in."

She glanced around. The rest of the class watched them. Embarrassment crawled across her entire body. "No, I was focused on this." She pointed to the clay in front of her.

"I noticed." His thick brows were still pulled together with the remnants of the pain she'd caused, but he no longer rubbed his knee and eased toward her. "You seemed absorbed in your work. That's why I came over to see what you were creating."

His clay, cedar wood, and bergamot scent teased her. His dreads were pulled up in a loose bun that should have looked silly. Smoky dark eyes, the tight, stain splattered t-shirt, and masculine ease combatted any thoughts of anything being remotely silly about this man.

Damien slid into the space between her and Larry to get a better look at the lopsided creation in front of her. Her side tingled as if he'd touched her even though he hadn't. She scooted away. She didn't want to tingle because of him.

"I'm just playing around," she said, feeling foolish for not at least trying to make something recognizable.

"The class is a joke to you?"

Her eyes shot up to his. "No."

The corner of his mouth lifted. Humor brightened his eyes. "Calm down. I'm only teasing."

Heat spread through her face again. "Oh, I didn't know you were capable of teasing."

"I'm capable of a lot of things." He indicated with his head toward her clay. "What is it?"

Her previous idea of saying she was listening to the clay seemed trite with him now. "I don't know. I can't figure out what to make." She glanced around at the other people at her table. Mostly bowls and asymmetrical plates.

"Is it you?"

She shrugged. "More than likely. I always get in my head and it causes me to overthink."

"No, I mean is the person you're making, you or someone else?" His finger ran across the edges of her work.

Nicola frowned. "I'm not making a person."

"That's what it looks like."

Nicola studied what she considered to be an elongated star-shaped lump and tried to see what he saw. She tilted her head to one side then the other. Now that he mentioned it, her work did kind of look like a really bad gingerbread figure.

"I don't know who it is," she mumbled.

"I think it's you," he continued. "A self-portrait."

Nicola didn't bother to suppress her disbelieving snort. "I look like a gingerbread person?"

He chuckled at her response. She liked his laugh. He gave her a once over. "I don't know. You don't have the stiff arms for a gingerbread figure."

Nicola laughed and shook her head. "Seriously, I wasn't making a self-portrait or anything. I was just playing around. Wouldn't that be kind of conceited. Making something in my own image the first lesson?"

"Not at all. Doing a self-portrait is often the hardest thing to do. You have to really look inside of yourself in order to be authentic. If you're choosing to really take a look at what's inside of you then that can be scary. It takes a brave person to take that first step toward self-discovery."

Damn, she hadn't expected him to get kind of deep on her. He studied her. No traces of sarcasm or joking in his features. Studied her as if he were trying to unlock her secrets.

She shook her head and broke eye contact. No, a guy who got as many panties thrown as him as Idris Elba was not trying to unlock her boring secrets.

"I'm not typically very brave," Nicola said.

"I'd bet you're braver than you think you are. Don't ever underestimate yourself."

Her gaze jumped up, but he was already turning away. "Mr. Goldberg, show me what you're working on."

She frowned, then focused back on her own work. Her heart rate had jumped in speed with his simple encouraging words. Here she was about to read something into it. Wonder if he was possibly flirting. Not that she'd flirt back, but she could at least keep the thrill of having him flirt with her close through the upcoming weeks as she tried to figure out how to make Desiree's perfume more exciting. Instead, he was just giving generic encouragement. Encouragement he more than likely gave to every other student who took a class at his studio.

No need getting all excited. Damien Hawkins did not have time to flirt with or entertain the fantasies of the wide-eyed and thirsty women who inevitably joined his classes. She would focus on what she was here to do. Learn to open another creative outlet. Further her skills. Not fall for a guy like Damien.

Her grandfather called when she got home later that night. It was nearly nine and he didn't typically call this late. Correction, he didn't typically call out of the blue at all.

She raised a brow and hurried to answer his call. "Hello?" She picked up the remote lying next to her on the couch and turned down the television.

"Nicola, I found a show!" he announced in an excited tone.

"A show?" She relaxed a little. He didn't sound as if anything was wrong. Thank God. But the jubilation in his voice still made her wary.

"A magic show!" He spoke the words in a hurry-up-and-catch-up voice. "I was down at the senior center the other day. I started going every once in a while, for the card games.

Your grandmother said the people there were nice. Well, they wrangled me into taking her place on the board, so she should have said manipulative. Anyway, I saw they were having sign-ups for a talent show this spring. I figured, what the hell, and signed us up."

The congratulations on the tip of her tongue were stymied by his words. "Us? Wait a second, Grandpa, what do you mean us?"

"You're going to be my assistant, aren't you?"

Nicola sat up straight. "Since when did I become your assistant?" The pitch of her voice rose with each word.

"Since you convinced me that your grandmother must have wanted me to keep doing magic. Every good magician has a lovely assistant. Why not my favorite grandbaby?" The grandfatherly guilt oozing through the phone was strong.

"Don't try to butter me up with flattery." Nicola folded her knees up and wrapped an arm around them. Despite his obvious attempt to guilt her into participating, she smiled. She couldn't remember her grandfather being this excited about anything.

"I'm not trying to butter you up. I'm your grandfather and I can tell you what to do. Now come up next weekend and we can start practicing."

Nicola cringed. "I can't come up next weekend. I've got plans."

"Make it work, Nicola. Remember, you're doing things you normally wouldn't do." No more guilt, this time his words were edged with the don't ignore my command she was used to.

"Being in a talent show at the senior center is not on my list," she countered.

"Maybe, but spending more time with your family is. This is how I want you to spend time with me. Are you going to do it?"

She was about to argue when an idea struck. One that would either get her out of this completely or have the potential to be good on film. "Only if you let me have cameras at the talent show."

"Deal!" he said faster than she expected. "It may be my ticket to stardom. Thanks, Nicola. See you this weekend."

With that he hung up, and Nicola was pretty sure she'd been played.

Chapter 10

"Well, how did the class with your crush go?" Shonda asked Nicola the next day as they had lunch at Maggiano's.

Nicola had spent the entire morning tweaking the formula on the samples she'd gone over with Desiree. To be sure, she hadn't missed anything, she'd also gone to the original brief and started up a new mixture. Nicola planned to overnight some of the samples for Desiree to try while on tour. She didn't want the process to slow down, or for Desiree to come back and hate everything with little time for Nicola to make adjustments.

When Shonda called and asked her to lunch, she'd considered saying no. In the end, staying cooped up in her lab wasn't going to make her find something brilliant any faster. She needed the break and, in an effort to do better, she took the break.

"It wasn't class with my crush." Nicola pulled off a piece of the bread on her plate and dipped it into the olive oil mixed with cracked pepper. The smell of pepper, garlic, and yeast made her mouth water. She'd burned off the granola bar she'd grabbed from the stash LeShawn kept in the office and two cups of coffee she'd had for breakfast hours ago. "It was just a pottery class."

Shonda wiggled her perfectly arched brows. "Taught by the guy you've been Instagram stalking for almost a year."

"It's not Instagram stalking I'm—"

"Admiring his work. Yeah. I've heard you say that," Shonda said in a no-nonsense tone of voice. "According to Quinn, you were all the way undressing him with your eyes at the art society luncheon the other day."

She considered tossing a piece of the bread at Shonda, but she was too hungry to waste it. "Will you two stop! Damien is a professional. I'm taking a class at his studio. Which is being taught by one of his apprentices, for your information."

Shonda's shoulders hunched. "You mean he doesn't come through at all."

"He did last night, but he won't come through every class. He's really busy and focused on his own projects. Which makes sense."

"You sound disappointed."

"A lot of the people in the class are disappointed." Herself included. But after last night's flirting that wasn't flirting, she hoped he didn't come through often. No need to give herself further opportunities to make a fool of herself.

Shonda let out a huge sigh and sat back in her seat. "Quinn is going to be upset. You know she's expecting you to sleep with Damien before the class ends."

Bread stuck in Nicola's throat. Coughing, she picked up her water glass and took a long swallow. "You and my sister will be disappointed. Damien is not interested in me."

"You don't know that."

"I do. There are absolutely no sparks there."

Not on his part at least. No way was she telling her friend

or sister about his lack of passion comment. Sure, he'd given her a compliment last night, but that was related to her lopsided creation. Nothing flirty or sexy about their interactions. For all she knew he had a girlfriend. He'd never posted anything like that, but his page was devoted to his art. He obviously liked to keep his personal life private. Which meant he could be married with five kids.

The thought made the bread feel like a lump in her stomach.

"Fine, I'll let you live in that fantasy Miss I'm Blind to Flirting. Why don't you tell me about what you're going to do next on your list?"

Another topic she'd prefer not to talk about. "I don't know. Stacie is getting really anxious for me to pick something for them to record. So far I haven't done anything really inspiring or exciting." She hadn't told Stacie about the magic show yet because she still hoped to convince her grandad to let her off the hook. Doubtful, but a woman could dream.

Shonda sat up straight and her eyes brightened. "You can go with me and Quinn to Cancun."

"I thought you two were going this weekend?" She was disciplined enough to not sound salty about Shonda and Quinn's plans to vacation without her. As much as she knew a trip to Cancun would make Stacie and the rest of the *Your Morning Wake-Up Call* team get excited, Nicola couldn't be out of the office right now. Not with the Desiree project ongoing.

Shonda's head fell back and she groaned. "It didn't work out," she lowered her head and met Nicola's eye. "My ex wants to be uncooperative and say he can't watch the kids. I'd call BS, but I know this really is the busy time for him at work. We've decided to put it off for a month or so. Which means, now you can go."

She was about to say no. Already all the things she needed to get done on top of the project for Desiree popping in her head. They'd received briefs from half a dozen other potential clients who wanted them to make perfume. Not to mention the normal, year-round projects such as the seasonal soap scent she was working on. Tia could handle some of the work. Especially now that they had interns, but she couldn't delegate everything to the other perfumers.

Nicola could envision Tia and LeShawn's eye roll if she gave that excuse in the office. Wasn't the point of her agreeing to do the stuff on her list that she had to stop making excuses to avoid doing things she really wanted to do? To say to heck with the schedule and take some risks?

"You know what. Let's do it. Schedule the trip and I'll go."

Shonda's eyes narrowed. "For real?" Nicola met her eye and nodded. Shonda clapped her hands and shimmied in her seat. "Great! Quinn is going to be so excited. We are going to have such a great time."

The waitress came with their lunch. She placed their plates down and refilled their drinks before leaving. They took a moment of silence before digging in. She'd ordered lasagna, one of her favorite foods, and as expected, it was delicious. Her original plan was to order a salad, but that wasn't what she wanted. She was living her best life and all of that.

"I want to do everything you did on spring break in college," Nicola said after swallowing a bite of food. "I missed it the last time and you had so much fun. I don't want to miss out this time."

"Okay, but I'm too old to take a row of lemon drop shots." Shonda pointed her fork at Nicola. "We'll have to take that off the list."

Instead of agreeing, Nicola shook her head. "Nope, shots and everything. We're going to have a great time."

"If that's the case, why do you sound afraid?" Shonda asked, grinning.

"Because this is crazy and I wish they never saw my list, but I've got to do something, so why not take shots in Cancun."

"Don't worry," Shonda said. "This really is a great idea. You need to get out and live the life you recreate in a lab. Stop focusing on capturing perfection in a bottle. Get out and smell the roses, spring rain, and mountain streams you imitate."

Nicola scrunched up her nose and shook her head. "I've never made a mountain stream. Streams don't smell nice."

"You know what I mean. You'll have fun while bringing attention to Queen Couture. This is a win-win."

Nicola nodded. "You're right. This will be good." She sighed. "But the Cancun trip is months away. Stacie wants something now."

Shonda gasped then gave Nicola a sly grin. "You know who I saw the other day?"

The you're never gonna guess slickness in her friend's tone made Nicola nervous. Far be it from the universe to not throw Nicola another ridiculous surprise. "I don't know, but I'm assuming you brought this up because you have a point."

"I saw Bobby Bradford the other day."

Nicola shook her head. "No. Do not go there."

Bobby Bradford was the guy she'd been crazy in love with in college. The one who'd also gotten married a year after graduation. The guy she always regretted never going for because Quinn swore Bobby had been just as crazy about Nicola as she'd been about him.

"Yes, I'm going there. I saw the list."

Her fork dropped to her plate with a loud clatter. "How did you see the list?" Her high-pitched shriek drew the attention of people sitting at the table near them.

"It's posted on the *Wake Up Call* website."

"What! No!" Nicola covered her face with her hands. Why would they do that? Had she agreed to that?

"It's okay, just a few things. Mostly the same stuff they mentioned on the show. And asking out Bobby Bradford was on the list."

"No, it's not," Nicola said. She was certain no names were involved related to the items on her regrets list.

"Asking out a guy you like and not ignoring the signs is on the list. And we both know Bobby is *the guy.*"

He was. She couldn't ask Bobby out. "He's married."

Shonda shook her head. "They split. I saw something he posted on Facebook about a year ago."

"Are you sure?"

"Yes, pretty sure."

So, Bobby was divorced. Maybe the woman he'd gotten with a year after college hadn't been the one for him. Obviously, if they weren't together anymore. What if this was her second chance? What if this was the universe saying go for it?

"He's back in Atlanta?" Nicola asked.

"Yep, just moved back. Gave me his number and said to hit him up sometime. Right after asking about you."

He asked about her? The knowledge shouldn't have made her feel like grinning or sent bubbles of eagerness through her belly. Why not call Bobby? He *was* the one who'd gotten away. She had no other prospects in her life. Nothing would happen with Damien. That had been just a silly admiration. Whereas Bobby was real, and probably put back in her circle by fate.

Nicola sat back and sipped her water. "Okay. Give me his number."

★ ★ ★

She waited until she was back in her office before giving Bobby a call. Her hands were slick. Her stomach clenched as if she were driving a hundred miles an hour down a busy highway. Heart pounding and breathless. She hadn't seen or spoken to Bobby in years. He might not even remember her.

Except, Shonda said he'd asked about her. He did remember her. That didn't mean he was still interested. A lot of time had passed. For all she knew, Bobby might still be married with kids by now.

He wouldn't have given his number to Shonda or asked about you if he were married. Would he?

Only one way to find out. She dialed his number and hit send before she could think about it anymore. She'd already paced her office a dozen times.

"Hello?" A curious baritone came through the phone.

Her heart did a flip. Her stomach did, too. She wasn't sure if it was excitement or nausea. "Hey, Bobby Bradford, this is Nicola King. I got your number from Shonda."

Two seconds passed when Nicola wanted to drop through a hole to the center of the Earth before he spoke again.

"Nicola, hey girl! How have you been?"

Her shoulders relaxed. He remembered her. Good first step. She paced the room. "I've been good. Really good."

"You still working in chemistry?"

Her cheeks hurt from her grin. "Yeah, still doing that. How about you?"

"I work quality control for a pesticide manufacturer. Still some chemistry, but mostly the boring administrative stuff."

He spoke in a self-depreciating manner. Bobby had gotten awesome grades in school. If he was working in chemistry, she didn't doubt he was leading up whatever section he worked in.

"Cool, sounds great."

"Actually, it's really boring."

She let out a stiff laugh. "Okay, sounds terrible." Could she get any worse at flirting?

He laughed as if he appreciated her silly joke. "It's good to hear from you," he said warmly. "I remember how much fun we'd have when we worked in chemistry lab together."

"I know. All those late nights." She cleared her throat. Now or never. "So, Bobby, are you seeing anyone?"

"Why?" he asked quickly.

"I was just curious," she replied feeling defensive. Had she crossed the line too soon?

"There's usually more than curiosity behind those types of questions. Tell the truth. Why did you ask?"

Nicola took a deep breath. Now or never. "Okay . . . I was wondering if you were free to hang out sometime."

"Hang out? Like college?"

Why was he making this so hard? "No, like a . . . date."

"Sure. When?"

There. She'd done it. Asked a guy out and the world still spun. Time ticked on. The sun kept shining. Her heart slowed down. She wanted to laugh and spin in a circle. This had been super easy. Why had she waited so long?

"How about this weekend?"

"What time?" He sounded excited.

Her confidence soared. She'd asked out a guy and he was excited about going out with her. "I've got to go to Aiken on Saturday to help my grandad, but we can meet for drinks or coffee on Sunday."

"Drinks sounds great. Text me the place and I'll meet you there."

"Great. I'll do that." She did a hip shimmy and opened her mouth to let out a silent, jubilant scream. She was going out with Bobby Bradford!

"I can't wait to see you." His voiced dipped an octave.

Shivers went down her spine. "Same here."

Their call ended and Nicola clapped her hands. This scratching things off her list thing was turning out to be a pretty damn good idea.

Chapter 11

Her grandfather's excitement hadn't diminished by the time Nicola arrived at his place on Saturday morning. He waved her in and pulled her into the living room. There, all of the items from his box upstairs were laid out on the couch and the coffee table.

"I got everything cleaned up and ready to go," Jeremiah said. His dark eyes were bright as he examined all his props. "I wanted to make sure everything still looked good. Of course, if you think we need to get matching outfits or something. I thought maybe purple sequins or—"

"No matching outfits." Nicola picked up his cape and sat on the couch. She spread the satin material out over her legs. "And no sequins."

"Why not? Most two person acts try to match each other. What are you going to wear on stage?"

She honestly had not thought that far ahead, but she didn't plan to wear matching outfits. When she'd mentioned the magic show to Stacie at *Your Morning Wake-Up Call* after telling her about Cancun, the producer had loved both ideas. Nicola had agreed to let her brief stint into the world of magic be filmed for prosperity, but that didn't mean she had to get up there looking like a disco ball.

"I was thinking black pants and a button up white shirt. Simple and classic, without taking any of the attention away from you."

Her grandfather frowned for several seconds before nodding. "I guess that's fine. Though I liked the idea of us doing something snazzy. Since I'm coming out of retirement, I want to make sure I return to the stage with a big splash."

"Have you already figured out what tricks you're going to do."

He held up a finger. "I don't *trick* people. Magic isn't about doing tricks. It's about creating illusions. Making the mind see things that it can't comprehend."

"Oh, well excuse me, sir," Nicola said raising a hand to her chest. "I didn't mean to insult your work."

He rolled his eyes. "Laugh all you want. When we finish, it'll be to a standing ovation. I used to always bring people to their feet when I performed."

She hoped he didn't get his hopes up too high. Nicola loved a good magic show as much as the next person. If she could remember attending a magic show. She had seen them on television before, and they always seemed fun. But those shows were put on by famous and skilled magicians. People who'd worked on their *illusions* for years. Her grandfather hadn't done a single magic trick in thirty years. She doubted they'd be booed off the stage at a senior center show, but that didn't mean they would also get a standing ovation either.

"What illusions have you put together?" she asked instead. Focusing on the show instead of her grandfather's visions of fame.

"I found my old notebook." He picked up a composition notebook. The pages were yellowed with age. "It's got some of my oldies but goodies in here. I was also going to check out YouTube."

"YouTube?"

"Yeah, your sister told me that you can find instructions on how to do anything on YouTube. She's right. I even fixed my dishwasher last month thanks to that site."

"Grandpa, why are you fixing your dishwasher? You can get someone to help you with that."

"I can also do things myself. What do you want me to do? Sit up in this house twiddling my thumbs?"

She didn't want him fiddling around with heavy appliances or cutting his grass in ninety-degree heat. He was right about needing something to keep him busy, but the last thing their family needed was for him to get hurt doing things around the house that would strain him.

"You're not twiddling your thumbs. You're focusing on a magic show. The best magic show ever, therefore, the next time something needs to be done around here you should call me or Mom. We'll help you figure out how to get it fixed."

"I'm not too old to take care of myself."

"No one said you were. Now, can we get back to the show? Tell me more about what you found online."

That took the disgruntled look off his face. He shifted over to sit next to her on the couch and opened his notebook. "First, let's go through some of my basic illusions."

He smiled and told her stories about where he'd first performed some of his illusions when he was younger. He'd started off doing magic for birthday parties and eventually, thanks to the jokes he'd tell, did shows at business and other corporate events. They went through posters he'd saved announcing his shows and even a few pictures of him on stage.

"Man, Grandpa, I still can't believe it." Nicola held up one of the polaroid pictures of her grandfather. He wore the cape and a black and white tuxedo. In his hand he held cards as he performed one of his card tricks. A huge smile creased his younger face. The joy in what he was doing was apparent even in the still shot.

"Why not?"

"Because, this was obviously a big part of your life at one time. You never once mentioned it."

He shrugged. "The kids weren't interested in my magic. Your mom and her brother and sisters were embarrassed. They couldn't stand it when I tried to entertain their friends who came to the house."

"Why didn't you show me and my cousins when we came along?"

"I figured you wouldn't be interested either." He took the picture from her hand and studied it. "By then magic was just a distant memory."

"How about I invite everyone to the show," Nicola said. The idea striking her instantly.

"Everyone like who?" he asked suspiciously.

"Mom, Auntie and Uncle, Quinn and my cousins. The entire family. Let's invite them to your reintroduction into the world of entertainment. Let's show the family how brilliant you are."

"You haven't even seen me perform. How do you know I'm brilliant?"

She squeezed his arm. "Because I'm brilliant, and I am descended from you."

"Silly girl." He brushed her hand away and stood, but not before Nicola caught the smile on his lips. "Want something to eat?"

"Sure."

Jeremiah headed toward the kitchen. Nicola picked up

the few scattered pictures and programs from his past. He stopped at the door. "You can let them know about the show, but don't make it a big deal. I don't want the family to feel obligated to show up."

"I won't."

He nodded. "Good. Not like I need all of y'all there getting in the way anyway. I like my privacy." He went into the kitchen grumbling the entire time about how family always showed up and made things complicated.

Nicola grinned and shook her head. Looks like her family would get an up close and personal seat at her public debut. She didn't care. She'd also get her mom and Quinn to bug everyone to show up for the show. Looks like the family she was going to spend more time with was going to expand.

Chapter 12

The next morning, Nicola woke up and started her normal routine. She showered, dressed, checked emails, and thought about what project she was going to work on in the lab that morning. She'd lost an entire working day on Saturday with her grandfather.

Not that she regretted it in the least. He'd tried to act annoyed as she'd called Quinn and her mom to get them on board with inviting the rest of the family to his show. Yet, she'd caught the gleam of joy in his eye whenever he didn't think she was looking.

For all the fun she'd had yesterday, she really needed to get caught up today. Especially since she was meeting Bobby later that night for drinks. She'd mentioned the date to Stacie, who asked about bringing cameras. Nicola expected Bobby to say no, or even cancel when she'd called to confirm the date and mentioned the cameras. Instead, he'd seemed excited about the idea of being on television. She was officially excited.

She scanned her kitchen for her keys. The quicker she got to the lab the quicker she could get back here and prep for her date. Her keys lay on the kitchen counter in a perfect ray of sun shining through the window. Nicola picked them up. The warmth of the sun warmed the back of her hand even through the window.

She looked outside. The morning was bright and clear. Few clouds in the sky. Birds flying around. If she went out there, she'd hear the sound of someone's lawn mower going. See her neighbors sitting on their porches drinking coffee.

A perfect Sunday morning. How many times had she told herself she would take off work and go to the Sunday morning farmers market? Just as many times as she'd talked herself out of going because there was work to do. Or an event to attend. Or she'd decided not to go because Quinn didn't *"do"* farmers markets, or Shonda had her kids and didn't want to bring them with her.

Not today. She didn't want to go to work. She didn't want to spend this beautiful Sunday morning hanging out in a lab. Making things that smelled like flowers, nature, and tropical vacations. She would do something different today.

She wasn't even going to call Quinn or Shonda for backup. She was a grown woman and could go to the farmer's market on her own. She clutched the keys and strode out the door with purpose.

She was proud of herself until she had to find a parking space. Never venturing to the market meant she hadn't realized how crowded this place could get. She eventually found a parking space, then had to walk too many blocks from her car to the market for the black flats she'd planned to wear to the office. Her sneakers were at work, the only place she'd needed comfortable shoes so far.

The beautiful rays of sunshine that had driven her out in the first place felt like burning laser beams as she walked. Sweat beaded on her skin until her blouse stuck to her back. She needed something to drink and settled for an overpriced bottle of water from one of the food vendors.

She sucked down the lukewarm water. What the hell had she been thinking? Obviously, not how miserable the farmers market could be on a hot Sunday in Georgia.

Taking a deep breath, she decided to try to make the best of things and enjoy the day. She strolled through the vendors. Admiring in the craft jewelry, locally sourced food, fruits, and vegetables. Though she tried to be optimistic about her jaunt out to do something different, she couldn't ignore the growing discomfort in her feet. The sweat continuing to trickle down her back. How long the lines were to purchase any of the items she was interested in. The market was crowded with people everywhere.

Hot and tired, Nicola was ready to go back to her car when a painting of a bright sunflower in a store window behind a bowl she recognized as Damien's pottery caught her attention. She walked toward the store window. The name Sienna Sun Gallery and Lounge was painted in bright orange letters on the door. Intrigued, Nicola wandered inside. The air conditioning in the gallery hit her sweat-slicked skin and sent a wonderful chill over her. A welcome relief after her trek through the Sunday farmers market. The lights were bright and highlighted the happy and colorful paintings on the walls. Shelves with decorated wine glasses, books, handmade crafts, and pottery filled the space.

"Good morning!" the young woman behind the counter called to her. "Let me know if you need help finding anything."

"Thank you, I will," Nicola replied.

There was a door to a large space connected to the gallery. A stage was on the far end, round tables in the center, and couches along the wall. More artwork hung in that space.

"We have music and dinner in there every night on the weekends," the woman said from the counter. "You should come back and check out one of our shows."

"Maybe I will." She mentally added that to her list. Maybe

this would be a good date spot if things worked out with Bobby.

No maybe—this *would* be a good spot. He'd always seen her in class or in a lab. They talked chemistry and occasionally movies or television. He needed to see her in a more laid-back setting.

"What time is the show tonight?" she asked.

"We start at eight."

Nicola wandered away from the show room and over to the display of Damien's pottery. His classic pieces with the signature blue-grey and marbled orange glaze.

"Those are great, aren't they?" the woman said. "We're the only local gallery allowed to sell his pottery."

"It is beautiful. I'm actually taking the class at his studio right now."

"Oh, that's dope! How do you like it?"

She looked forward to the next class and had thought a lot about what she would work on next. This time she would surrender to whatever her mind wanted to create while working with the clay as she did when she first started making scents. For all her scoffing about Fran's comment that they would find themselves with the clay, she was doing just that.

"I'm really enjoying it."

"I'm glad to hear it," a caramel-smooth male voice answered.

She spun around. Her purse bumped into a podium and the vase on it wobbled. She and Damien both lunged forward to stop the catastrophe. The tips of their fingers brushed as they steadied the stand. The touch rattled her just as much as she'd rattled the podium.

"You're really good at sneaking up on me," she said.

Damien's smile was a flash of white teeth against his brown skin. The beginnings of a beard darkened his square jawline. She didn't like beards, typically, but she liked the way his facial hair framed his lips. "You're really good at getting lost in your thoughts and tuning out the rest of the world."

"What are you doing in here?"

He pointed over his shoulder to the lounge area. "Visiting with the owner. He's a friend of mine. Another friend is playing in the show tonight."

She wasn't surprised to find out he had friends here, considering this was one of the only places to purchase his pottery away from his gallery. "Are you coming back for the show?"

He shrugged. The thin material of his black t-shirt strained with the casual movement. One thick silver chain rested around his neck. "Thinking about it. You?"

"Thinking about it," she replied.

He scratched his chin and nodded. "Now tell me. What are you doing in here?"

"Part of my list. No working on Sunday. Go out and enjoy the farmers market." Except now she was sweat-stained and tired while he looked perfectly comfortable and incredibly desirable.

"You haven't been before?" He asked as if it was everyone's duty to attend the farmers market.

"No, and I can't say I'm enjoying it much now." She shifted her purse from one shoulder to the next. "I came in here to cool off. I think I'm going to hike back to my car and call it a day."

He shook his head. "Nah, you can't do that. If you're going to take off and enjoy the day then you need to do that."

"I'll be fine. Plus, I saw some of the farmers market. It's not really for me."

He hitched his head toward the door. "Come on. I'll show you around."

"You don't have to do that."

"I know I don't, but I want to." His lips lifted in a smile.

There was a flutter in her chest. Well, when he asked like that, with that smile, and those eyes, how could she say no?

He took her to nearly every booth at the farmers market and knew almost every vendor there. Most greeted him by first name. Damien told her about the various crafts, foods, or jewelry the people sold. His knowledge about the differences with each of the people out there impressed her.

The weather was still hot, but Damien continued to cool her off with frozen lemonades, ice cream, and other treats as they walked and talked.

"You come here every weekend." It wasn't a question. There was no way he could know so much without coming out regularly.

"Most weekends when they have it. The art community is closely knit. I get to know other artists because being around other creatives helps to replenish my well."

"I never thought of it that way," Nicola said. "I'm always isolated in my lab. Making things that people love, but lately it hasn't been as easy."

"You obviously must be doing pretty good if you were able to get Desiree's attention."

She stopped walking along the busy street to raise a brow at him. "Oh, so you do pay attention to the world of fashion."

He grinned and waved a hand. "I only looked you up because you're in my class. I take an interest in all of my students."

"Okay, sure," she said with an eye roll even though his answering chuckle made her stomach feel squishy. In a good way.

"On the real," he said as they continued walking. "You should consider coming out more. Being around other people making things. You're an artist, too."

"Not hardly." She'd never thought of herself as an artist. A biochemist who happened to stumble into the glamorous world of perfume making, but not an artist.

"You are. You make perfumes and colognes and if I'm right, no two are the same. Which means you have to create something new every time you go into your lab. Art takes many forms. It doesn't have to just be on a canvas or with a lump of clay."

She was silent for a few moments. Considering his words. "You know you were right the other day."

"Right about what?"

"When you said I didn't have the passion in my voice about what I do."

He stopped again and placed his fingers on her arm. Regret deep in his eyes. "Hey, I was out of line for going there. I didn't mean to make you doubt yourself."

"I don't know if it's doubt, or more like fear. Maybe one day people will realize I'm a fluke. I got lucky with one magic formula. How can I possibly sustain it?"

She'd gotten lucky. Lucky no one knew how she really came up with their signature scent. Lucky no one had caught on that every time she went to make another perfume she wondered if this would be the one that tanked. That everyone would finally see she didn't belong. That she'd never belonged.

Damien lightly tapped her arm getting her attention after her mind had wandered into hidden pockets she tried not to delve into. "You have sustained it. From what I can tell about you, you're doing a damn good job making perfumes."

"You really did look me up?" The idea made her feel a bunch of things she probably shouldn't be feeling.

"I really did." His answer was slow and deliberate. As if he couldn't believe he was admitting as much.

She started walking again before she assumed he was flirting. "I'll think about what you said about being around other creatives. I meant what I said back there. I'm really enjoying the class."

Damien's long legs easily kept up with her. He walked close enough for her to breathe in his earthy scent and occasionally brushed against her arm. "Thank you. Even though we can't have as many classes as Fran would like, I think the smaller classes make it easier for people to connect with what we're trying to do."

"I wasn't sure I could become one with the clay like she said."

"Sounded silly, huh?"

Nicola laughed. "Honestly, yes."

"Don't you do the same thing when you're working on a project? Don't you put a piece of yourself in every scent you create?" The question was serious, although he didn't sound as if her earlier laughter had bothered him.

When she felt comfortable with a briefing she received. When she could visually see what the client wanted and the scents just came to her. That's when her work was the most fun. When she became one with her project. "I guess I never thought of it that way."

He tapped his forehead "I know what I'm talking about sometimes. You're a creative person. Expressing yourself through other outlets not only gives you a new experience, it also opens your mind to things you may not have considered before. That's why I try to spend time with different people. Learn what makes them tick. What's visually appealing to them. It helps me as I go back into the studio and work on the next piece. I bet that if you spend more time out of the lab, reconnect with your creative side. Replenish the well, then you'll be even better back in the lab."

She nodded, but didn't answer. Wasn't that what she was doing with her list? Reconnecting and reliving her life. Rediscovering what she liked in order to help her create the essence of perfection in a bottle.

They kept walking down the street. Silent while she let his words sink into her brain. What he said wasn't revolutionary. She'd known that on some level. Everyone knew that. Get out, live life, find ways to care for yourself to avoid burnout. The advice wasn't new, but her drive to actually listen to the advice this time around was new.

"Damien!" a voice called out.

They both turned toward the voice. An older man with a bright smile wearing a butter-yellow shirt with salmon-colored shorts strolled their way. Damien grinned as he walked over to meet the man, and the two of them hugged.

"Louis, what are you doing here?" Damien said.

"You know every time I'm in Atlanta I have to come through here," Louis replied. "I hoped I'd run into you."

Louis looked over Damien's shoulder at Nicola. Damien turned her way. "Louis, this is Nicola. She's in my current class."

Louis reached out a hand. "Nice meeting you."

"Likewise." Nicola shook his hand.

"You're still teaching classes, too, huh," Louis said. "You started with that wheel in your garage and look at what you've accomplished. I saw Shante last week and we talked about how well you're doing."

Damien's body stilled. The smile on his face turned brittle. "Much to her surprise." There was a coolness in his voice now that hadn't been there before.

"Not at all. She knew you'd do great with your pottery. Told me herself. She wishes you well." Louis kept up the cheer, either oblivious to Damien's discomfort or choosing to ignore it.

"I'm sure she does. Look, Louis, it was good to see you, but I've got to get back to the studio."

They hugged again before Damien indicated for her to follow him back the way they came. She shouldn't ask. It was none of her business. Damien didn't owe her any information about his personal life.

"Who's Shante?" The words tumbled out.

"My ex-wife."

"Oh." Explanation given. She didn't have to know more. Obviously, his ex was still a sore spot. "I take it you two don't talk much."

"We don't talk at all. Five years ago, she decided she wanted to live in another country. My pottery was just taking off. I wanted to stay. She insisted she had to go. That she couldn't live her entire life in the Southern United States."

"She left you?"

He shrugged. "Left me sounds harsh. I told her I couldn't leave right now. She said she didn't want to be tied down with a husband back home. After that, the divorce was very quick and very amicable."

Except she heard the pain and disappointment in his voice. Did he still love her? Did his ex-wife still love him?

"It's for the best," he said. "I love my work. I don't want to be tied down either."

"I say the same thing," Nicola replied. "I don't want to get tied down. I love my work."

Damien focused on her but kept walking. "But?"

Her face heated. Embarrassed but somehow feeling okay telling him anyway. "But I have to tell someone I love them. It's on my list. Tell someone I love them. Which means... I guess I need to try one day."

"You've never told a person you loved them?"

"Just my family, but not in a romantic way. It's always seemed too much of a risk."

"It is a risk. That's why I'm not putting myself back out there." He shook his head. His face resolute and determined. "Tried marriage and am not planning to go down that road again."

She understood the resolve in his voice, but that didn't stop her from being disappointed. She'd been right. Damien Hawkins was not a guy she should even consider dating. He was divorced, probably heartbroken, and obviously still upset about the way his marriage ended. She was trying to focus on positive things in her life. Not trying to fix the heart of a man who was giving off clear *I'm not relationship material* signals.

"I don't know," Nicola said. "I'd like to at least try being in love at least once. Which is why I'm going on a date tonight."

He did a double take. "You are?"

"Yes. With a guy I was once afraid to ask out. I called him up and we're going out tonight. Maybe it'll be my chance, you know." She infused her voice with the hope that blossomed out of the disappointment of knowing Damien Hawkins wasn't the man for her.

The corner of Damien's lips tilted up in a half smile. "I hope it is. You seem like a cool woman, Nicola. I hope you find happiness."

Chapter 13

"What are you wearing?"

Nicola glared at Quinn's name on her car's console. She was on the way to meet Bobby for their date and decided to call Quinn. In hindsight, she should have known calling her sister before a date wasn't the best idea. She should have called Shonda for emotional support. Shonda was good at being her "hype man," whereas Quinn was good at making Nicola feel like a social outcast.

"Why do you care what I'm wearing?"

"Because, you were once super into this guy. I'm trying to make sure you don't walk in there looking either too desperate or too boring."

Nicola gritted her teeth. She knew how to dress for a date. It hadn't been that long since she'd gone out. "It's too late now to change. I'm almost there."

"I can probably tell you how to fix things if you've messed up," Quinn continued. Her freight train of advice unable to stop once it barreled down this track. "So, stop being difficult as hell and tell me what you have on."

Nicola sighed and rolled her eyes. "Fine. I'm wearing a black cocktail dress. Nothing too sexy or too formal."

"Which dress?" Quinn shot back skeptically.

"The one I wore to the fashion week luncheon."

"That Calvin Klein dress?" Quinn did not sound impressed.

Nicola glanced down at her dress. She looked good in this dress. "What's wrong with that?"

"Nicola, nothing is wrong with it, but it's... I don't know."

"You just said I shouldn't be too sexy or too boring. This dress is very nice." The black sleeveless dress fit her upper body, flared out at the waist and stopped right above her knees. It was all black except for a white horizontal stripe across the skirt.

"You could have at least shown some cleavage." Quinn tossed out. Disappointment heavy in her voice.

"You're making no sense. Now you say I need cleavage. I don't know why I called you."

"At least tell me you're wearing heels."

She wasn't. She'd chosen a cute pair of flats with black sequin accents. No need to make her sister completely freak out. "Will you stop. What I'm wearing is fine."

There was the rumble of a deep male voice in the background before Quinn said, "Okay, I'll be right there. Just finishing up with Nicola."

"Is that Omar? Tell him I said hello."

"Girl, I left Omar at home. I'm here with Joseph. We're meeting with some of his colleagues to talk about the ad campaign."

The guy from the nightclub that Quinn had been talking to. Nicola glanced at the clock. "It's eight in the evening."

"All work isn't done between nine and five." Quinn chuckled as if Nicola was clueless. When it came to Quinn and what was cool, Nicola was clueless. "You of all people should know that. Look, just try not to spend the entire night talking about chemistry. Ask him lots of questions about himself. Get him talking and then ask more questions. That works with men. It makes them think their life sounds interesting even when it isn't. Smile, don't do that frowning analytical face you do when something doesn't make sense, and if he tries to kiss you at the end of the night let him. It's been way too long since you've gotten any, and you might as well screw Bobby."

Nicola gripped the steering wheel. Might as well screw Bobby? Would it even come to a discussion of them having sex? She shook her head. She would not let Quinn get into her head. This was Bobby. They'd had an easy friendship in college. If she just relaxed then things would go smoothly.

"Geez, any other great advice for your socially awkward sister."

"Nope, that's it." Quinn replied, sounding pleased and ignorant of the sarcasm in Nicola's voice. "Call me when it's done. If I don't answer, text. I may be here a long time and want to make sure you're okay."

"You call me, too. You shouldn't be out late with strangers."

Quinn laughed. Nicola felt as old-fashioned as that statement made her sound. "Okay, I'll text you later. Good luck."

The call ended and Nicola took a deep breath. If Quinn's advice was anything to go by, she might need a whole lot of luck.

There was one cameraperson waiting on Nicola outside of the restaurant. She'd opted out of going back to the spot next to the art gallery. She didn't want to risk running into Damien. This reconnection was going to be awkward enough with the camera there filming them as if they were on a reality show. She didn't need Damien's raised brow and cocky smile to be a bigger distraction.

"Are you Darcy?" she asked the woman with the camera.

"I am." Darcy held out her hand to shake Nicola's. She spoke with a broadcaster's voice. Her hair was cut in a stylish bob and a big, perfect smile creased her face.

"Great to meet you," Darcy said. "We aren't going with a big crew or anything. I know this must be hard enough for you. Tackling all your regrets with a camera watching. It'll just be me going with you and only my camera to try and make it less stressful."

"I appreciate that." The words were polite, but as Darcy lifted the camera to her shoulder Nicola's throat nearly closed up. "Are you going to start recording now." She glanced left and right at the other people on the street in front of the bar. Her face burned with embarrassment, even though most people ignored them and kept it moving.

"Just a quick pre-date interview. That's why I asked you to show up first. Set it up and tell us why you decided to call Bobby and ask him out."

Nicola licked her lips and squeezed her purse instead of fidgeting with her clothes. She'd done hundreds of interviews for magazines and trade journals and had just been on national television. There was no need to be nervous. Except, this interview was specifically to get deeper into her personal life.

Darcy lifted the camera. A laser red light came on. "Say your name and spell it so that I can check the sound."

Nicola gave her name and spelling. Darcy nodded and grinned. "Great. The sound is good. Now repeat my question in your answer. Introduce yourself and tell me why you called Bobby."

Taking a deep breath, Nicola focused on the red light. "Bobby is on my list because I worked with him for years in chemistry lab while we were in college. I had a pretty big crush on him, but I was always too nervous or unsure about asking him out. Even though I'd suspected he was interested. After graduation, my best friend told me Bobby confessed he'd felt the same, but by then he'd moved to San Diego and I was coming to Atlanta. After that, I regretted never asking him out. That's what went on my list. Don't be afraid to ask out a guy you like. When I heard Bobby was back in town and asked how I was doing, I decided to shoot my shot."

Darcy stopped filming and grinned at Nicola. "That's fantastic, Nicola. I know this is a small thing compared to others on your list, but how many times have I waited for a guy to show he's interested instead of just speaking up. I think it's really cool that you're doing this."

"It's not that big of a deal. Most women aren't afraid to ask someone out."

"But for those who are, this may give them a boost."

Nicola hoped so. She was afraid most viewers would look at her fear of asking a guy out and think she was old fashioned. That she wasn't a modern woman. Would they understand that for Nicola, someone who'd never felt like she'd fit in, asking a guy out had been as scary as being stranded in the middle of the ocean surrounded by sharks?

Nicola's cell phone buzzed. She pulled it from her pocket to find Bobby's number. She smiled as her nerves jumped.

"Bobby? Hey."

"Hey, Nicola, I just got here. I'm heading that way. Are you there already?"

"Yeah, I'm standing in front of the restaurant."

An ambulance went down a side street. She heard the echo in Bobby's phone. She turned around to look for him. It didn't take long to spot him. He must have recognized her at the same time, because he smiled and lowered the phone from his face.

Bobby hadn't changed much. He was about ten pounds heavier, but the extra weight only filled in his build. Gone was the fade he'd worn in college, replaced with a smooth bald head. A full, well-groomed beard covered his jaw. When he hugged her, his body was warm and solid. He smelled of sandalwood and spice. A competitor's cologne.

"You look great," Bobby said after he pulled back. His eyes trailed up and down her body several times.

"Same to you."

Darcy spoke up. "Can you do that again. I didn't have the camera up."

Bobby glanced at Darcy and her camera. "You're hiding my face, right?" That was the one thing he'd asked for when Nicola mentioned the camera.

Darcy nodded. "As promised."

He grinned, gave Nicola another once over, licked his lips, then winked at Darcy. "Alright. As long as my face is hidden. That's cool." There could be a number of reasons he wanted his face hidden. The top of the list being he didn't want his personal life on display. The thought that lingered in her brain was that he didn't want to be seen on television going out with her.

Bobby leaned in for another hug. With this one, he squeezed her a little tighter and several seconds longer before letting her go. Nicola tried to smile as Bobby wrapped an arm around her waist and led her toward the front of the restaurant.

"I'm so glad you called me," he said. "I'd hoped to look you up once I got back in town. You know I really had a thing for you back in college."

A hint of relief washed through her. Okay, maybe he wasn't embarrassed to see her. She tried to relax even though he clutched her close against his side. This was what she'd wanted, kind of. He seemed just as excited about this chance for reconnection as she was. Maybe this was going to turn into something. They'd start dating. Things might get serious. They'd take long weekends out of town together, and she'd start to look forward to leaving the lab early instead of spending so much time there. Her chance to tell a guy she loved him.

"I didn't know you had a thing for me back then," she said once they were seated at the bar and had ordered drinks. She tried to ignore Darcy as she set up her camera to focus on them. The people outside didn't seem to care, but those inside watched her and Bobby with blatant curiosity.

Bobby turned completely toward her. He lifted his drink and slowly wrapped his lips around the tiny straw protruding from the glass. His eyes never left her face the entire time. If the move was supposed to be sexy it failed. She bit the inside of her mouth to stop herself from laughing.

After taking a long sip, Bobby let the straw slip through his lips. "You always seemed kind of hands off. Focused on work all the time. I was sure you'd turn me down."

Nicola hoped he wasn't attempting to be seductive and that was just the way he drank from a straw. Then again, maybe she didn't. "I never got the feeling you were into me," she said. "If I would have known, I would have asked you sooner."

"Then maybe I would have married you." He reached over and squeezed her arm. His eyebrows wiggled.

Nicola's eyes widened and she leaned back. "You think?"

"Yeah. Marrying you would have been the right decision. No drama. I bet you wouldn't give me a hard time about who I'm talking to and where I'm going. Would you?" He grinned and sucked on the tiny straw.

"I don't know. Would I need to give you a hard time about that?"

Bobby laughed, put his drink down, and took her hand in his. His hands were wet from the condensation on the glass. "No, you wouldn't. You see, I'm not that type of guy. I'm a one-woman man. Once I give my heart to a woman I'm not going anywhere. That's what I always thought about when I thought about you. Being with someone real. Someone who wants the same things out of life."

Nicola pulled her hand from his. "That's cool. What have you been up to since college?" she asked, hoping to steer the conversation away from marriage. She supposed she should be flattered he'd once thought about what it would be like to marry her, but he spoke about marrying her as if she'd be more support than partner.

"Working," he said. "That's all I have time for. Work and then I go home. I need a break from all that. Don't you?"

"I do. It's one of the reasons I agreed to do this. I want to spend some time having fun and enjoying life."

"Me too. I knew this was fate when you called me. That it was time for my life to turn into something great." He took her hand again.

Nicola looked into his eyes and relaxed. She wouldn't get her hopes up, but maybe things with Bobby would turn out well. "We'll see how things go."

"I know they'll go great." Bobby lifted her hand and brushed his lips across the back.

"Oh, hell no!" a woman yelled from the other side of the room.

Bobby stilled. He dropped her hand and sat up straight. He rubbed the bridge of his nose. "Damn."

Nicola leaned toward him. Worry replacing her earlier unease. "What's wrong?"

"That's my wife."

"Your wife?" Nicola jumped up from her seat. She looked in the direction of the angry outburst. A woman charged in their direction. Rage in her eyes.

"Bobby, I know your ass isn't out here in these streets again. Not when I just had to finish antibiotics from you burning me just a few weeks ago." The woman reached them and slapped the back of Bobby's head. "You are a jerk." She turned her glare on Nicola. "And who the hell are you?"

Nicola raised her hands. "Someone who did not know he was married." Separated her ass. She was going to kill Shonda. Never again would she rely on social media statuses when it came to people's relationships.

Bobby's wife lifted her hand and wiggled the finger with a ring on it. "Hell yes, he's married. Been married for seven damn years. You ain't about to take my husband."

"You know what. You can have him. I don't want a thing to do with this."

Bobby pleaded for Nicola to stay and for his wife to calm down as Nicola grabbed her things and rushed out of the restaurant. Darcy chased Nicola out of the restaurant. Her entire body was on fire. Anger and embarrassment were a toxic mix in her stomach. Making her feel sick. She never should have done this. What was she thinking? Fate hadn't brought Bobby back in her life. Now she was humiliated for the entire world to see.

"Nicola, wait!" Darcy called.

"I've got to go."

"No, listen." Darcy grabbed her elbow. "I won't use this at all. I promise. We won't even bring it up. I'll tell the network he didn't show up or something."

Nicola placed a hand over her face. This had to be the worst night of her life. She'd been the other woman. No matter that he hadn't really answered her question about being single when they'd talked. How dumb was it for her not to insist on a straight answer? "That's great. They'll think I was stood up."

"It's either that or let them know he tried to play you," Darcy said in a no-nonsense voice Nicola couldn't ignore.

He had tried to play her. She wanted to go back in that restaurant and slap the back of Bobby's head, too. All of those you wouldn't question me comments he'd thrown out. He'd thought she was naïve. Easily manipulated. Easy to play. She dropped the hand from her face and glared back at the restaurant. "You know what. Let the world know. Maybe it'll save the next woman he tries to lie to."

Darcy shook her head. "I won't use it. I promise."

Bobby and his wife came out the door. They were arguing. Bobby caught her eye and looked like he wanted to head her way. Nicola's stomach clenched. No way was she going to get pulled back into that drama.

"You know what, do what you want," she said to Darcy then hurried away before she cried. This was why taking risks was absolute crap.

Chapter 14

"Don't you dare laugh!" Nicola pointed at Mr. Goldberg sitting across from her in the Tuesday afternoon pottery class.

They were still making things by hand and not throwing on the wheel. Mr. Goldberg had decided to be original, his words, and make a miniature sculpture of his dog. Nicola was sticking with bowls. The smell of clay and glaze had taken some of the tension out of her neck and shoulders when she'd walked into the studio that afternoon. Maybe that's why she'd lost her mind and decided to tell Mr. Goldberg about her disastrous date with Bobby.

"What did you do when she slapped the back of his head?" Mr. Goldberg wiped a tear from the corner of his eye. "I would have loved to have seen that."

"It wasn't funny. It was embarrassing." But as she re-told the story she could see some of the humor in the situation.

"Would you prefer if she hadn't shown up and then you would have continued to date a married man? Maybe even fallen hard for the guy?"

"No. In fact, I don't know if I really would have gone for

the second date. There were red flags. He was kind of creepy with the way he eyed me like a piece of steak. Plus, the questions about if I'd harass him about where he went and what he was doing."

Bobby had given off enough bad vibes to make her wonder if she'd romanticized their friendship back in college. He'd been a brilliant chemistry major, but he'd also been a member of one of the most popular fraternities on campus. She'd been a little dazzled that someone as popular as him had been interested in her. A side effect of being the uninteresting one in the family for years.

"Then I suggest you laugh at the humor in the situation and shake off the embarrassment," Mr. Goldberg said. "He was the screw-up in this situation, not you."

"When you put it that way." Nicola thought back to the guilty expression on Bobby's face when his wife had yelled from across the room. The corner of her mouth lifted. "It was kind of funny. He did look like a kid caught doing something he wasn't supposed to."

"The other day I caught my grandson on the video game right after my daughter told him to get off. When I walked in the room the boy looked like he'd been caught stealing the crown jewels." Mr. Goldberg held up his hands, his eyes wide and his mouth opening and shutting like a fish. "Mom didn't...I thought...but I..." He started laughing. "He couldn't even get out a good excuse. In the end he just tossed the controller aside and stood with his head down. Caught in the act."

Nicola placed a hand over her mouth, but that didn't muffle her snort of laughter. "Yeah, that's about how Bobby looked when his wife slapped the back of his head."

"See, I told you there was humor in all situations. So, what happened next?"

"Nothing really. She turned on me, but I quickly shut that down. I told her I didn't know he was married, and she could keep him. Then I walked out with my head held high. They were screaming and yelling in the background."

Darcy had called her again to say she wasn't going to show the clip. Nicola had thanked her. In hindsight, even though she'd originally wanted them to humiliate Bobby the way he'd humiliated her, she'd changed her mind. She just wanted to be done with him and not provide proof to the world of her embarrassing encounter.

"Good for you!" Mr. Goldberg lightly slapped her arm with the back of his hand. "See, classy woman with a classy exit. His loss."

"You're right. His loss," Nicola said, nodding. For now, she'd put telling someone she loved them at the bottom of her list of things to get done.

They'd both turned back to their projects and were silent for several minutes when Mr. Goldberg asked. "When is your next date?"

Nicola nearly pinched a hole in her bowl. "With Bobby?"

"No, with a new guy, or gal. I don't want to paint you into a box."

Nicola chuckled. "Don't worry. I've painted myself into a box. The I'm happy to be single box. There will be no next date."

"Why not? Because of one jerk?"

"Because it's too much. The drama of dating. I can have fun doing the things on my list without going on multiple dates."

Without risking further embarrassment. This entire ordeal was about living her life to the fullest. Not about finding true love. If that even existed.

"What about your list and doing everything on it?" Mr. Goldberg asked.

"There are other things on my list I can do." She could still do something to prove her life was about more than creating the fun scents of the world without actually going out and experiencing the things she imitated on those briefing documents.

"But don't give up on dating. Everyone needs someone in their life. Even if it's just for sex."

Nicola's jaw dropped. "Mr. Goldberg!"

He shrugged and added the tail to his dog. "I'm not lying."

Damien walked into the room then. As if the utterance of the word sex had summoned a man who inspired sexual thoughts. He'd shown up for the second class last week as well. Like then, Fran seemed surprised he was there. He scanned the room and stopped when his gaze landed her and Mr. Goldberg. He returned her smile, which hadn't gone away since Mr. Goldberg made her laugh, and walked over to their table.

"What's so funny over here?"

"Just telling Nicola not to let one bad date get her down," Larry said.

Damien's laser sharp eyes focused on her. His dreads were pulled up in a loose knot at the top of his head. His light grey t-shirt was spattered with blue, green, and orange stain along with the ripped jeans. The scent of clay clung to him and combined with his own woodsy scent.

"Your date didn't go well the other night?"

She considered kicking Mr. Goldberg for spilling the beans, but it wasn't as if her bad date was a trade secret. She'd seen a few other members of the class chuckle to themselves as she'd told him her story. "Fortunately, it did not."

"Fortunately?"

She pinched the sides of her bowl to try and evenly distribute the clay. One side was definitely thicker than the other. "Yes, turns out my date was married. His wife showed up. I got lucky that I found out sooner rather than later."

Mr. Goldberg leaned over. "And I'm telling her that she has to get back out there."

"And I was telling him that I'm in no rush." She replied with raised brows.

Damien placed his hand on the back of her chair. He didn't touch her, but the movement brought him slightly closer. Her skin tightened. The essence of him was so tangible and real he might as well have touched her. "Sorry to hear about your date, but you're right, you were fortunate to find out. You deserve a man who'll treat you like the queen that you are."

She glanced at him from the corner or her eye. "You think I'm a queen? Is that something you say to all women?" She didn't mean to let the skepticism come out in her voice, but no man had called her a queen. After the blowup with Bobby, she was feeling extra critical of male attention. Wasn't that just some line wannabe players tried to use?

Damien leaned in a smidge closer. "No, I don't tell that to all women. And, yes, I do think you have the grace, poise, brilliance, and beauty of a queen."

Nicola sucked in a breath. Heat spread through her chest, up her neck, and across her cheeks. Was he serious? He looked serious. No traces of laughter or gaslighting in his expression or tone.

Why would he say that? Did she care? God, she was falling back down the Damien thirst trap. This man had disavowed relationships in her presence just a few days ago.

"Well, that sounds like an invitation to ask him out on a date," Mr. Goldberg said with all the subtlety of a bucking bull in a library.

Damien dropped his hand from her chair and took a step back. Nicola shook her head and tried to appear unfazed.

"I wasn't trying to hit on her."

"He was just being nice."

They spoke at the same time. Damien rubbed the back of his neck and gave her a sideways smile. "I'm going to check out the other students."

"Yeah, I need to get back to this." She focused on her bowl and didn't look up as Damien hurried away. *Dear God, let me erupt into flames of embarrassment right now.*

"He likes you," Mr. Goldberg whispered.

"No, he doesn't. He's just being nice." And just announced to the entire class that he wasn't hitting on her.

"You said that already."

"I know what I said. I said it because the words still stand. Damien is cool. I've got four more weeks in this class and then I won't see him again."

Mr. Goldberg's lips twisted as if he were holding back words, and thankfully he did. Nicola went back to her bowl. She didn't look Damien's way again as he strolled through the studio and gave feedback with Fran on the various artwork. Damien was divorced and had made it very clear at the farmers market he wasn't even trying to get involved with anyone. She could admire his arms, legs, eyes, and that mouth from afar, but there was no way she was going to get caught up in thinking he might be interested. She had bigger things on her plate. Starting with picking the next item on her list.

Chapter 15

Quinn saved Nicola from having to think too long about the next item on her list. After Nicola told her sister about the disastrous date with Bobby, Quinn immediately went in with her signature brand of commentary.

"I always knew he was a liar," Quinn had said. Amazing how she'd never brought that up before. "Forget him. I know exactly what you're doing next. Remember when that prince guy wanted you to pet his tiger?"

"Yeah, why?"

"Well, he's in L.A. this weekend for a party. We're going."

Nicola had burst into laughter. "I am not going to L.A. for a weekend."

"Yes, you are. His tiger isn't here, but I worked it out for you to get a behind the scenes tour at the L.A. zoo. You're going to hang out with a prince and pet a tiger this weekend. I don't give a damn what you say."

Despite all her arguments and reasons why, Nicola found herself on a plane to L.A. with her sister Friday morning. A hundred arguments for why she shouldn't skip town ran through her head, but she ignored every one. Every once in a while, Quinn did something elaborate but sweet that reminded Nicola of why she and everyone she knew couldn't help but love her sister's vibrant personality. For Quinn to go through this much effort to help Nicola check items off her list meant her sister cared.

She hadn't told the producers at *Your Morning Wake-Up Call* because she was pretty sure whatever celebrity party her sister had finagled their way into did not want outside cameras. She'd take her own pictures and videos to send to them later.

She'd even purchased a new dress for the trip. One that Quinn had begrudgingly approved after Nicola unpacked it the night before. She'd figured her sister would approve when she'd gone against what she typically would have worn. The sleeveless orange dress fit her body like a glove and had a skirt that was sheer from her knees to her ankles with a split down one side. She wouldn't admit that part of her was uncomfortable stepping out in the bright dress, but another part of her, a small happy part of her, also felt sexy. Something she hadn't felt in a long time.

"You might get more numbers than me tonight," Quinn said as she passed off her keys to the valet attendant in front of the night club where the party was being held.

There was a line of cars behind theirs. Paparazzi snapped pictures of the various celebrities going in and out. Some even stopped to answer questions. From what Quinn had told her, the night club was a frequent spot for celebrities, but tonight the crowd was expected to be bigger. Who wouldn't want to party with a prince?

"Why would you get numbers," Nicola asked. "You're married."

Quinn rolled her eyes. "Omar knows I do this. Besides, I'm not getting numbers to use them. I'm just wondering if I still have what it takes. I've been on the shelf too long."

"On the shelf. What does that even mean?"

Nothing about Quinn seemed remotely shelf-like. Tonight, her skin glowed and her curves in the black and gold sleeveless party dress she wore drew the eye of nearly every man and woman they passed. Her hair was jet black, sleek, and shiny in a ponytail that brushed her mid-back, and her makeup impeccable. On the shelf was not a phrase that described Quinn.

"I don't know. I feel stuck. I married Omar so quickly when I was young, because..." Quinn's mouth snapped shut. She sighed and waved a hand. "Doesn't matter. All I'm saying is yeah, I'm a rich man's beautiful wife, but that doesn't mean I still have what it takes to draw a man's attention. There's no guarantee I'll be with Omar for the rest of my life."

Nicola stopped walking and she grabbed Quinn's arm. "Wait! What do you mean? Are you thinking of leaving him?"

Quinn pulled out of her hold and lifted one shoulder. "I told him that, but we'll see. I just said it to see if he'd even care."

Quinn turned toward the bouncer at the door controlling the people going in and out. Nicola stopped her again.

"Hold up! You can't just throw that out there and keep it moving. What did he say? Are you serious?" Nicola wasn't close to Omar, nor liked how he used Quinn as a prop, but she'd had no idea her sister was considering leaving.

"It's no big deal. He said girl, you know you ain't leaving me," she lowered her voice in an imitation of Omar. "Then I was like, you right, and that was it."

Her tone was light and flippant, but Nicola heard the frustration beneath. Making it hard to tell if her sister really wanted to leave Omar or if what she said was true and she'd only wanted to get a rise out of him.

"So, you aren't serious?"

Quinn avoided eye contact and pulled her ponytail over her shoulder. "I don't know. I guess I'm staying. Now come on before everyone gets up in here. I think we have VIP, but I want to make sure."

Quinn grabbed her hand and pulled her to the door before she could ask anything else. Quinn had completely bypassed the line. Nicola was sure that if Quinn had dragged her all the way out there to L.A., their name was on the list.

Nicola's head spun as Quinn confirmed they could enter. Quinn was a flirt and complained about her husband no worse than any other person Nicola knew in a relationship, but she hadn't gotten the feeling that Quinn was unhappy. She'd always seemed to relish her life as Omar's trophy wife.

She wanted to ask more questions and get to the bottom of what Quinn meant. But that wasn't how their relationship worked. She loved her sister. She'd always have Quinn's back and knew her sister would do the same, but they stayed out of the major details of each other's personal lives. They didn't talk on the phone every day, tell their deepest secrets, or ask for advice about what to do next. Typically, any advice given was unsolicited. If Quinn decided to really leave Omar she'd tell Nicola, but if she was considering the option she would keep her thoughts to herself.

Their names were on the list and Quinn was on the VIP reservation. When Nicola heard the name of whose party they were a part of, she had to stop her sister again.

"Nathaniel Jones? How on earth did you get to be a part of Nathaniel's VIP section at an L.A. party?" Nicola asked.

Nathaniel was an R&B singer who was fairly new to the world of superstardom, but he'd been producing independent records for years. After a performance on the Grammy's followed with a Superbowl appearance, the man was everywhere.

Quinn shrugged as if it were no big deal to be joining the party. "I've been following him on Instagram for years. The other night he slid into my DMs and asked me to come out. I said yes when I found out who would be here."

"Why was Nathaniel Jones sliding into your DMs?"

"That new swimsuit picture I posted. The one I told you to like. He commented and shared, then it was shared even more, and before you know it, gossip accounts were buzzing. My number of followers jumped through the roof. The least I could do was come out. Now come on."

Nicola followed and before long they were cozy on a couch with glasses of champagne while Nathaniel Jones flirted with her sister. Nicola wasn't star struck. She'd made perfumes and scents for rich people long enough to know that acting star struck wasn't a good look unless you were dealing with the super conceited. While she still couldn't believe her sister had gone from posting a picture to hanging out with R&B's latest *it* star, she wasn't surprised. That type of stuff just happened to Quinn.

After an hour of sipping champagne and pretending to have fun while she watched Quinn flirt with Nathaniel, Nicola acknowledged she was bored. She stood and Quinn finally stopped giggling with Nathaniel to look at her.

"Everything okay?" Quinn asked.

"I'm good. Just going to walk around a little."

Her sister grinned and waved her on. "Okay, have fun, and flirt a little bit."

Nicola gave her sister a tight smile instead of rolling her eyes and walked out of VIP.

Quinn hadn't said anything more about the Prince of Marobi being here tonight, and after seeing her sister and Nathaniel she wondered if that had just been an excuse to get Nicola to come. Before labeling her sister a liar, she decided to investigate and see if there were any royal people in the other VIP sections.

She hadn't seen him since his people asked her to make the perfume for his younger sister. If he were there, she wouldn't be able to just walk up to him, but she might be able to get to one of his people and find out if the princess still liked the perfume. Two trips around the club resulted in no prince and Nicola's feet hurting from her heels.

She spotted Quinn and Nathaniel on the dance floor. As much as she wanted to be mad at Quinn for dragging her to L.A., Quinn's bright smile as she danced made Nicola smile in return. Quinn was beautiful, and her enthusiasm for everything she did drew people to her. A circle formed around Quinn and Nathanial to watch the two dance.

Part of Nathaniel's popularity was how well he choreographed his shows, but Quinn was able to keep up with the singer's moves as they did an impromptu dance-off to the beat of the music. Quinn glowed beneath the lights in the club. Her ponytail flipped from side to side with her uninhibited movements and her dress slid up with each sensual twist of her hips.

The song ended and the crowd cheered. Nathaniel wrapped an arm around Quinn's waist and pulled her against his body. They hugged and laughed then turned to bow to the onlookers. Nathaniel leaned in and said something in Quinn's ear. Her sister's smile broadened, she glanced at Nathaniel and nodded.

A sinking feeling went through Nicola's stomach. Whatever he said could be completely innocent, but she'd seen that look in her sister's eye. It was the same look she'd had when she'd first seen Omar, and told Nicola, "See that man over there? I'm going to sleep with him."

Her sister may have been thinking about divorcing Omar, but they weren't divorced yet. Nicola was not about to be the one to look the other way if Quinn wanted to hook up with someone else. She didn't want to know if Quinn stepped out on Omar. She wasn't good at lying, but plausible deniability she could pull off.

She hurried over to Quinn before she could disappear in the crowd with Nathaniel. "Hey, I'm not feeling so good. Do you mind if we head out early?"

Quinn's brows immediately drew together, and concern filled her face. "Yeah, sure."

That's what she loved about Quinn, no matter how different they were, her sister wouldn't leave her hanging or allow her to leave the club without her. "Sorry to pull you away like this."

"It's okay, I'm getting tired, too." She glanced over her shoulder to Nathaniel. "Hit me up later?"

He rubbed his chin and grinned at Quinn. "Most definitely."

Her sister winked then led Nicola out of the club. Once they got the car from the valet and were on their way back to the hotel, Nicola spoke up. "You sure you're okay with leaving the party early?"

"Yeah, I had fun. Didn't you have fun?" Quinn grinned and bobbed her head to the music playing through the radio.

Watching Quinn dance had been fun. Sitting in VIP listening to Nathaniel's entourage talk about nothing, not so much. "I never did see Prince Mandell. Are you sure he was supposed to come?"

Quinn pulled her shoulders up and gave Nicola a sheepish smile. "Oh . . . yeah . . . about that. He wasn't coming."

Figured as much. "Then why did you tell me he'd be there?"

"Because I knew that would be the only way to make you come. The tiger thing tomorrow is true though."

"Why did you need me to come. You don't typically drag me to parties."

Quinn sighed and rolled her head in a circle. "Omar was tripping when he found out I was coming out here. He's all up in my business after Nathaniel's comments on my photo blew up."

"Are you telling me I'm your decoy?"

"No, he just knew I wouldn't do anything stupid if you were here."

"Were you planning to do anything stupid?" Why had she asked that? She didn't really want to know.

"I had no plans to do anything stupid. Nathaniel's cool. That's all. I just wanted to chill with an R&B star and let him buy me champagne. That's all."

That she could see. Not many people would turn down the opportunity to party with a celebrity. Especially, if that celebrity sought them out via social media. Still, she would have liked to know the real reason for the sudden trip. "Okay, but you should have just told me. Not make up stories to get me out here."

"My bad. I know. I promise nothing but the truth from now on. But, for real, you get to pet a tiger tomorrow. How awesome is that."

Some of her sister's enthusiasm infected Nicola and she grinned. This is why she could never stay mad at Quinn. Every day was a rollercoaster of emotions with her. "I guess it is pretty awesome."

"Hell yes. I'm the best sister out there."

"You're a'ight."

They laughed and talked about the party on the way back to their hotel suite. Once there, Nicola was exhausted from the three-hour time difference and the club. When she said she was going to bed early, Quinn didn't put up a fuss. They both took off their makeup, put on pajamas, and got in bed.

Nature called at three a.m., pulling Nicola from sleep. On the way to the bathroom, she glanced into Quinn's bedroom, but her sister's bed was empty. Frowning, she tiptoed into the room. "Quinn?" she called.

No answer. A note rested on the pillow.

If you see this know I couldn't sleep and went downstairs to read. Didn't want to wake you. Call if you worry.

Nicola read the note three times, then placed the note back on the pillow. She shook her head and went to the bathroom. A part of her wanted to head downstairs to see if

Quinn was really reading in the lobby. Another part of her chanted plausible deniability.

Two hours later, Quinn quietly entered the suite. Nicola pretended to be asleep. Didn't call out to ask if Quinn was tired now. Didn't think too hard about not seeing a book in Quinn's hands as she tiptoed past Nicola's open door.

Chapter 16

They arrived at the zoo just before noon. Like the night before, their names were on a special list and she and Quinn were immediately met by one of the directors and the veterinarian in charge of the large cats, Barbara. She was a tall woman, thick with muscle and dark blonde hair pulled back into a ponytail. The director thanked Quinn and Nicola for their patronage and interest in the zoo. Based off her words, Nicola assumed Quinn paid a large amount of money for this experience.

"How much did this cost?" Nicola whispered to Quinn as they rode the golf cart with Barbara through the zoo.

"Don't worry. It's for you."

"How much?"

Quinn pushed her shades up the bridge of her nose and sniffed. "Stop counting my coins and enjoy yourself. You're knocking something huge off your list. I'm only trying to help."

After that Nicola kept her mouth shut. They were escorted into what looked like large veterinarian's office where the big cats were examined and cared for. Barbara gave them a behind-the-scenes tour of the food prep area, the machines they use to treat the animals, and where they handled emergency situations in case the animals needed help quickly.

Nicola's excitement grew during the tour. The female tiger at the zoo had recently given birth to cubs. Nicola and Quinn watched with grins on their faces as Barbara and her team examined the cubs and the mother. The entire experience was so amazingly unbelievable. Nicola knew she'd never forget the feeling or the smell of the clean musk of the animals as the vets worked with them. Never in her life would she have imagined she'd one day be behind the scenes at a zoo, or that she'd feel such tenderness in her heart watching the mother tiger with her cubs.

She didn't pet a full-grown tiger, thankfully, but she was able to hold and bottle feed one of the cubs. The warm weight of the animal that was so young but still bigger than any cat she'd ever held was a humbling experience. She laughed, and her eyes prickled with tears as she cared for the small creature. She didn't care how much Quinn paid for the tour, she was just grateful that her sister had given her the opportunity to have such a fantastic experience.

"Hey, thank you for that. It was really cool," Nicola said hours later as they rode to the airport to catch their flight back to Atlanta.

Quinn had hired a car to drive them back and they were both settled in the butter-soft leather seats in the back of the car. They'd ridden in silence for most of the ride. Quinn enamored by her phone as she posted pictures and video of their time at the zoo; Nicola lost in her thoughts about the amazing experience they'd just had.

Quinn glanced up from her phone. "It was cool, wasn't it?"

"I know I gave you a hard time about the money, and I still want to know how much so I can at least pay you back something, but it was by far the most awesome thing I've done."

A perfect way to bounce back from the disaster that was her date with Bobby. Once again, excitement about doing items on her list bubbled up. Staying away from any personal things on her list was the best thing to do moving forward. Focus on fun, not on matters of the heart.

"Well, you have plenty of time to do more," Quinn said. She held up her phone showing Nicola a picture she'd taken of her feeding the tiger cub. "I got some really good pictures and video you can send to the show."

"I'm glad you stayed on top of that. I didn't even think about capturing anything for television. I was so excited to actually hold a tiger cub that I forgot the reason why I was there in the first place."

Quinn slipped her phone back in her purse and pulled out a bottle of water. "How are you feeling about everything? The list getting out and everyone seeing that part of you?"

Nicola sighed and let the joy of the day fade just a little with the reminder of why she'd ultimately gotten in that room in the first place. "I'm still not cool that the list was sent to them. The date with Bobby was horrible, and even though they promised not to show it on TV, I'm sure I'll be asked about it. But, overall, doing the things hasn't been too bad. I'm spending more time with Grandpa, and the pottery class is cool."

Her grandad had called her on Wednesday insisting they have weekly conference calls about the magic show. Nicola had agreed, even though the calls would mostly be her grandfather telling her what she needed to learn and asking for updates on the rest of the family attending the show.

"You did call Aunt Kim and Uncle Carl to make sure they were coming to the show?" Nicola asked.

Quinn rolled her eyes but nodded. "I did. Mom called

and delivered her own form of guilt trip. Don't worry. The family will be there. If anything, to see Grandpa Jeremiah do something as out of character as magic."

Nicola laughed. "Believe me, he's very excited about it. You won't be disappointed."

Quinn shrugged and looked doubtful, but kept any other verbal concerns to herself. "Have you asked Damien out yet?"

The words were tossed out casually. As if Nicola asking out Damien was a forgone conclusion. There was no way Nicola was going to put herself out there like that. Damien had been very clear that he was not interested. In her or relationships.

"Not happening. Damien's cool. I like him and he comes into the classes every once in a while, but other than that, nothing romantic is happening."

"Oh really, because Shonda mentioned something about a farmers market stroll you had with him."

"That was an accident," Nicola said in a rush. "We bumped into each other. We also bumped into one of his old friends who mentioned his ex-wife, which practically made Damien's eye twitch with irritation. She did a number on him and now he's all anti relationships. Not going there."

Quinn cringed. "A man with baggage is not fun, but at least his issues are out there up front. Now the decision whether to avoid him completely or go in with your eyes open. You never want to get involved not knowing what you're getting into and being stuck."

Her sister told no lies. If Damien were interested, Nicola wasn't sure what choice she'd make. The smart choice would be to avoid completely. She had enough work dealing with her own baggage much less bringing a guy into her life with his own.

The problem with that thought was who didn't have baggage? Everyone had something in their past. Some more traumatic than others, some more hurtful that others, some maybe not big in her eyes but the size of a mountain to them. How they dealt with that baggage was the real thing to consider. Did you walk into things with someone who could handle it, or wind up stuck with someone who couldn't, or worse, wouldn't.

The divorce conversation she'd had with Quinn the night before popped back into Nicola's mind like a meddlesome neighbor who couldn't stay on their side of the fence. Had Quinn known what she was getting into when she'd married Omar? Was she no longer willing to deal with whatever challenges they both faced? It wasn't her place to ask. Nicola should mind her own business, but, like that neighbor, she couldn't help herself.

"What book were you reading last night? I need some suggestions to download while we're on the plane." She pulled out her phone and opened her book reading app.

"You don't like to read what I read."

"But whatever you're reading must be good. It kept you in the lobby for a few hours." She didn't mean to, but her tone rose at the end of her sentence making her words more of a question than a statement.

Quinn quirked a brow and smirked at Nicola. "Is that what this is about? If you want to know if I was really downstairs reading all you have to do is ask. You don't have to pretend as if you're looking for a book. We both know you're going to fall asleep on the ride back." Quinn pulled her cell out again.

"Okay, fine, what were you doing down there?" Nicola asked.

Quinn didn't look up from her screen. "Reading."

Considering she hadn't seen Quinn with a book, reading device, or heard her sister talk about a book in nearly a decade made Nicola suspicious. "You promise."

With a huff, Quinn lowered her phone and glared at Nicola. "Why do I need to promise? Shouldn't you trust me?"

Nicola licked her lips and shifted in the seat. Plowing past her discomfort she continued. "I do trust you. I just don't want you to get into anything that's going to hurt you."

"What could I possibly get into?"

Nicola thought of her sister dancing the night before. "Nathaniel?"

"Seriously, Nicola?" Quinn laughed. "You think I snuck out and spent the night with Nathaniel?"

Heat spread in Nicola's cheeks. Her stomach twisted with guilt for throwing out the suggestion, but now that she'd put it out there she wasn't going to back down. If Quinn was unhappy Nicola wanted to know. She wanted to help. She owed her sister that much.

"I don't know. Did he pick you up or something?"

"Don't you think if I'd gone back out with Nathaniel someone would have seen and it would be all over the gossip sites?" Quinn said as if she were talking to a fool.

"Not if he's discreet."

"So, now I'm Nathaniel's hidden away mistress? Come on, Nicola, I know you and the rest of the family think I'm a screw up, but I wouldn't do that."

The truth was, Nicola had no way of knowing her sister wouldn't do that. "You said you were thinking of leaving Omar."

"It was a thought. Married people have these thoughts all the time. We got into a fight before I came, and it made me mad. That's all. I wouldn't mess up my marriage by cheating. Do you know I get nothing if I'm caught stepping out on Omar? Nothing." She put the tips of her fingers together forming a zero with her hands. "I'm not ruining my life for a few minutes in bed with another man. Not even Nathaniel."

Even if she didn't believe Quinn was above stepping out on Omar, she did believe Quinn wasn't willing to sacrifice the life she had. Quinn had money working for Queen Couture, but Omar was a self-made multi-millionaire who didn't mind spending his money spoiling Quinn and showering her with gifts. Her sister loved the comforts that came with being married to Omar. Guilt swallowed the rest of the curiosity in Nicola. "I'm sorry. I shouldn't have said anything."

"No, I'm glad you said something. At least I know what you're thinking of me," Quinn tossed out. "What everyone thinks of me. I get it from Omar, I should have expected to get the same from my family."

She placed her hand on Quinn's arm. "Hey, I mean it, I'm sorry. It was wrong and stupid of me. Honestly, I was jealous."

Quinn cut a glare at her from the corner of her eye. "No way?"

"Yes. You're so out there. You aren't afraid of anything, and you've got superstars sliding into your DMs with requests to see you. I've got their people sliding in my DMs asking if I can make a special soap for their friends attending their latest baby shower. One thing this entire business with the list has taught me is that your life is so much more exciting than mine. My hesitancy to do anything even remotely fun was splashed on the news for everyone to see. I'm the boring one with a great imagination, so I imagine my sister is spending the night in the arms of a handsome, successful, famous singer while I'm lying in a cold bed alone."

The words rushed out on Nicola. All of them true and the closest she'd ever come to spilling her heart to Quinn. The closest she'd allowed her sister to get to knowing how much Nicola had always wished she'd had a little of Quinn's spark. The reason she'd snatched some of Quinn's shine so long ago and both loved and hated how that shine had gotten her where she was today.

Quinn chuckled and then took Nicola's hand in hers. "Okay, you're forgiven."

Nicola shook her head and silently laughed. Relieved Quinn had responded lightly instead of taking this conversation someplace deeper. Her deepest regrets were already on display for world examination, she wasn't ready to reveal even more. Not even to her sister. "Thank you."

"And your life isn't boring. You have a wonderful job, you are a wonderful person, and everyone loves you. That's all that matters."

Nicola squeezed Quinn's hand back. She felt terrible for accusing Quinn of sneaking out. For projecting her own jealousy onto her sister. Whatever Quinn did or didn't do in her marriage was her business. From now on she'd be a good neighbor and keep her insecurities to herself.

Chapter 17

Nicola spent the week trying to play catch up on her projects. She'd sent the video of her feeding the tiger cub along with a few pictures of herself to *Your Morning Wake-Up Call*. She'd received an excited reply then was gently reminded to let them know about the things she planned to check off her list. That way they could be there with a camera.

Stacie urged her to pick something else. Instead of telling Stacie she was only doing fun, nonpersonal items, she convinced Stacie to focus on the trip to Cancun with Quinn and Shonda and the magic show with her grandfather. Though she figured Quinn and Shonda expected it, Nicola made a mental note to tell them the trip was now scheduled to be recorded. She was sure they'd love that.

By the time her grandpa called on Wednesday for their weekly magic show call Nicola wondered just how silly she was going to look on stage.

"I need you to be my date on Saturday night," Grandpa Jeremiah said immediately after her greeting.

Date? Her grandpa hadn't shown any interest in going out and socializing since their grandmother died.

"Date where?" she asked.

"Don't worry about all that. Just be at my place by six thirty on Saturday."

"Hold up. I need more than that. How do I know what to wear if you don't tell me where we're going?"

"Just wear something you'd wear to church," was his exasperated reply. "Okay. See you then." He hung up before she could ask further questions.

Her mom had given her no better idea of what was going on with her grandfather when she asked, so Nicola put on her Sunday best and drove to Aiken on Saturday afternoon instead of working on her projects.

She'd also avoided her mom's telephone calls along the way. It hadn't gotten past Adele that Nicola had sent more fragrance samples to Desiree. She'd asked if everything was okay, and Nicola swore they were, but her mom wasn't a fool. If the fragrance was in the bag more samples wouldn't be needed.

Nicola hadn't heard back from Desiree about the latest tweaks. Nicola chose to take no news as good news, and put it out of her mind. Yes, she probably should be in the lab today working on other projects, but her grandfather needed her. For what, she didn't know, but that didn't change the fact that he'd called for her help. Plus, she'd stayed until midnight last night going over notes and aromas for another project with Tia. One afternoon shouldn't kill her career.

When she arrived at her grandfather's place his front door was open. He waved at her from behind the screen before hurrying out and locking the door before she could get out of the car good.

"What's the rush?"

"You're late," Jeremiah replied. He moved down the driveway to her car.

Nicola checked her watch. It was five forty-five. Her grandpa had said he wanted her here by six thirty.

"You said to be here at six-thirty."

"No, no, no, the thing starts at six thirty. I want to get there early so we can get a good seat."

She was pretty sure he'd said six thirty, but he already seemed nervous, so she didn't bother to argue. Nicola sighed and sat back in the driver's seat. He opened the passenger door and slid in. The smell of his cologne, one she'd created, filled the car. He wore a pinstripe blue suit with a navy tie, the hair on the sides of his head were slicked back, and he wore the gold watch Nicola had given him for Christmas two years ago.

Her grandfather handed her a piece of paper. "Put that address in your phone or whatever. It'll tell you how to get there."

"Care to tell me what we're going to?" Nicola punched the address into her car's GPS. The calculations estimated it would take fifteen minutes for them to arrive.

"You'll see when we get there."

"Grandpa, really? You can't give me a hint?"

"Just drive. How was your trip out to L.A.? Your mom told me you and Quinn went out there. You kept your sister out of trouble?"

"I don't have to keep Quinn out of trouble. She knows how to take care of herself."

Her grandfather snorted. "I saw the pictures of her dancing with that singer guy. She better watch out before Omar starts to get suspicious."

She cut her grandfather a look as she maneuvered out of his neighborhood. "There is absolutely nothing to get suspicious of. She helped me out. I'm trying to have more fun and she arranged a trip for me. I got to feed a tiger cub. She worked that out for me."

"No kidding?"

Since he sounded impressed, Nicola told him about the trip to the zoo, and the fun she and Quinn had on the behind the scenes tour. She still felt guilty for assuming her sister had stepped out on Omar. If she could keep the rest of the family from going in on Quinn for something she hadn't done, then she would.

As much as she sometimes envied how quickly people liked Quinn, Nicola was glad she didn't get that kind of attention. Being the quiet sister worked to her advantage and allowed her to focus on her work. That was much more important than having people scouring through every detail of her personal life.

The GPS led them to a hotel downtown. Nicola parked in one of the guest spaces then raised a brow at her grandfather. "What's going on?"

"Just come on."

He hopped out of the car and walked to the front of the hotel without waiting on her. Nicola turned off the ignition and got out. She hurried to catch up with her grandfather, but he kept shushing her as they entered. Once inside, he greeted the people behind the desk.

"Yes, I'm here for the speed dating event."

"Speed dating!" she said, grabbing the arm of her grandfather's coat.

He shook her off. "You heard me." He smiled at the woman behind the desk. "It's here right?"

"Yes, sir, you're in the right place," the desk clerk said with a bright smile. "Through the lobby and to your left. It's in the meeting room down there. They have signs set up."

"Thank you."

Nicola bit her tongue as she followed her grandpa away from the desk and through the lobby. Sure enough, there were signs leading the way to the *Lucky in Love* dating event. Nicola grabbed his arm before he got to the registration table.

"Grandpa, stop and explain right now."

Her tugged away then smoothed a hand over the front of his suit jacket. "Fine. I didn't tell you because I knew you'd say no."

Hell yes, she would have said no. She wanted to still say no and drag him out of there. "Why are you doing speed dating?"

"I'm trying something new. Your grandmother made me promise to be happy after she died."

Nicola pointed at the line of people at the registration desk. "Speed dating makes you happy?"

She wanted her grandad to be happy, too, but not like this. How was he going to find someone even a bit as sweet and funny as her grandmother at a speed dating event? And who did speed dating anymore anyway?

As if thinking of him on a dating site would be better.

"Doubtful," he answered shrugging. "But talking and spending time with a woman will make me happy."

"What about the senior center? Can't you meet a nice woman there?"

He scowled and shook his head. "I don't feel like trying to meet anyone down at the senior center. Every woman down there knew your grandmother. She said be happy, not fool around with one of her friends. Besides, I thought this would be good for both of us. You need to get out there after that fiasco with that Bobby fellow."

Dear Lord, how did her grandfather know? "How do you know about that?"

"Quinn calls me every Sunday. She told me." He said the words as if she should have expected the news to come from Quinn. Quinn was the last person she expected to tell her grandfather anything about her personal life.

"Quinn calls you every Sunday? I didn't know that." She didn't think Quinn would even remember to call every Sunday.

She often forgot to call Nicola on things. "Did she start after grandma died?"

"No. She's done that for years. I'm surprised you didn't know. Either way. You're taking risks. I'm trying to meet a new lady. Come on. Maybe we'll get lucky."

He turned and strolled over to the registration table with a huge grin on his face. Nicola stood next to him and accepted her badge and information packet while she let her grandfather's words sink in. If she hadn't already felt like she wouldn't be winning any prizes as the world's best granddaughter, she'd figured she would at least score higher than Quinn.

Quinn had called Grandma and Grandpa every week. Gave them updates on what was happening. Since when had Quinn become so considerate? Since when had Quinn been more considerate than her?

Guilt immediately followed the thought. Quinn wasn't as close to Nicola as everyone assumed they would be as sisters, but she did love their grandparents. Quinn's dedication only added to Nicola's regrets for not being there for her grandmother more at the end. For not being there for anyone the way she probably should have been.

They were signed in and led inside where a group of people mingled. Nicola got a glass of wine and drank it slowly. Though the idea of downing it quickly seemed pretty good. She was driving back to Atlanta tonight so no matter how much she didn't want to do this, she couldn't ease the swirl of her emotions with alcohol. She could take pictures for the show, then immediately canned that thought. One dating disaster was enough.

Her grandpa's excitement grew with each passing minute. The one bright spot of the event. He clapped when the hostess told the group about all the many happy matches that were made between people who came to their programs. Their success rate was mostly due to their choosing the right people to attend, and how they offered a more personal experience than dating apps could provide. Nicola barely kept herself from rolling her eyes, but she was trying to be supportive.

She sat through the ridiculous speed dating. Forced herself through the various small talk and quick dating questions. The men ranged in age from younger than her to her grandfather. Mostly men from Aiken and the surrounding areas. She felt no spark with any of the guys, and even if she had a few interesting minutes of conversation with a couple of the men, she didn't plan to follow up or ask for future dates. Nothing real could come of this. The entire event was just a ploy to get single desperate people into a room and make them believe they could find true love. True love wasn't found on a speed dating circuit.

On the car ride back, her grandfather nearly burst with enthusiasm at the prospects from the night. "That was a lot of fun. I met some fun ladies."

Nicola sucked her teeth. Supporting her grandfather was one thing. Letting him think any of the ladies there were serious contenders for step-grandmother was another. The women were nice enough, but none were in his age range. Plus, she'd overheard some of the other conversations, none of those ladies were half as fun as her grandmother had been.

"Seriously? Come on, Grandpa, you can do better than the women that were there."

"Why do you say that?"

"Because, you and Grandma were together for years. Do you really think you're going to find something long-lasting and serious at a cheesy event like that? If you really want to meet a nice woman you can spend your time with, then you need to go more traditional. Church, volunteer organizations, mutual contacts."

"What makes you think you can't find something real at speed dating? They've had a sixty percent success rate with matches." He tossed back the sales pitch they'd sat through as if it were a convincing argument.

"That's what they tell people to make them feel lucky. I wouldn't trust them. It's reeks of fakeness. You deserve better."

She felt his glare before he pointed an accusing finger her way. "You know what. That's your problem."

"What are you talking about?"

"You think everything is supposed to go a certain way. You don't just relax and let things happen. Even with this doing things on your list, you're only doing safe things. Take a pottery class. Come visit me. Ask out a guy who you already knew would say yes. You're too scared."

"I'm not scared. I'm practical." And none of the things she'd done had been exactly easy or convenient for her. Small steps for some were huge for others. Why didn't anyone understand that?

"You're scared," he argued. "Have been ever since you were younger. Your grandmother may have let you sit in your perfect orderly box and praise you for it, but I'm not her."

"Grandma appreciated me for who I am."

"Your grandmother felt sorry for you. She knew you were too timid to spread your wings and fly, so she made you feel special about the things you did love. Everything doesn't fit into a perfect box you know. Everything doesn't have to be just right or go the way you planned. Life isn't one of them designer fragrances you whip up in a bottle. It's a bunch of messy, scary things that you make the best of. The sooner you learn that, the better."

The anger in his voice snatched away the hurt his words had caused. *She made you feel special about the things you did love.* The safe, boring, expected things Nicola clung to. The things she knew she could do instead of the things she never believed she could do, but also envied Quinn for being able to go for them without hesitation.

"I didn't mean any harm, Grandpa," she said quietly, hoping to end the conversation. Not wanting to reflect on how her criticism of his speed dating was just another projection. Another way for her to take her own insecurities out on someone else.

"Well, next time think before you speak. I had a good time tonight and you're ready to take away my joy. Instead of doing that, why don't you find some joy of your own. It might do a lot better than you trying to do some things on a damn list."

They didn't talk the rest of the way. At his place, she asked if he wanted her to come in, but he said no. Nicola watched him get out of the car and go inside without a backwards glance. Her stomach was in knots. Guilt squeezed her like a vice. She'd ruined her grandfather's day and had no clue how to make things better.

Chapter 18

Nicola headed to her parents' place the next day. At least once a month, she made the trip to her parents' house to discuss where the company stood on various projects, including going over the latest with packaging and promotion for upcoming fragrances and timelines for potential new projects. All of this was under the guise of a family Sunday dinner. Really her mom just wanted the family to huddle and discuss business away from the office and the other directors of Queen Couture.

Nicola used to wish her mom would ask her to come over to hang out and just catch up on life, but that wasn't the nature of their relationship. Her mom and sister were more alike and hung out together for shopping trips, spa days, and brunch with their various society friends. Nicola was more like her dad, who was happiest in his study or at his office on Morehouse's campus where he taught business classes.

Her parents lived in a beautiful penthouse atop the epicenter in Midtown. They'd moved there three years ago when her mom decided they needed something modern and sleek.

Their previous home had been a gilded shrine to the beauty industry, complete with knockoff art and plush furniture.

As a kid, the word gaudy would never have crossed Nicola's mind when it came to her home. That's what her mom liked and had raised her and Quinn to believe was beautiful. Nicola had loved the place and thought her home mirrored her mom's glamorous career. Until her thirteenth birthday party, when she'd worked up the nerve to invite friends from school. Not just her friends from the math team and the gifted and talented program. She'd invited Whitney Sullivan. The new girl at school whose mother was a fashion contributor for multiple magazines and had quickly become the most popular girl in school. Nicola had hoped if she could show Whitney how cool she was then others would agree.

It had been the best birthday of her life. Everyone *oohed* and *ahhed* over the gold crown molding, pink carpeting, and abstract paintings. Her mom had let them all get makeovers and try on clothes. For once, Nicola hadn't been the nerdy girl, but instead the cool, beautiful girl.

That lasted until Monday morning. When Whitney announced to everyone that Nicola's house looked like a unicorn exploded and covered everything in glitter and gold. Whitney, who of course knew what was fashionable because of her mother, knew bad taste when she saw it, and Nicola's mom had bad taste. The words did their magic. Nicola was no longer the smart kid, which she'd hated, she became the smart kid with a gaudy family.

She wondered what Whitney Sullivan would say now. Nicola, her mother, and Queen Couture couldn't be called any of those things. Immaculate, sophisticated, stylish were all words that described the neutral colors, floor to ceiling windows, and modern décor of her parents' penthouse. Nicola had never told her mom what Whitney and the kids at school said, but since then she had tried to sway her mom's choices.

Which resulted in being called judgmental long before her grandfather had accused her of the same thing the night before.

Nicola no longer cared what the Whitney Sullivans of the world thought, but she tried to avoid being an easy target of criticism. She'd walked away from her focus on medical research to make her family's business one of the most highly respected in the industry. While she still wondered what would have happened if she'd gone on into biomedical research, she was proud of what she'd done for Queen Couture.

Her dad answered the door before she could ring the bell and looked startled to find her on the other side. Her dad was only a few inches taller than her, slim, with a pleasant face and a perpetual what-can-I-say smile on his face. The expression he'd worn whenever his mom demanded something new for the house, Quinn asked for money to buy a new outfit, or Nicola brought home another stellar report card.

"What are you doing here?" her dad asked. He smiled and stepped back so she could enter.

"Family dinner, remember? Where are you going?"

Her dad's dark leather messenger bag was slung over his shoulder and he wore his favorite camel colored fedora and a light jacket.

"Oh, that. I'm going to the office. I've got some papers to grade and your mom is on another level in there talking about the perfume for that singer."

Nicola wrinkled her nose. On another level? She really hoped her mom hadn't gotten wind that Desiree still wasn't one hundred percent satisfied with the fragrance.

"That's why I'm here. To settle her down. Will you be back soon?"

He was already shaking his head. "It'll be a while. Me and Doctor Griffin are going to watch the game after I finish up." He leaned in and kissed her cheek. The scent of ink, papers, and pine came with him. "I'll see you the next time."

"Okay, Dad," Nicola said with a smile. She'd bet money her dad had not forgotten today was family dinner day and that he was making his great escape before she and Mom got lost in a conversation related to perfume making. "Love you."

"Love you, too. Oh, and good work with your grandfather. I know your mom thinks it's a waste of time, but I'm glad you both are getting out and doing more stuff. Can't wait for the magic show."

Nicola's smile froze. She wondered if Grandpa Jeremiah would call this Wednesday to talk about the magic show. Nicola was going to give him a few days to calm down. He might need a few days to get over her scoffing at speed dating. She still didn't like the idea of him dating that way, and if he needed time she'd wait until he was ready to talk to her again. If hiding from or deflecting uncomfortable emotions were an Olympic sport, her family would all have gold medals.

"I can't wait. Thanks, Dad."

He left and she locked the door behind him before going into the kitchen where she knew her mom would be. The savory smell of Indian food greeted her. Not cooked by Adele, but ordered and delivered from her favorite restaurant. Another reason her dad dipped out, that wasn't a favorite of his.

Her mom stopped setting food out on the table and gave Nicola a quick hug. "Right on time. Always punctual. That's one of the things I love about you, Nicola."

"Thanks, Mom." She didn't know any other response to that.

"Your sister is coming by," Adele said as if she wished that weren't the case. "I told her she didn't have to, since your dad is going out, but she said she didn't mind."

"Why would you do that? Even though she doesn't do as much work for Queen Couture, she's technically still on the payroll."

Nicola hung her purse on the hook outside the kitchen then came back in to wash her hands.

"I'll admit, she was useful once," Adele said as she continued to unpack the food. "Now, she's more likely to bring scandal than anything."

Where in the hell had that come from? She pulled a towel from the drawer and dried her hands. "Quinn isn't scandalous."

"She had a legitimate chance at being a real model, instead she lowered herself to posing half naked online. I call that scandalous."

"First of all, have you seen what makes up the average perfume ad these days? Nothing but half naked models. Second, can we not bash Quinn? She's doing her thing and no matter what we think of it, it's working for her."

Nicola hated to admit it, but her sister's unconventional career path was putting her in contact with people Nicola never would have expected. As much as she might wish Quinn would work full time for Queen Couture, the fact that her sister was influential couldn't be ignored.

"Fine. Fine. Come in here and let me know what you think about the bottle design concepts for Desiree's fragrance."

Adele threw the bag the food had been delivered in into the trash then walked toward the hall. Nicola followed her mom down the hall to her home office. Sunlight filtered in from the floor to ceiling windows that overlooked Midtown Atlanta. The various awards and accolades Queen Couture had received surrounded a framed poster of Triumph, their hallmark fragrance. The one that had saved the company. The other wall was covered in various portraits of her mom and dad.

"You're already doing bottle designs? We haven't finalized the juice yet."

"I know. You're running behind, Nicola." Adele shifted through various papers on her desk and held up one print.

"I'm not behind."

Her mom placed one hand on her hip. "You think I don't know about the additional samples you sent Desiree."

"I wasn't hiding that from you." She just didn't want her mom to worry.

"I didn't say you were. The guilty person always cries the loudest," her mom said with a shake of her head. "I know you'll get it right. That's what you always do. I also know celebrities can be finicky. I need you to be ready to make any changes she wants. I know you're off doing that list thing, but don't forget your responsibilities."

"You told me to go on the show."

"I didn't say agree to do another project that has nothing to do with making perfume," her mom admonished. "There will be plenty of time for living life after you make Desiree happy. Now, come here and look at these. I spoke with the designers and we're thinking of something bold and out there for Desiree's perfume."

That did not sound like the classic and timeless fragrance Desiree wanted. Nicola moved closer to her mom to look at the picture. "I don't know about that. Desiree specifically said she wanted this to be a timeless fragrance. Not something that will smell like a fad or that'll be forgotten in two years. She wants it to connect with the women who wear it no matter their age."

"Which is why we need a bold, unforgettable bottle."

"Or, we go with something simple. Something that doesn't say we're trying to razzle dazzle them with fancy packaging. The juice inside is what counts."

"Oh, you always want to turn down my ideas. You're always so practical." Her mom's shoulders slumped, and she pulled the print closer to her chest.

"My practicality is what helped make Triumph. I know what I'm talking about with this design."

With a heavy, you're-killing-me sigh, her mom held out the paper. "Just look at these. You might change your mind."

Nicola looked at the sketches and bit her lower lip. A microphone, one that mimicked a CD, and a final design that made Nicola tilt her head to the side. That couldn't be what she thought it was.

"You can't be serious."

Her mom's eyes sparkled with delight and she clasped her hands together in front of her chest. "Desiree is about music and sex appeal. I think these would be perfect, but I really like the third one."

The third one looked like a man and woman having sex. The woman's legs were bent and wide. The man pressed against the woman's body. Their faces entwined in a kiss.

Nicola shook her head and dropped the picture. "No. We aren't going with any of them. Who drew these? Ramon? If so, I'll call him and tell him that this isn't going to work. Don't worry about it, I'll handle the design."

Adele snatched up the paper. "No, you won't. You worry about making the juice. I can work with Ramon on the design of the bottle."

"If this is where you're going with the idea then we aren't going to go with them. This isn't what Desiree is going for."

"You're doing it again. My poor mom is going to embarrass me with her over the top ideas. Let's downplay her and go with my boring idea instead."

"If you care to admit it, my boring," she did air quotes with the word, "ideas have worked out."

"You're embarrassed by my ideas."

"I'm not. I just don't think this is the right direction." Desiree may be sex appeal and excitement, but she was also not going to go for a bottle that mimicked sex.

Quinn came into the room. "What are you two arguing about now?"

Her mom's eyes lit up. "Aha, if anyone will get it then Quinn will. Come over here and look at these bottle designs for Desiree's perfume and tell me what you think."

Quinn came over and looked at the pictures.

"I told Mom—"

Adele snapped at Nicola. "Hush, don't interrupt. Let Quinn make her own option."

Quinn tilted her head to the left then the right. "I don't know if this will work."

Adele's excitement deflated. "What? I thought you'd love it. You're all about being sexy."

"I am," Quinn agreed. "But this isn't what I remember Desiree saying she wanted. She didn't want a bold in your face fragrance, she wanted something more... old school."

Adele threw up her hands. "Nicola got to you. That's what this is."

"No she didn't, Mom. Don't be dramatic." Quinn grinned. "If you want, I can give you a few sketches, or work with the artist on the design. That way you don't have to."

Adele snorted. "Do you really think I'm going to put you in charge of a project this big? No thank you. Nicola, you can talk to Ramon and have him work up some other ideas."

Quinn's mouth tightened. "But Nicola is busy making the perfume. Why not let me help? I'd like to help."

Adele patted Quinn's cheek. "You just need to focus on giving me my first grandchild. Not worry your pretty head about this."

Adele's cell phone rang in the kitchen. "That's probably Ramon now. I told him I was showing you his sketches, Nicola. He was curious about what you had to say." She hurried out of the room to answer.

Nicola looked at her sister. "I really don't mind working with him on the design."

"Aren't you tired of having to fix everything for her?"

Quinn sounded irritated. "I work in the marketing department. I'm supposed to coordinate this stuff while you focus on making the perfumes."

"Well, it's not as if you've been doing a lot in the marketing section lately," Nicola shot back. "Besides, it helps when I'm involved in the process from start to finish."

Quinn flipped her hair over her shoulder. "Because you're a control freak."

The words hit too close to the sore spot Nicola had from her fight with their grandfather and Adele's judgmental comment. "No. I just like to see a project through. Mom knows that. Plus, you're busy."

"Not that busy." Quinn walked over and met Nicola's eye. "Let me do the bottle design."

There was a quiet plea in her sister's words. Nicola wanted to say yes. She owed Quinn, after all the stuff her sister had done for her. Knowingly and unknowingly.

The Desiree project was just too important. She couldn't turn something this big over to her sister. Quinn would want to help out today, but tomorrow she'd be on to the next thing. The next R&B star sliding into her DM's and another trip to L.A., Vegas, or Hawaii. Then the bottle idea would be forgotten, and Nicola would be stuck pulling that together and working on the perfume anyway.

She shook her head. "I've got it."

Quinn sucked her teeth. "Typical."

"You can help with another project. Look, we're doing the summer scent for the Forever Young line. It'll need a new look. You can help with that."

Forever Young was a clothing store that catered to women in their early twenties. The mass-produced clothing was cute and sexy, but cheaply made. It was one of their less prestigious but lucrative clients. If the scent failed or the bottle was a mess it wouldn't be too much of a loss. The company tended to try things that were considered trendy and then discarded them with the next season. Quinn couldn't mess that up.

"Are you kidding me?" Quinn's voice was like a pane of frozen glass. "Do you think you can tide me over with your low budget client?"

"Forever Young isn't a low budget client. They have stores across the country, a major following, and are one of our biggest distributors."

One of Nicola's juice blends, a basic fragrance with orange blossom, rose, and a hint of musk, was in such demand that Forever Young made it their signature scent instead of rotating it out it after a season. Forever Young's perfume line was a huge part of their current profit.

"You also give the seasonal projects to the new perfumers who intern in your lab," Quinn said, her back ramrod straight and her eyes fierce. "You let them test the waters there knowing if they mess up it won't be too much of a problem. I've heard you say this numerous times over the years. I know you're trying to make things better, while just giving me a get over it project."

"Quinn—"

Quinn held up a hand. "Save it, Nicola. I know you love me and all, but I also know that no matter how much you complain, you love being the darling star of Queen Couture. I get it. You created the best-selling perfume. You're the expert. Not me. I expect that from Mom, but I'd hoped you would at least acknowledge that back then, Mom asked us both for help. I could have just as easily created Triumph and you know it."

The words stabbed right into Nicola's defenses and twisted through her like a knife. The turning point in their roles in the family. Their mom had asked them both, but she'd believed Quinn would be the one to make something useful. They'd created separate blends, but often talked to each other about how to tweak their formulas. Then one night, for reasons Nicola didn't know, Quinn had shown up at the lab drunk and accidently ruined her sample. That was also the night Nicola realized what she needed to do to make Triumph. Nicola had thrived while Quinn floundered.

If only that was the real version of the story.

"I do know that," Nicola said, all of the guilt and frustration of that night so long ago heavy in her voice. She knew better than anyone that Quinn was smart enough to handle this project. "Look, if you want—"

"Stop. Don't say anything we'll both know will just be another way to patronize me. You can continue to be the savior of the family. I know the role I'm supposed to play. Don't lose any sleep over me. I'll be over it in the morning."

With that, Quinn walked out. Nicola was about to follow when her mom called. "Ramon wants to talk to you, Nicola."

There was what she should do and what needed to be done to keep things on track. She would talk to Quinn later. For now, she had to keep things going.

"Coming, Mom."

Chapter 19

The conversation with Quinn hung over Nicola like a thick cloud the next day. She couldn't focus and went back and forth with herself. Quinn was her sister. She knew Quinn was smart, and more capable than most people realized. If anyone knew how smart and intuitive Quinn was, it was Nicola. The only reason Quinn didn't know how much she influenced the company was due to a fuzzy, next day memory, provided by a hangover.

Nicola couldn't think about that now without regret fogging her brain. She needed to get lost in something. Making Desiree's perfume was not going to help clear her mind. Desiree's agent had emailed that Nicola was "on the right track" with the latest samples. Back to the drawing board. The only problem was that Nicola didn't know what other colors to draw with.

She ruled out staying in the lab, being mad she couldn't think of anything, or going home and drinking wine with the hope alcohol would inspire something. She could look at her list of things to do when she finally had time for a life, but that would only create a sick knot in her stomach as she relived the embarrassment of having her list read on television. So, she opted for something else. Free creative time at the pottery studio.

Fran mentioned the free time after the first class. Sunday, Monday, and Friday, for a few hours when Damien wasn't working, students could come in and work on their pottery. She needed a creative outlet. Since her ability to make the perfect perfume was stunted at the moment, she could at least put her hands in clay and hope something came of it.

She arrived at the studio, grabbed an apron, and settled in at one of the corner tables. There were only two other students from the class taking advantage of free studio time. A sister pair who'd been very excited about making their own bowls and vases for family members. She wasn't surprised they took advantage of free studio.

Nicola spoke to them briefly, but mostly she wanted to do something with her hands. She decided to practice the braided bowl technique Fran had shown them in the last class. Something that was relatively simple but still required focus. Eventually her mind cleared as she rolled the clay in to long thin strips, braided the strips together, then layered the braids on top of each other to make a bowl. Once that was done, she felt creative, and used a scalpel and cut leaf shapes to go around the edge.

She sensed Damien as soon as he entered the studio and wasn't surprised when he came to watch her work. She'd had a feeling he would come talk to her. She liked what he smelled like. That familiar mix of clay and mint with his own cedar undertones. She'd be able to recognize him in a room of a thousand people.

He didn't speak when she looked up at him. He studied her bowl. Nicola had been so into making it, she'd been meticulous with her work. She'd hoped this bowl would be perfect. The best thing she ever made. Now that he stood over her. The expert in pottery. Her bowl seemed disproportionate.

"I know. I should try to keep the braids better aligned."

Damien shook his head. "Actually, I was watching your hands while you worked. I think you'll be good on the wheel."

A flutter in her chest. She should not be so flattered by an off-hand compliment, but she hadn't been praised much lately and decided to enjoy the feeling. "You were?"

"Yes. Want to try?"

"Of course I would." They weren't going to start on the wheel until next week, but Nicola wouldn't turn down a chance to start early.

He nodded. "Good. Let's do it."

Visions of the movie *Ghost* crept into her mind as she followed him to the wheel. Her hands sliding across the slick surface of the clay. Damien sitting behind her. His strong arms wrapped around her as his fingers entwined with hers to show her the way.

Nicola shook her head. She was in her feelings after the arguments with her grandfather and sister. Now was not the time to have romantic fantasies about a guy who was clearly not into her.

Damien pointed to one of the potter wheels and told her to sit. He dropped a lump of clay on top and the bucket of water next to her. He did the same at the wheel next to her then sat there.

"Now follow my instructions."

Nicola tried not to let her disappointment show. So much for a sexy *Ghost* recreation. Damien's demeanor screamed instructor, not romance. She just had to get this damn crush on him to go away.

Damien talked her through the steps of centering the clay

on the wheel. She focused on getting her hands set up correctly so she wouldn't push the clay off the wheel. Damien's voice provided low and steady instruction as she worked on creating a bowl. Bringing her back to center whenever she got frustrated or made a mistake that threw her work off balance. At the end of his lesson she had a small, somewhat symmetrical dish with an exaggerated rim that she thought was one of the most beautiful things she'd ever created.

"I did it!" she said admiring her work on the shelf with other items waiting to go into the kiln for setting.

"You did. That's a good start. You'll be able to give your classmates help when the rest of them start on the wheel tomorrow."

Damien smiled at her as he wiped excess clay off his hands with a towel. She tried not to notice how great his arms looked in his clay splattered grey t-shirt.

"I think I'll avoid giving instruction. I tend to make people mad when I give suggestions."

"Does your instruction come with a dose of condescension?"

She followed him to the sink where he turned on the water and pumped soap into his hands. "Are you saying I'm condescending?"

"I'm asking if you give advice because you want to help or if you give advice because you think you know better. There is a difference."

She pumped soap into her own hand and washed hers after he pulled his hands from the water.

"I'm trying to help. I'm always trying to help." Her tone was sharp.

"I didn't mean to hit a sore spot."

Hard not to. Her sore spot was pretty big right now. "Do you always make broad assumptions about people's lives?"

Water hit the side of her face. She gasped then turned to

him. His lips trembled with a suppressed smile. His dripping wet hand lifted to fling water at her.

"Did you just flick me with water like we were kids?" She tried to sound affronted, but laughter crept into her voice.

"I did," he grinned as if he dared her to challenge him. His grin did strange things to her mid-section.

"Why?"

"Because I could tell you were about to get back in whatever funk brought you in here today, and I didn't want that to happen."

She snatched the towel out of his hand to dry hers. "So, you act like a kid?"

"Did it work?"

She glared then flicked her fingers at him, splashing his face with several drops of water. "What do you think?"

"I think." he reached over and ran his thumb across her cheek, "that even when you have clay on your face and are throwing water at me, you're still cute."

Nicola forgot to breathe. The edge of his nail gently scraped off the dried clay. She felt the tickle of his touch in every nerve in her body. Her heart constricted. Heat spread through her face. He'd moved closer. Not so close that she was crowded, but close enough to make her want to wrap an arm around his waist and curl into his chest.

She turned her head and took a step back. "Don't. I can get it off." She used her damp hand to wipe at the spot he touched. The spot that still tingled.

Damien slid back. "I'm sorry. I didn't mean to make you uncomfortable."

"Look, Damien, I'm just . . . the thing is I'm not good with reading signals, so I don't want to mix up anything with you. I know you're not interested, and I'm trying not to read too much into our relationship. I mean friendship."

There she'd said it. Gotten her big old embarrassing crush

out in the open. She was going to be brave and daring and give him the *I like you but it's okay if you don't like me we can still be cool* speech.

She dared a glance at him. His eyes were wide. Lips slightly parted. Oh, crap, she'd made it worse. Embarrassment burned her stomach like a hot poker.

She turned to run away. Damien's hand wrapped around her elbow. He pulled her back until her chest touched his. "Who said I'm not interested?" his voice dipped low.

She couldn't believe it. *Was he interested?*

"You said you didn't do . . . that you were only being nice."

His hand rested on her hip. His head dipped lower. "That was me trying to put up a front. Believe me, Nicola, I'm very interested."

Her heart beat so hard she was surprised it hadn't burst. Her breath stuttered out. "Oh well, in that case . . ."

Her lips parted just as his head lowered, and his lips pressed into hers. The kiss was hesitant. Questioning if he should continue. For once, Nicola didn't worry about being too aggressive. She lifted her chin and slid her tongue against his full bottom lip. Damien didn't need any more coaxing. He pulled her tighter against him. Both of his arms wrapped around her until she was engulfed by his arms, his kiss, his scent.

Her hands were still damp. She wanted to dig her hands through his hair, or under his shirt. Yeah, under his shirt would be really good. But she didn't want to break up this fantastic moment with cold wet hands. She wrapped her arms around his neck but held her hands away from him.

Damien obviously had no qualms about the dampness of his hands because his roamed up and down her back. Wetting her thin shirt so the heat of his palms burned straight through her. So hot, she wanted to take off all her clothes.

Make love in a public place.

One of the things she wanted to do. One of the things she'd had the chance to do once in college before her practical mind convinced her smart girls did not have sex on the quad. She could make up for that now. Right now, with Damien.

Then what?

The question made her pull back quickly. Her breathing hard and ragged. He didn't want a relationship. He didn't believe in love anymore. She wanted him. Wanted to do this, but she had to think about it. Had to get her bearings straight. Was she really ready for a quick love affair? Would she be able to stop herself from falling in love with Damien?

Chick yeah! Both Quinn and Shonda's voices screamed in her head.

"I should go?" The words came out like a question. Even though her brain tried to say she needed to slow down before she was headfirst in a situation she couldn't handle, her body was like go for it right now!

Damien's hands slowly slid from her back to her hips. They rested there lightly. Just enough pressure to pull her back if she leaned in or let her go if she pulled away.

"Can I see you again?" Damien asked.

"You'll see me tomorrow. I have class."

He grinned and his dark eyes sparkled. He was so friggin' cute. Her heart felt tight in her chest. "Can I see you again outside of class?"

Hell yes, but she couldn't be too eager. She had to be sure about this. "Maybe. Sleep on it, and we can talk tomorrow."

He nodded and let his hands drop from her hips. "Fair enough."

"I'll see you tomorrow," she said.

"Looking forward to it."

She grinned as she left the studio. Her world was rocked

off its axis, but life outside of the little corner where Damien had kissed her went on as normal. The sisters had left earlier. Free studio time was over, so Fran had cut out too, but outside of the studio cars drove, the sun was setting, and the birds chirped. Everything was so normal and completely changed at the same time. Good. She wanted to keep this memory hers for a little longer. Savor the moment. Her own secret thrill.

Chapter 20

Damien didn't come through to observe the pottery class the way he typically did. Nicola tried not to show her disappointment as she and Mr. Goldberg chatted about his grandkids while they sat next to each other making bowls on the pottery wheel. Nicola kept her private lesson with Damien the day before to herself.

They'd only kissed. It wasn't that big a deal. They'd made no promises. None of that lessened how much she wanted to see him.

She'd halfway convinced herself not seeing Damien was a good idea when he strolled in at the end of the class while everyone cleaned up. He didn't come directly to her. Instead, walking around and making observations on everyone's work. He approached Nicola and Mr. Goldberg last then asked innocuous questions about their bowls.

"Hey, Nicola, can you stick around for a few minutes? I want to run something by you," Damien asked after giving them suggestions on ways to ensure a more even distribution of the clay in their work.

"Sure, let me put up my stuff."

"I'll be in my office."

She nodded and worked with everyone else to clean their area and put away their creations. Outwardly, she was cool and calm as the class chatted and complimented each other on their work. Inwardly, Nicola's heart beat erratically and her skin tingled with expectation.

Her mind considered various topics he might want to discuss. The kiss yesterday. Whether it should happen again. What if he wanted to apologize and say it was a mistake? What if he wanted to kiss her again?

By the time she waved goodbye to the rest of the class and knocked on Damien's door her palms were sweaty and her nerves on edge. No matter what he said she would be cool. She wouldn't get her expectations up.

"Come in," Damien called.

She entered and was surprised to discover his office was larger than she expected. He had room for a sturdy wooden desk, a display case filled with various pottery pieces and pictures she assumed were of him with friends and family, and a blue loveseat next to a table with a one-cup coffee maker with a rack of coffee pods next to it.

Damien got up from behind his desk and walked over to one of the lounge chairs. "Have a seat. Thank you for sticking back."

"No problem." She didn't know what else to say. *Are you going to kiss me again* is what she wanted to say, but that didn't seem like the best icebreaker.

"I wanted to ask you about your list."

Nicola plopped down in the chair. "My list?"

"Yeah, you trying things you haven't done before."

If he had wanted to kiss her again this was not the way to set the mood. "What about it?"

"I've got an idea of something you can try. Something we

can do together." He ran his hands over his ripped jeans. His sexy dark eyes watched her steadily.

"Well, that's not exactly how it works. I'm supposed to pick things already on my list. Not add new things."

The corner of his mouth tipped up ever so slightly. Her stomach clenched. "Well then how about you consider my request anyway."

Somehow, he made the words sound sensual and heat pooled in her lower belly. "Okay, what were you thinking?"

"Would you like to go kayaking with me this weekend?"

She watched him for several seconds. Waited for the laughter followed by an "I'm kidding." It didn't come. She raised a brow. He mirrored her movement.

"Kayaking?"

He nodded slowly. "That is what I said."

"Like... on a river kayaking?"

This time he smiled, and it took him from gorgeous to heart stopping. "That's typically where people go to kayak."

Was he crazy? There was not a single cell in her brain that thought getting into a tiny boat and going in the middle of a raging river was smart. What if she fell in? Sure, she could swim, but she only swam in pools and only when she went on vacation. Which meant she hadn't swam in... she calculated the time since her last vacation. Four years.

They'd only kissed once and the man was already plotting ways to kill her off.

"I'm not sure," she said in a measured tone.

"Think about it. It'll be a lot of fun. Plus, I overheard you talking to Mr. Goldberg about needing something interesting for *Your Morning Wake-Up Call*. What's better than choosing something that takes you out to experience nature?"

She had a magic show and a trip to Cancun lined up for television and they seemed just fine with that. "Why would you ask me to go kayaking? I thought you asked me in here to talk about our kiss last night or something."

He ran a hand over his mouth and leaned back. “I was going to eventually get to that.”

“And your lead in was kayaking?”

He shrugged. “I haven’t asked a woman out on a date in a while. Would you have preferred dinner and a movie?”

She would have, but the words died in her throat. A date. He was asking her out on a date.

“You don’t date.” The words rushed out.

“I also don’t typically kiss a woman then ask her to go kayaking, but here I am.” He infused enough humor in his voice to make her smile.

Okay, maybe she could try kayaking. It was not on her list, but not being afraid to try something new when asked was on there in one version or another. A vision of icy cold water, crocodiles, and snakes falling from trees floated across her vision. She shivered and considered suggesting the dinner and movie idea until she met Damien’s dark eyes. The spark of anxious hope in them. He sat stiff and unsure. Was he nervous about asking *her* out?

Nicola straightened and nodded. “Why not. Let’s go kayaking.”

Damien’s body eased and he shifted out of his seat to kneel in front of her. Nicola easily rested her hands on his broad shoulders. Unwilling to ignore her temptation to touch him. His hands pressed lightly against her waist as he eased her forward.

“Were you worried I wouldn’t want to go?” she asked. Her ever blunt self reared its ugly head again.

“I was worried you’d say no in general.”

Really? Damien Hawkins, rising art celebrity and big-time internet thirst trap was worried she wouldn’t want to go on a date with him? Pre-list she would have said no. Pre-list she wouldn’t have signed up for his class. Pre-list she would have enjoyed watching the muscles of his hands and arms work beneath his skin as he created something on the potter wheel and posted the video on social media. Daydreaming about his artsy sex appeal while simultaneously thinking a guy like him was not dateable.

His fingers lightly played along her side. Sparks of electricity shot out with each soft touch. Now, with Damien in front of her, seeing the vulnerability in his eyes as he'd asked her to do something as out of her world as kayaking, she was once again grateful that she'd been pushed into doing things on her list.

"Well," she said, being bold and cupping the back of his neck. The thick weight of his dreads brushed her hand and she loved it. "I don't typically kiss a guy then say no when he asks me out the next day. Especially when he kisses as good as you do."

The heat in his gaze could melt polar ice caps. "Then I guess I better kiss you again."

Nicola went straight to Shonda's place after forty minutes of bone melting kissing with Damien in his office. He hadn't pushed her for more, and even though her body screamed for more, her brain held back. She needed to think. Her personal life wasn't supposed to blow up like this, she still had Desiree's perfume to figure out, there was her fight with Quinn to fix. Now wasn't the time to start a hot affair. Was it?

Shonda would help her figure this out. Her divorced best friend was actively and aggressively dating. Not to find a new husband, but to find out what was out there and what she did and didn't want to deal with after being married since she was twenty-two. Shonda could instruct her on how to enter the realm of no-strings-attached love affairs. That's all she had time for right now.

Her heart plummeted when she pulled into Shonda's driveway. Quinn's car was parked outside of Shonda's garage. What was Quinn doing there? They hadn't seen each other since the disastrous dinner at her parents' home. Now she was hanging out at Nicola's best friend's place?

She considered backing out and leaving. Quinn would decimate the little bit of self-esteem Nicola had in whatever it was she was doing with Damien with her unsolicited advice and assumption Nicola would mess things up. The curtains fluttered and she knew she'd been spotted.

Shonda answered the door. She held a wine glass in her hand and hip-hop music played in the background. "Hey! I didn't know you were stopping by. We just got back." Shonda hugged Nicola then pulled her in.

"Got back from where? It's Wednesday. Where are the kids?" Why hadn't they called her?

"Their dad wanted them to go to bible study with him and stay at his place. Now that he's suddenly found Jesus and decided to be sanctimonious, I agreed to let them go after Quinn asked me to the Women's Empowerment Network's monthly meeting."

"She's going to that?" Nicola followed Shonda into the house.

"She's on the board. Didn't you know that?"

She had not known. "Oh, yeah, I forgot."

They went down the hall into the family room. Shonda's home had an open floor plan that allowed conversation and people to flow easily from the kitchen to the family room. Quinn sat on the couch where she sipped wine and flipped through one of Shonda's many photo albums. In a world of online posting and hundreds of digital pictures on a phone, Shonda was the one person Nicola knew who routinely printed her pictures and put them in frames and albums.

"Shonda, I'd completely forgotten about going to that all white party. That was really three years ago?" Quinn said not looking up.

"Hey, look who's here," Shonda replied.

Quinn glanced up. Her smile didn't falter. Her body

didn't tense up. Her eyes didn't frost over, but Nicola could still sense her sister wasn't entirely happy to see her.

"Nicola, what brings you out on a Wednesday night?" Quinn asked sweetly. Too sweetly. Almost mockingly.

Nicola didn't take the bait. "I just finished pottery class. Thought I'd come through and hang out with Shonda and her kids for a little bit before going home."

"I'm glad you're going home instead of going back to the lab," Shonda said. "That class is doing you good. You used to work until this late at night."

Shonda went into the attached kitchen and picked up a bottle of wine. She pointed at Nicola and raised a brow.

Nicola nodded. "Just one glass. I'll work late tomorrow. I got behind with the trip to L.A. I'm still catching up."

Quinn held up a hand. "My fault. I'm a bad influence."

"I didn't mean it that way," Nicola said. "I'm just saying I need to catch up." Remind herself of her responsibilities when her body still hummed from her time with Damien. A guy like that could become a big distraction.

"No offense was taken," Quinn replied. Her phone chimed and she glanced at the screen and grinned. "I guess your busy schedule means you can't go to Cancun."

Shonda brought over the glass of wine and Nicola took it. She sat on one of the leather lounge chairs and took a sip. "Of course. I can't wait."

If it weren't for the promise to the television show she'd bail on the trip. They were leaving in a few weeks and she really couldn't afford to take off right now, but the smug tone in Quinn's voice meant her sister expected her to change her mind. Maybe even wanted her to change her mind.

Shonda sat on the arm of Nicola's chair and gave Nicola a one-armed hug. "See Quinn, I told you she was still going."

"Yay," Quinn said with a tight smile before dropping her phone and flipping through the pictures.

Shonda squeezed Nicola's arm. A silent plea. Quinn may

have already filled her in on their argument. Shonda was now pushing for a peace offering.

"Why didn't you tell me you were elected to the Women's Empowerment board?" Nicola asked.

Quinn shrugged. "I couldn't believe it myself. It just kind of happened."

"I knew you were a member, but it's really great that you're taking a leadership role." Did that sound preachy? She didn't want to sound preachy when she talked to Quinn. She wanted Quinn to do well. To not feel like a disappointment when Nicola knew she wasn't.

"One of my followers was attacked by a guy who thought the way she dressed was invitation enough for his advances. When she commented on one of my posts, I got mad. Then I found out that the Network was trying to help her find a lawyer. I stepped in, and then started helping them with other cases."

Shonda nodded. "Your sister has gotten the Network a lot of attention and new donors. They're able to help many more people now."

Pride at her sister's efforts filled her chest. "I remember you talking about that. That was almost two years ago. I didn't realize you stayed involved. I thought..."

"That I was just using my status as trophy wife to sell products online? Turns out selling products can translate to selling people into giving to a good cause."

She opened her mouth to defend herself. Shonda placed a hand on her shoulder. Did her small be nice head shake. Nicola sipped her wine then took a deep breath.

"You should tell Mom you're on the board," Nicola said.

"I told her." Quinn flipped a page of the photo album. "She didn't seem impressed."

"Why not?"

Quinn looked up from the pictures in her lap and nailed

Nicola with a hard stare. "It was right before the Desiree announcement. She was preoccupied."

Nicola glanced away. This upside-down world they lived in made her uncomfortable. Quinn's accomplishments getting ignored because of Nicola. Her mom downplaying one sister to uplift the other. Just like their childhood, except now the roles were reversed. Reversed because of a miracle in a bottle Adele believed Nicola made on her own. When without Quinn, the miracle may not have happened.

Shonda, bless her soul, felt the tension and broke the silence. "Nicola, how's the pottery class going?"

"Pretty good." The low hum that had disappeared as she talked to Quinn returned as memories of her kiss with Damien resurfaced. "Really good."

Shonda moved next to Quinn on the sofa. Her eyes were wide, and she elbowed Quinn and grinned. "Oh no. Do you see that smile? Something has happened."

Quinn's icy stare melted away. She crossed her legs and leaned forward. "Oh yeah. There's definitely a story behind that look."

Nicola sipped her wine. Her face was on fire. "It's nothing."

Shonda shook her head and pointed a finger. "Don't even come at me with that. Spill it. I know you're dying to."

She was, and even though she didn't want to talk Damien with Quinn, maybe doing so would melt some of the frost between them. Let Quinn see how helpless she was when it came to dating, and maybe she'd forget about being mad at her.

"Fine. Damien finally kissed me."

Quinn and Shonda clapped their hands. Shonda spoke first. "I thought this was a never gonna happen situation."

"I did too," Nicola said. "But I went to the studio the other day and he kissed me. Then tonight, he asked me out."

Quinn lifted a shoulder "At least he asked you out."

Shonda gripped her wine glass and grinned. "When and where?"

"He wants to go kayaking." She tried to infuse her voice with excitement. A *yay I'm doing something fun* type enthusiasm.

They didn't buy it. Shonda's nose screwed up and she leaned back. Quinn's lips parted in a disbelieving gasp.

"Girl, didn't you see *Bird Box*?" Quinn shot back. "Do you want to fall in?"

Laughter bubbled up in Nicola. Leave it to Quinn to say something silly. "We won't be going down blindfolded. And the last time I checked there are no monsters out there."

Quinn shook her head and leaned back. "Are you going?"

"I am." She straightened her shoulders. "I'm doing new things, remember. This will be fun."

Quinn snorted.

Shonda placed a hand on Quinn's knee and laughed. "Stop. It's cool to try new stuff. Besides, a date is just an interview for the next date. If she does fall in, then she knows not to go out with him again."

"Will you two stop saying I'm going to fall in. It'll be great. It'll be fun. It'll be an adventure!"

Quinn giggled. Shonda joined in. Nicola rolled her eyes, but her lips twitched. "It's going to be a disaster, isn't it?"

They all broke out into a fit of laughter.

Chapter 21

Instead of dragging a *Your Morning Wake-Up Call* camera person on her kayaking adventure, the local affiliate outfitted Nicola with a portable camera to get all the action. The thing was attached to her helmet and ready to go. She'd asked Damien to not mention that this was a date while she wore the camera. Just two friends on an outing to keep their personal relationship out of the news. He'd agreed, but for a brief second, she'd wondered if her request bothered him.

Now, as they stood on the edge of the river listening to instruction on how not to die on said river, she couldn't think any more about if his feelings were hurt by her request. She was about to canoe down the river. Thankfully, Damien had insisted they do a two-person boat instead of putting her in a kayak. Apparently canoeing was easier.

She doubted that.

"Are you sure you don't mind that I picked this?" Damien leaned over and asked.

"Not at all," Nicola said with a forced smile.

She tugged on the red life jacket and tried not to look terrified. She glanced over at the swift current in the river and swallowed hard. Their guide for the tour gave information about how the trip would go. The more he talked, the more she questioned her ability to swim. She would survive if she were dumped in the middle of the pool. Getting dumped in the middle of a river. That was a whole other story.

"I didn't know you were the outdoors type," she whispered back.

Don't say no to new experiences. If she survived, this would be an awesome story.

Damien leaned in closer to her, making their side conversation less likely to interfere with their tour guide's instructions. "I took a canoe trip a few years ago. I did it on a whim when I saw it advertised online. I didn't think I'd like it, but it was great. Once you're out there in the middle of the river the sights and sounds of the city just fade away. It's nothing but you, nature, and your thoughts. It's a good way to get grounded again."

"Is this your typical first date choice?"

He chuckled and damn if he didn't look cute doing so. Even though his dreads were pulled back and the helmet they'd given barely fit over his hair he still managed to look sexy. Or maybe her hormones and a memory of how well he kissed made her immune to anything that could take away from Damien's obvious sex appeal.

"Not typically. Not at all. I haven't been on a date in a while."

"How long is a while?"

"Since my divorce." He glanced away then.

Five years. He said he'd been divorced for five years. She tried not to think about the type of pressure that statement came with. Tried and failed. If she was the first date in five years would he be okay with her directing whatever they were doing down the no strings attached road?

"If you fall in the water don't panic."

The voice of their guide snatched her attention. Her gaze swung to their guide. Fall in? Don't panic? Four words that should not be spoken in the same sentence. Falling into a pretty big river should require a modicum of panic.

"If you fall in, raise your hands and feet toward the surface," their guide continued. "With the life jackets on you'll float, and someone can easily pull you out of the water."

Nicola leaned toward Damien. "Is he serious? Are we expected to fall in?"

Damien chuckled. "Nah, he's just going over the rules. Like a flight attendant on a plane."

"I think I have a bigger chance of falling into this river than being in a plane crash."

Damien placed a hand on her shoulder and squeezed. "You'll be fine. You're in the canoe with me. I know what I'm doing."

Nicola nodded stiffly and listened to the rest of the in-case-you're-about-to-drown instructions. Damien hadn't taken his hand off her shoulder. She liked the feel of him holding her. His body firm and warm against her. His hand a reassuring pressure with the occasional squeeze whenever their guide talked about what to do if something went horribly wrong on the tour.

A few minutes later they were all in the canoes heading down the river. Nicola turned on the camera when they started. The group didn't talk much as they paddled. Their guide pointed out interesting birds and plants along the way. Occasionally, Damien would chime in and point something out to her like the family of turtles on a log or the fish swimming next to their canoe. He'd been right. It was kind of peaceful and fun.

"What do you think?" he asked.

The water was calm but steady. The current strong as it guided them and the rest of the tour. After fifteen minutes of no disaster in sight, Nicola's shoulders relaxed. "This is nice. Thank you for bringing me out here."

"Would you want to come back?"

"I think I might."

She glanced over her shoulder at him in the back of the canoe and caught his smile. He looked as if she'd just made his day. If coming out here with him resulted in that kind of reaction maybe she'd buy a canoe and they could come out every weekend.

"That's cool," he said. "I wasn't sure if you'd be into this or not."

"I'm trying new things."

"I did that," he said. "After my divorce. Went out and tried new things. It's how I ended up on the river in the first place. My ex said I was stuck and comfortable with the way things were and that she didn't want to be comfortable. She wanted the discomfort of being in an unfamiliar environment."

"That sounds . . . interesting." She slowed her rowing and turned off the camera as she listened. The producers didn't need to hear the details of his personal life.

"Yeah. She wanted to move to Barcelona. Read an article about how you can live there on two thousand a month or something. My studio was just starting to take off, and I didn't want to go. I thought Barcelona was just a whim of hers. Then one day she was on a plane and I had an It's-me-not-you letter left on the bed. Divorce papers came six months after she left."

Nicola sucked in a breath. Her chest tightened at the pain that must have caused. "Damien, that's terrible. I'm sorry."

"I was too. Then I realized maybe it was for the best."

"That's really mature of you." She wasn't sure if she would have handled a breakup like that so easily. Marriage was supposed to be a partnership. A lifetime of we're in this together.

"Yeah, well, I wasn't grown up about it at first. I was hurt. Angry. Really angry. My friends all told me afterwards that they knew she was selfish. That she wasn't the right person for me."

Her hands tightened on the oars. "Don't you hate that? How friends tell you how horrible the person was after you break up?" The way Quinn said she'd always known Bobby was shady after he'd embarrassed Nicola on their date.

"I do hate that, but I get it. You don't want to ruin your friend's happiness." He sounded as if he didn't quite believe his own argument.

"You know what, ruin mine." She started rowing again. They were lagging behind the rest of the group, but she didn't mind. She liked being able to talk to Damien without everyone else around. "I'd rather know how my friends really feel than hear their *I told you so* later."

"And what if your friends say you shouldn't date me?"

It wasn't her friends who'd say that. What would he say if he realized she was telling herself not to date him? Not to get too attached or distracted with him. "Are we dating? I thought we were just making out in corners."

His laughter was like a warm breeze across her skin. "Oh, you got jokes I see."

She was a master of avoid and deflect.

"Hey guys," their guide called. "Up ahead are some class one rapids. Not very dangerous, but still a challenge for new paddlers. We can go up on the banks and walk down to where they are so you can see before we go. That way, if anyone doesn't feel comfortable tackling the rapids, they can meet us on the other end."

The group maneuvered to the banks and secured the canoes. Nicola turned the camera back on as they walked a few feet downstream to where the water was choppy with a few white peaks as the river rushed through the rocks. Nicola's eyes got wide. Okay, it wasn't exactly white-water rafting, but she also wasn't sure if she could maneuver them through that. She looked at the other newbies in the group and all of them were excited.

"Anyone want to walk past?" their guide asked.

A bunch of negative head shakes. These people had to have lost their minds. Not one other person in the group seemed afraid to tackle the rapids. Which meant she couldn't be the only person scared. No way was she going to be that girl.

"Are you sure?" Damien asked once again with a reassuring shoulder squeeze. "We don't have to do it."

His mouth said that, but she saw the anticipation in his eyes. The rising joy of tackling nature. If she said no, he'd be okay, but then he'd judge her. She'd be boring Nicola afraid to try anything new. She'd gotten this far, the guide said they were class one, which had to mean not dangerous. *Please, God, let that mean not dangerous.*

She balled her hands into fists that she tried to pump with excitement. "Yeah, let's do this."

Her show obviously worked, because Damien grinned and squeezed her shoulder again before they all trudged back to the boats. Everyone chatted excitedly as they climbed in and got back on the water. The calm sound of the river gave way to the louder sound of faster moving water. Each dip of her paddle into the water revved up her heart another beat.

Yes. I can do this. Just follow the people in front of us. Damien will do most of the work in the back. Okay. Almost there. Man, that water sounds loud.

The current picked up and they were there. The front of

the canoe dipped down and then back up. She gripped the paddle. Fear and exhilaration sent adrenaline surging through her system. She could do this. She would make it. Nicola versus river, and she was going to win!

The paddle slipped in her hands. The canoe rocked harder, dipped then popped up. She wasn't sitting anymore. A brief sense of weightlessness overtook her as she flew out of the canoe before cold water engulfed her.

Oh God. I'm going to die!

She panicked. Her heart hammered. Her eyes were wide open and burned. The light from the surface blending into the darkness of the water. She flailed her arms and legs. Searching for something solid to save her.

Hold your arms and legs up. Someone will get you.

The instructions came back to her. She forced herself to relax and held up her arms and legs. Sure enough, she floated. Strong hands gripped the front of her life jacket and hauled her up. Damien wrapped her in his arms. She gripped him for dear life.

"I've got you," he whispered in a shaky voice. "Don't worry. I've got you."

Everything after was a blur. She was deposited back into the canoe. Everyone made sure she was okay, but after the excitement died down, the tour continued as if she hadn't nearly drowned. The fear she'd felt was replaced with embarrassment. Her wet clothes, workout clothes and not the wet suits the experienced paddlers wore, were heavy and cold. When the guide stopped to point out a bald eagle, she wanted to throw a brick at his head. She wanted out of the boat, not to do more sightseeing.

Damien patted her back. "We're almost done."

He sounded guilty. It wasn't his fault she'd fallen in. She should have agreed to walk the bank instead of tackling rapids. Even baby rapids, when she'd never canoed before.

"It's cool. I've never seen an eagle." She said between chattering teeth. She tried to look at the eagle with an expression of wonder and appreciation.

Damien chuckled. "Okay, I know where the tour ends. Let's go ahead and get you out of here."

She couldn't hide her gratitude, so she didn't even try. "Bless you."

Chapter 22

The ride back to her place was miserable. Despite Damien turning on the heat, the cold dampness of Nicola's wet clothes seeped all the way into her bones. That and the smell of the river: mildew, fish, and sulfur had her dreaming of an hour-long hot shower.

"Are you okay?" Damien asked again as they pulled into her neighborhood.

He'd asked the question a dozen times since getting in the truck. She should be happy he even cared enough to ask, but she knew the real reason. Just to make sure she wasn't about to freak out the way she wanted to. He probably couldn't wait to get her out of his truck. She couldn't do something as simple as canoe down a river. Everything she'd tried to do on that damn list resulted in some type of disaster.

Maybe she just had to face it. She wasn't cut out for an adventurous life. She was the uninteresting, sensible one. She pulled at her damp t-shirt. The uncoordinated one. Pretty soon everyone, including Damien, would realize the image of levelheaded sophistication she'd tried to portray was just that. An image.

"Nicola?" Damien asked.

She gave him a tight smile and nodded. "I'm good."

His hand tightened on the wheel. His shoulders rose and fell with a silent sigh. She could practically hear the disappointment in his brain.

He pulled in her driveway a few seconds later. Nicola unhooked her seat belt and opened the door before he'd gotten the vehicle in park. "Thanks for the ride. You don't have to come in."

Damien switched the gear to park and turned off the truck. "I'm not going to just drop you off and go away."

"It's no big deal really. I'm good."

"I'd like to make sure you're okay."

"I am okay. Just wet and ready for a shower. Besides, I know you probably have other things you'd like to do."

"I'd like to take care of you," he said. He got out of the car while she sat there stunned. Take care of her?

A few long strides brought him around to the passenger side. He opened her door but didn't let her out. One long arm rested on the door the other hand pressed against the side of his truck. Concern filled Damien's chocolate brown eyes.

"Look, I know you probably can't wait to get away from me, but I feel terrible about what happened. It was stupid of me to take you out on the river when it was obvious you don't like doing stuff like that. I thought you'd like trying something new since you were doing that list thing, but I should have known you wouldn't have been into that."

"You feel terrible?"

That was not the reaction she'd expected. She'd expected him to be embarrassed by her falling in. Annoyed with her inability to first admit she'd been afraid to do the rapids, and second that she'd risked both of their lives by not speaking up. But that's what she did. Kept things to herself. Tried to pretend things were okay, and plunge ahead.

"I won't take you out there again." His voice was strong and determined.

"You're not mad at me for falling in?"

His head drew back. Confusion flashed across his features. "Why would I be mad at you? I thought you'd be mad at me?"

She placed a hand on her chest. "I'm the idiot of fell in trying to impress you instead of walking along the bank like the guide offered."

His lips drew up in that smile that almost made steam rise from her wet clothes. "You were trying to impress me?"

"I thought you'd think I couldn't hang or that I was afraid." She hadn't wanted him to see her fear.

He reached forward and took a wavy strand of her hair between his thumb and forefinger. The two cornrows she'd put her hair in for the trip had unraveled after her impromptu diving lesson. Now her hair was a crinkly, damp, hot mess of curls around her head.

"I was worried you'd be more upset about your hair."

Nicola rolled her eyes. She slapped his hand away. "I can wash my hair. I'm just glad you fished me out of the water. I could only imagine my family's reaction if I would have drowned. They'd probably say it served me right for trying to prove I can be interesting."

The smile on his face fell away. His eyes hardened. Long fingers closed around the hand resting in her lap. "Don't joke about that. When you went under… that was the scariest moment in my life. I'd never forgive myself if something happened to you."

Emotion vibrated in his voice. Her stomach quivered. Heat flooded her chest and neck. If she were a romantic person, she'd think he felt something for her. Something bigger than the sizzling kisses and casual dating scenario she'd envisioned. Something that should have sent off warning bells of upcoming distractions but didn't.

"Is that why you were so heroic and quickly saved me. To avoid a lifetime of guilt."

"That was part of the reason." Some of the humor returned in his eyes, but a glint of something else was there too. Something hotter.

Nicola eased a little closer to him. "What's the other part?"

Damien nudged her knees apart until his hips settled between her thighs. He gently cupped the back of her neck. "I'd miss you too much. That happens when you start to care about a woman."

Her eyes widened, and her heart became a pounding hammer in her chest. "Starting to care?" Caring wasn't supposed to come into this. They'd kissed twice. Only had one date. He'd pulled her from the river.

He lowered his head closer, paused. "Nicola."

"Yes," she whispered. His lips were so close to hers. His scent, clay and fresh air, and temptation, overpowered any remnants of the river.

"Stop overthinking."

His lips covered hers. Damien's lips heated her as he placed soft intoxicating kisses on her lips, her cheeks, down her jaw to her neck. The chill to her bones vanished. She didn't want slow and easy. Her body itched to get closer, or maybe that was the wet clothes. His teeth nipped her lower lip. Fire flared in her midsection. No, that itch was not wet clothes.

Nicola's fingers found their way beneath his shirt. Damien sucked in a breath. The hard muscles of his stomach clenched. The hand gripping her hip pulled her closer to him.

A horn honked. Nicola and Damien jumped. They stared into each other's eyes. Their breathing ragged and heavy. She'd forgotten they were outside. Sitting in his truck for everyone in her neighborhood to see.

A breeze swept over them. Damien shivered. He wasn't as wet as she was. He'd worn the right clothing for a river trip, but he must be just as anxious to shower and change as she was.

"I should take a shower," she said.

Damien nodded. The ponytail he'd pulled his long dreads into was loose. Partly from pulling her from the river. Partly from her fingers gripping his head and pulling him into her.

"I bet you are ready to go inside and rest." The low rumble of his voice vibrated through her.

Resting wasn't the only thing she wanted to go inside and do. She took a deep breath. Called on the courage and confidence she'd seen in Quinn and Shonda over the years.

"You can join me." Her voice didn't shake. She sounded like a bad femme fatale movie cliché with her throaty proposition. If he laughed, she wouldn't blame him. Okay, maybe she would, but she'd at least understand.

Damien swallowed hard. "You have no idea how much I'd love that."

Later that afternoon Nicola sat at her kitchen island sipping hot chocolate out of a mug and watched Damien make pancakes at her stove. His clothes were in her dryer. The dryer cycle ended at least an hour ago, but he still wore her fuzzy bathrobe and nothing else. Not that she complained. The belt barely kept the pink and purple polka dot robe closed over the long lean muscles of his body. Which meant she got enticing glimpses of Damien's thighs, abs, and other attributes.

Those glimpses combined with a newfound sense of going for what she wanted—maybe because she hadn't drowned in the river—resulted in her not only making love with Damien in her shower, but also in her bed and again on her sofa. Her hair was still a frizzy mess, but she didn't care. She doubted she'd ever be able to come into her house and not think about all of the ways Damien had made her tremble.

She wore a light grey tank trimmed in lace with a pair of matching shorts. A gift from one of her lingerie clients. She didn't typically buy cute pajamas, but the way Damien had licked his lips when she'd come into the kitchen in them earlier made her consider filling her drawers with nothing but cute, lace trimmed pajamas.

He'd surprised her by cooking. She'd offered to order something, admittedly too tired after the day to even consider touching her stove, but he'd said he wanted to do something nice. The warmth of the cocoa filled her and contentedness seeped into her every pore. A sexy man making food, preparing hot chocolate and walking around her kitchen barely covered in a fuzzy bathrobe was definitely something worth being content with.

"What are you smiling at?" Damien asked. He hadn't looked over his shoulder and continued making their food.

"How do you know I'm smiling?"

"I can feel it." He winked at her over his shoulder.

Her stomach flipped and she almost giggled. Almost. "You're feeling really cocky right about now."

"Why shouldn't I be? I saved a beautiful woman and then made love to her several times. I think I have a right to be cocky."

Nicola laughed. "Maybe I'll fall in a river more often if this is the treatment I get."

He plated their pancakes and brought them over. He'd

also found the pack of bacon in her fridge and cooked it. He brought that over to the island, too.

Damien cupped her neck and pulled her closer to him. He buried his nose in her hair. Which he'd washed for her. *Swoon!* Then kissed her. "Please don't ever fall into the river again."

"I won't," she said hearing the trace of fear in his voice. "Though, I'm not used to being spoiled like this. What's a woman got to do to get this type of treatment again?"

She tried to keep her voice light. Even though the question was serious. Was this just a one-time thing? Her initial plans had wavered. Maybe it was just the excitement of the day, maybe because she really did want more with Damien.

"Just invite me over." He let her go and sat next to her.

Nicola's pulse jumped. Had they crossed over into a relationship? "You want to come over again?"

"Of course, you didn't think this was a one-time thing." His eyes widened and he studied her. "Wait, did you want this to be a one-time thing?"

The way he said it, as if the idea hadn't occurred to him until just now, made her stomach tighten. Was he serious about making this attraction between them something deeper?

She focused on drowning her pancakes in syrup. "I don't know. You were the one who said you didn't do relationships."

"What if I did do relationships?"

She shrugged, even though her pulse pounded in her ears. She didn't have time to start a serious relationship. She was meeting with Desiree's manager next week. If the singer still wanted changes. Nicola had to make them and get things right as soon as possible. That meant long nights at the lab working on various combinations. Not cutting things short to be with a new boyfriend.

Despite all that her heart answered instead of her brain. "I'd be okay with that."

He took the syrup from her and covered his own pancakes. "So would I."

She heard the smile in his voice. She glanced over at him with a half grin. "Then we're a couple, huh?"

He nodded. "I guess so."

That was easy. Too easy. Which meant her brain was ready to overanalyze the conversation. "Why?"

Damien cut his pancakes with one hand and took a bite of bacon with the other. "Why what?"

"Why are you suddenly okay with being in a relationship? You seemed adamant when we saw your friend the other week. Are you testing the waters with me? Am I rebound after your divorce? Because then I can prepare myself for..."

Damien dropped his fork and turned to face her. His brows drawn together. "For what?"

The fall out. The ultimate break up. The inevitable heartbreak. She'd done that before. Dated the guys who said she was too dedicated to her work. That she didn't spend enough time with them. That she wasn't fun or spontaneous.

"For what?" This time his voice was stiffer.

"I don't know. I just want to know where to place this relationship we're in." She kept her reply calm. She wouldn't give him the upper hand when they'd just started.

"Why? If we agreed we're together what else is there to categorize?"

She put her fork down and faced him, too. Better to get this laid out now versus later. "Because you seemed to be really hurt by your divorce. I just want to know how that's going to play with us."

"My divorce isn't about us. My wife decided she wanted something better and didn't need me anymore, so she split."

"What did she want that was better. You seem pretty great?"

He relaxed a little, but the tension around his eyes and mouth didn't go away. "She wanted to be independent. She said marriage tied her down. She wanted to live in Spain and the idea of having to consult with me about it irritated her."

"Then why did you two get married in the first place?"

He sighed and rubbed his temple. "We loved each other. Love makes you overlook the faults in someone else sometimes. I knew she was strong and independent. That's what made me fall in love with her in the first place. She didn't take shit from anyone. She was the CEO of a Fortune 500 tech company. She ate men more powerful than me for breakfast and let me know right from the start that her life would go on if I didn't meet her standards."

"She sounds rigid."

He chuckled and dropped his hand. His fingers brushed hers resting on the counter, and he absently rubbed the back of her hand. "Yeah, she was, but when we were together, she wasn't like that. She let her guard down for me. So, I let my guard down. We made it two years before things fell apart."

The pain in his voice was apparent. The guarded look in his eyes telling the rest of the story. He hadn't seen her leaving coming. He'd been blindsided and that had hurt. "I'm sorry."

He shrugged, swiveled in his chair, and ate some of his food. The awkward silence that followed made her want to rewind ten minutes. Her and her big mouth. Always having to know everything and be in charge. This was why Desiree hated the fragrance. Nicola couldn't just let go and accept things. She had to set rules and boundaries to everything.

"What about you?" he asked a few minutes later. When

she raised a brow, he raised his. "Your history. You made me spill my deal with my ex. Any ex-husbands, fiancés, or crazy boyfriends I should know about?"

Nicola shook her head. "Not hardly. I'm not the type of woman to inspire passionate emotions in men." She closed her eyes. Yeah, that's how you showed your new boyfriend he'd made a good decision.

"Shower, bedroom, couch."

She opened her eyes and saw he had three fingers raised. He let up a fourth. "I'm going to suggest kitchen counter after we eat. So, I don't believe you when you say you don't inspire passion."

Her face flamed. The sudden urge to shove the plates off the island and test his theory hit. She tamped it down. For now.

"Well, you're the exception not the rule. I've had a few relationships. None serious. All ended by the other party."

"Why?"

"Oh, the usual, it's me not you. Followed by, you work too hard. I'm not good enough for you, which I think was just said to make me feel better. And the one time I was told I act like I didn't need a man, so why should he stick around."

"Do you need a man?"

"No." The word was immediate. "Do you think I need one?"

He held up his hand as if fending off an attack. "I'm not saying that you do. You're obviously taking good care of yourself. But, if you'd let me, I wouldn't mind being the man in your life."

Warm tingles raced up her spine. She held back a Disney Princess-worthy sigh, but was pretty sure her eyes were doing that swoony thing she'd seen in movies. Slow and steady. That's how she'd move forward with this thing with Damien. She'd hold him close, figure out what they were doing before she opened herself completely, because right now, as he looked at her like she was beautiful and precious, she liked the idea of him being the man in her life.

"I think I'd like that."

The heat that flared in his eyes made her mouth go dry. Damien pushed their plates aside and stood. "Good. Now, if you're done." He lifted her and sat her on the counter. "Let's get to number four."

Chapter 23

Damien left the next morning, and Nicola decided she couldn't put off what she needed to do much longer. She skipped going to the lab and drove to Aiken to see her grandfather. He'd skipped their magic show call during the week. She wanted to apologize for upsetting him at the speed dating event and let him know she was still all in on helping him with the show.

If she didn't go see him, he would continue to push aside their weekly calls, assume she didn't want to be in the show and wouldn't bring it up when she eventually saw him at the next obligatory holiday dinner. They'd go on as if her attempt to help had never happened and he wouldn't be any ornerier towards her than he'd been before.

Nicola didn't want that to happen. He was her last living grandparent. Her grandmother had always been there for Nicola and she'd never gotten the chance to show her grandmother appreciation in kind. She wouldn't let her grandfather down. She wanted to continue to build their connection.

Which is why she spent the drive brainstorming ideas for their debut show. She was thinking matching outfits, of course, but also, she wanted something classic. Black capes and top hats weren't enough. Maybe she'd agree to the purple sequin he'd mentioned before. They also needed great stage names. Like "The Magnificent Jeremiah" or "The Fantastic Jeremiah and his *Grand*daughter." Emphasis on grand to add a little *umph* to the name.

She was well aware both titles were terrible. Being creative and naming things wasn't listed on her resume. She just hoped her grandad would be happy she was trying. That he'd forgive her for being a know-it-all the last time she'd come up.

Not assuming she could just pop up on him, she'd called when she'd gotten in the car and told him she was coming. Jeremiah hadn't sounded excited or annoyed by her plans, which she took as a good sign. When she pulled up to his house early Sunday afternoon, she was surprised there was a green Prius parked in his driveway. He hadn't mentioned anything about company.

She rang the bell and was even more surprised when a black woman who looked to be in her late twenties opened the door. "Hey, you must be Nicola. Come on in."

The woman's dark eyes were warm and welcoming. She was dressed casually in jeans and a teal-colored t-shirt with *Partners for Healthy Waters* written on the front. Her hair was cut into a sleek pixie cut and earrings made out of soda pop tabs dangled in her ears.

"I am, and you are?" Nicola walked through the door.

"I'm Valeria." Valeria's brows rose and she said her name as if Nicola should have immediately known who she was. "I'm helping your grandad with his show at the senior center."

"You are?" When had that happened? They'd only missed two weekly calls. That shouldn't have been long enough to get replaced.

"Yeah! I volunteer down there and when he told me you couldn't help anymore, I just couldn't let him drop out. Jeremiah is a sweetheart you know?"

You couldn't help him anymore?

They were going down the hall and entered the living space. Nicola stopped and took in the sights with her mouth wide open. So much for coming with ideas. Valeria, the super assistant, had her grandad's living room looking like the backstage of a theater. Jeremiah stood in the middle of the room. He wore a purple sequin suit that looked too big but had pins in it around the arms and legs. Other purple sequin material was scattered around the room. A video that explained magic tricks played on the television and a box of what looked like props sat in one of the chairs.

"Nicola," her grandfather said and grinned bigger than she'd ever seen him. "Sorry for the mess. Just move stuff around and find a seat."

Valeria hurried over to Jeremiah and tugged at the front of the suit. "Don't move too much. You'll poke yourself."

He scoffed. "A little pin prick won't hurt me."

"Maybe not, but there are a lot of pins in this suit. So, be careful." Valeria kneeled and worked on the hem of the pants.

Nicola eased farther in the room. A sinking feeling deep in her gut. "What's going on here?"

Jeremiah's grin didn't waver as he spoke. "Valeria works in the drama department at the high school and volunteers on weekends at the senior center. She said we could use these old suits for the magic show. How about that?"

That was the absolute last thing she'd expected. His apparent joy at having a new assistant made her heart twist painfully in her chest. One fight and he'd replaced her?

She wanted to snatch the sequined material out of Valeria's hands, yell at her grandfather, and demand that he give her an explanation. But the way he beamed down at Valeria killed any arguments Nicola had. He'd never beamed at her like that.

"That's great. I didn't know you needed a new partner?" Years of practice kept the hurt of rejection out of her voice.

"Well, I knew you were busy with that new perfume you're making. After the last time you were here, I realized you were right. I was wasting your time."

"I didn't say that?" Nicola shot a look to Valeria. Her replacement didn't look up.

"You didn't have to. I knew you had more important things to do than come up here and keep me company. I shouldn't have dragged you to that speed dating thing. So, I figured I'd find a new partner and you wouldn't be distracted."

Basically, I don't want to put up with you and your know-it-all ways, so I found someone more suitable.

"But I don't mind helping. I even thought up names for our act." Thankfully her voice didn't waver. Inside she felt lost. Like a kid forgotten at the store watching their parents drive off. Except, she knew Jeremiah wouldn't realize he'd left Nicola behind. He thought he was doing her a favor. She'd hurt his feelings, so he'd assumed she didn't want to spend more time with him.

"Oh, we have a name," Valeria said grinning. "Acts of Wonder by Jeremiah the Wonderful."

"That's a mouthful." And better than what she'd come up with.

"It sets the stage," her grandfather said defensively. "Valeria can get posters printed using her teacher discount. We're going to put them up around the center before the show. It'll build buzz."

Nicola bit her lip. She hadn't meant to sound judgmental, but it was hard to not be petty when she'd been tossed aside. She ran her fingers over the material of one of the outfits and tried to pretend as if she were okay with the change. She'd say something to Jeremiah later. She wasn't about to argue in front of Valeria. The woman seemed happy to help Jeremiah. If Nicola started an argument, then it would be another example of Nicola being judgmental about her grandfather's decisions.

"Sounds like you're good. But, you know I was still happy to help." There it was. The smallest of pleas in her voice. Damn, she hadn't wanted to give proof to how much being ditched by him was like a kick in the shins.

Her grandfather's brows drew together. "You aren't upset about me working with Valeria, are you? I mean, you always seemed to be more of a loner. Independent and everything. I didn't think you'd mind with all the other stuff you have going on?"

Except she had cared, and wanted to do this thing with her grandfather. Wanted someone in the family to be excited about needing her for something fun. Wanted to prove she could be there for someone in her family. That she wasn't completely selfish.

She shouldn't be disappointed. After thirty some odd years of being the one who was okay being left out, of course her grandfather wouldn't think she'd be upset. After all, she was the one who'd been okay when her family didn't show up for honor roll recognitions because she always made honor roll. She hadn't cared when they'd never gotten excited if she was elected into an academic honors society, because making good grades and getting in was a given. She'd gracefully said she didn't mind when she wasn't included in planning Quinn's wedding because she wasn't into that type of stuff. Why should she care now if her grandfather booted her out of his magic show for someone who had easy access to purple sequin suits and could print posters with Jeremiah the Wonderful at a discount.

Nicola did what she always did, smiled and acted like there weren't razor blades slicing across her heart. "You're right. It makes much more sense for you to work with Valeria."

He relaxed then pointed at the television. "Watch this. It's the big finale for our show. I found this video breaking down magic tricks on the internet."

Nicola sat in the middle of the sequins and pretended to be happy. "Sounds like you've got it all worked out."

"We do. You are still coming to the show, right?" he asked. "If you're too busy I understand."

"No, I'll be there. Remember I got all of the family coming."

"You sure?" he asked.

"Positively sure. Things will be said and done with Desiree's perfume by then." That was the one good thing out of this. The silver lining. She could devote more time to that. Time she could have spent today if she'd known she'd been fired.

"How is that going? Your mom said she didn't like the last sample you gave her?"

"Minor setback. You know me. I'll get it figured out." Earlier that week she'd made tweaks to the samples she'd sent Desiree in preparation for her meeting with her manager. She wasn't sure what feedback Desiree had, but she couldn't sit still and not try something.

"You always do." Her grandfather waved excitedly toward the screen. "Valeria, write this down. We can't forget this part."

Valeria laughed. "It's a video, Mr. Jeremiah, I can re-watch it. Now hold still while I get these pins in the pants."

Her grandfather settled but continued to beam at Valeria. Nicola's chest burned. She'd be okay. She always was. So she smiled, listened to her replacement's grand plans, and went over all the reasons why not being in a senior center talent show was actually great news.

She left her grandfather radiantly happy with Valeria and drove back to Atlanta an hour after arriving. He didn't seem to notice her visit was short or ask her to stay longer. Not that he needed her anyway. Not wanting to go home to be alone, or to call Damien and possibly appear needy after spending the previous day with him, she went to her parents'.

"Nicola, what are you doing here?" Adele asked after Nicola followed her into her bedroom. "I'm getting ready for a dinner party, so you can't stay long."

"Do I need a reason to visit my mom?" Nicola asked. She plopped down onto her mom's king-sized bed. Various discarded items of clothing littered the bed. Her mom was never neat when she searched for the perfect outfit.

Adele settled in front of the vanity in the corner. "You don't *need* a reason, but you also don't typically come over unannounced."

She glanced around the room. "Where's Dad? Isn't he going?"

"He's in the shower down the hall."

Nicola nodded and settled onto her side on the bed. Her dad used the guest bedroom closet and the guest bath for his stuff since Adele's stuff took over everything else. Sometimes Nicola wondered if he also slept in the guest bedroom, but decided never to ask. She didn't want to know that much or think about what it meant if he did.

Nicola jumped from the bed and crossed the room. "Want me to help with your makeup?"

Adele chuckled and waved her away. "That's cute. No, I've got it."

"You always let Quinn help you with your makeup."

"Well, Quinn knows what she's doing."

"I've worked in the beauty industry for years, Mom. I know what I'm doing." She picked up a bottle of Triumph and brought it to her nose. She still loved that fragrance.

"You can help me pick out a perfume for the night." Adele used a brush to smear primer on her face.

"Easy, you always wear our signature to dinner parties." Nicola set the crystal jar back on the vanity.

"It's a new classic, remember," Adele said proudly.

How could she forget. *Vogue* magazine giving their fragrance that title helped launch Queen Couture from potential failure to being one of the top names in fragrance. She didn't want to think about how she'd "saved" the company all those years ago.

"Did you know Grandad found someone else to help him with his magic show?" Nicola asked. She sat on the floor with her back against the wall where she could watch her mom apply her makeup.

She hadn't done that since she was a little girl. Her mom used to always drag her dad to fancy parties he'd rather not attend. He'd leave the bedroom and turn it over to the women in the house. Nicola and Quinn would sit in the corner and watch their mom do her makeup and hair. Quinn always providing suggestions that made things better. Nicola trying not to show how clueless she was when it came to applying makeup by pretending to read a book.

"Good for him," Adele said. "I told him you're too busy to be fooling around with his three-quarter-life crisis."

"Three-quarter-life crisis? What is that?"

"Well, he's seventy-five. Mom kept him straight during his mid-life crisis. What else is this besides a three-quarter-life crisis? Wanting to do magic shows and dragging you to speed dating events." Adele rolled her eyes then leaned in closer to the mirror as she applied foundation.

"How about he's trying to find something to be happy about now that he doesn't have Grandma. Besides, I wanted to help him out."

"Nicola, please, we all know you don't have time for silly things. You're more serious than the rest of us. Always with your nose in the book. He said you were angry after speed dating and I told him you were probably angry in general that you had to be pulled into his silly talent show."

"I wasn't angry. I was excited." She admitted. Her mom's assumption was probably what ultimately lead to Nicola being traded in for the handy and crafty Valeria.

Her mom laughed as if that were the funniest thing she ever heard. "Okay, Nicola. But in all seriousness, you really need to get to work on Desiree's fragrance. Her people called me on Friday saying they are really hoping to nail things down for your meeting this week. You can't get distracted by anything right now except making sure Desiree and her people are happy."

"I'm working on it." She would get this figured out.

"Well, work faster. Jesus, Nicola, you finally put all of that chemistry knowledge to a good use by making fantastic perfumes, and when it really counts you want to pout about not being in Dad's magic show, or run off to L.A. with Quinn for no reason."

"I'm doing stuff I never did before. Publicity, remember? And what do you mean finally put my knowledge to use? Mom, I graduated top of my class. I had an offer to work on my thesis with one of the best biochemical researchers out there. I could have gotten a job or worked on a research project that could have helped so many people. My knowledge was already being put to good use."

Adele sighed and leaned forward as she applied eye shadow. "See, there you go again, being dramatic. Sometimes I think you would have preferred working on some research project than actually lowering yourself to work in the beauty industry."

"I never said working here was lowering myself."

"Well, you also make it perfectly clear that your dream job wasn't here. I know you sacrificed what you really wanted to come help me turn this company around. That you think your research might have saved Mom. Well, guess what, it probably wouldn't have." Adele's hand trembled. She took a deep breath and lowered the brush. "What happened to Mom was unfortunate, and we both know that researching a cure isn't the same as finding one. I've come to terms that Mom is in a better place and no longer suffering. It's time you accept that, and stop acting as if working here is a step down from your lofty goals. We know you're smart, Nicola. You don't have to remind us."

Nicola drew her knees up and wrapped her arms around them. No matter how bad she felt, her mom knew how to add more guilt. "I am happy here. I wouldn't want to work anywhere else."

It was true. She'd had lofty goals of scientific discovery, but she didn't regret a day of working at Queen Couture. She loved working with her mom. Loved being a part of the world she'd never belonged to before. Only at times like this did she remember that she hadn't gotten there solely on her own merits.

"Well then prove it, by making Desiree's perfume. Quit worrying about what your grandfather is doing and quit following Quinn when she goes off on one of her flights of fancy and do what you're supposed to."

Nicola nodded. She absorbed her mom's words. Adele was right. She wasn't supposed to be having fun, traveling to L.A., or spending time on a magic show she hadn't really wanted to do. Her job was to be the top perfumer of Queen Couture. If she wanted to continue to be a person her family admired instead of ignored, then she had to make Desiree's perfume a success.

"Yes, ma'am. I'll get to work on Desiree's perfume tomorrow."

Chapter 24

When Damien texted asking if she was coming by the studio, Nicola only hesitated a second before saying yes. The visit with her mom had left her irritated and weighted with responsibility. Instead of spending the night thinking about how all her focus would need to be on creating Desiree's perfume, she decided to let the happiness that infused her from Damien's text wash away the lingering disappointments from her day.

By the time she arrived, the studio was closed, but Damien's truck was parked around back. She pulled out her phone and texted that she was outside. A few seconds later he replied to meet him at the side entrance.

He wore a t-shirt that was once white but had been stained with various colors, probably over several months. Dried clay splattered his arms and, God bless him, the grey sweatpants he wore. There should be warning signs posted when a good-looking man was going to be out and about attacking women's libidos by wearing sweatpants. His dreads were pulled back in a loose knot. The silver chains he wore tucked beneath his shirt.

Not caring about his stained clothes or the clay on his arms, she immediately wrapped her arms around his neck and lifted onto her toes to kiss him. Damien pushed the door closed and pressed her against it. She breathed him in. Felt settled by the certainty that he wanted her. That his hands on her body were just as desperate as her hands on his. After a day of rejection, his desire was like a balm to her scratched nerves.

Damien broke the kiss first. His breathing heavy and his eyes dark pools of desire. "You okay?"

The concern in his eyes made her throat constrict. No. This was not a time for emotions or crying. She had a man in her arms. A man for whom she actually inspired a passionate response. Now was not the time to cry about her family hurting her feelings. Desiree, Quinn, and Shonda wouldn't spend this time pouring out their emotions. Neither would she.

She reached for the waistband of his sweats and jerked them open. "I'd be better if you stopped talking."

His body shivered. Another question brightened his eyes. "What's gotten into you?"

"Damien." She leaned up and brushed her lips across his.

"What?"

"Stop talking."

His mouth opened. There was a battle in his eyes. Find out why she was all over him two seconds after coming into the building, or go with what she wanted. She slid her hand into the waistband, and sweet Lord he wasn't wearing underwear. Damien's body trembled and he stopped talking.

"Now are you ready to tell me what's going on?" Damien asked much later.

Nicola snuggled closer against him on the loveseat in his office. He lounged in the corner with his legs stretched out. Her back was against his chest. She didn't want to talk about what was going on. She wanted to bask in the glow of finally having had up-against-the-wall sex. Hard, passionate sex, which was a little difficult to coordinate, but still great. She tried to think of fragrances that represented those feelings. Those emotions. That's what she needed to make for Desiree.

Hard, something earthy, like nocturnally flowering Guettarda spruceana or a passionately sweet scent like ylang-ylang might work. Something difficult and uncoordinated. A scent that couldn't be easily wrangled in.

"Hey," Damien nudged her with the arm across her chest. "Stop thinking and start talking."

"Sorry, it's just work stuff."

"Things going okay?"

His hand trailed down her arm. Her body trembled. Damien pulled the thin blanket he'd had draped over the back of the chair over her.

"I've got a big meeting next week for Desiree's perfume. I'm worried we may lose the account," she admitted. "I've never lost a client before."

She said what she'd been afraid to say out loud before. If she didn't ultimately make Desiree happy then she could easily pick another perfume house to make her perfume. Queen Couture was financially stable enough to handle losing the account, but the backlash of being unable to meet Desiree's needs would affect them. Other clients may not consider them. Their quick rise in the competitive industry wouldn't mean anything if other celebrities avoided working with them.

"I thought you had that project locked in?" Damien continued running his hands over her. The slight movement hypnotic and comforting.

"Nothing is ever locked in when it comes to this industry. Desiree liked the original samples I put together, which means her lawyers are now talking to our lawyers to come up with a contract about licensing, usage of her name and things like that, but the final contract isn't signed. There's still time for her to walk away."

"Why would she walk away? She likes your samples, right?"

"She did, but I still haven't gotten it exactly right. I'm meeting with her manager in a few days. I'm starting to worry that I may not be able to do what she wants."

"What does she want?"

"Something edgy and exciting, but also classic and long lasting."

He lifted her hand and spread it out against his. "Sounds like a contradiction."

She grinned and watched him study their hands. He was touchy-feely. She never would have expected that when they'd first met. She'd never been touchy-feely and was surprised how much she liked his caresses and kisses.

"It is a contradiction." She threaded her fingers through his.

"Is that the problem?"

"No. I've had clients who've asked for random things to go together before. Last year I made a scent for a lotion that was called California Red Wine and Sunshine."

Damien's chest vibrated beneath her as he laughed. "What?"

"Yes! It was for a winery that sends special gifts to their patrons. The scent wasn't as hard to make as it sounds. I took the notes from the wine and synthesized citrus scents for sunshine."

"What you just said makes no sense to me, but it sounds like you are the expert they say you are." He kissed the back of her hand. Their fingers still joined together. "If you know how to synthesize sunshine, I think you can handle making Desiree's perfume. Are you sure you aren't too stuck in your own head and it's making it hard for you to trust yourself?"

She pulled her hand from his and stared at the ceiling. "You think I don't know that already. I'm trying. This shouldn't be a problem. I always figure things out. That's what I'm supposed to do. Figure everything out."

"Aha, now we're getting to the real reason you jumped me."

"Number one, I didn't jump you. And I'd think most men would be happy when their woman shows up and demands they take off their pants."

Strong arms wrapped around her, and he hugged her tighter. "You did jump me, and I am happy about everything that happened. I wasn't happy about the sad look in your eye right before you drowned your emotions with sex."

She cocked her head in order to look up into his face. "Are you analyzing me?" She couldn't believe he'd noticed.

"No. I recognize the signs." A history of dealing with someone who hid their inner feelings haunted his voice.

His ex-wife had done that. Hidden her thoughts until one day she packed up and left. She didn't want to be compared to his ex-wife. She wasn't narcissistic or overly independent. She was only independent because she had to be. It's what everyone expected her to be. She could open up and let people in.

"My grandfather dumped me," she said softly. "I was supposed to help him with his magic show at the senior center and he replaced me."

Damien shifted behind her. She turned to her side so they could look each other in the eye. He brushed her cheek with his thumb. "Ooh, baby, I'm sorry."

The empathy in his voice made her heart feel squishy. "Her name is Valeria, and to make it worse, she's kind of perfect to help him."

"How dare she be perfect," Damien said with mock outrage.

She knew he was only saying that to make her feel better, and it made her smile. "I know right. She works at the drama department in the high school. Got him a fancy costume and all these props. Just because I live an hour away, and don't have access to costumes, and can't come to all the rehearsals doesn't mean I was a bad assistant."

"Not at all, but maybe it's just easier with her there."

Nicola sighed. "I know. It makes sense. I'm busy with the perfume. I'm always working." All very legitimate reasons she shouldn't complain.

"But..." he raised a brow.

"But it was the way it happened. He just assumed I wouldn't care. My family always assumes I don't care. That all I want to do is work in the lab and be the fixer. Never the fun one. Never the one they can count on for anything other than solving a problem."

"There's nothing wrong with being a fixer."

"There's nothing great about being the one no one cares about. The one who doesn't need anything because she can take care of herself."

The one they assumed could always give a bit of herself without any expectation of receiving support in return. Her fault really. All her life she'd hidden how much she wanted to feel like she was a part of the family.

"Hey, tell your family how you feel. Ask for help sometimes. If you never show that you need something, then they'll assume you don't."

"It's not that easy." She couldn't show her family she was afraid of messing up all the time. That half the time she wasn't sure if she was making the right moves. That even when they thought she'd made the right moves, she hadn't. Then what would she be in the family? She couldn't go back to being ignored, or worse, scorned after everyone learned the truth.

Damien kissed her temple. "It is that easy. That's what family is for." He was quiet for several seconds. Nicola watched the conflict in his eyes, the question of how much more to say, before he spoke again. "After my divorce, I was so angry. I couldn't even appreciate the success I'd made of the studio. My big brother and little sister took me out and basically told me to get over myself. Stop acting like the forgotten middle child and celebrate the good stuff in my life."

"Did that work?"

He shook his head, but his lips lifted in a wry smile. "It pissed me off more, but then my mom called all excited about seeing one of my pieces discussed on some television show. It was the first time she'd called excited about something I'd done. I know my parents love me and they want the best for me, but my brother is the successful heart surgeon, my sister is a school superintendent who gave them their first grandchildren. I was just the artist."

"You're not just an artist." Her voice was fierce. No one was ever *just* anything. The feeling of being *just a* fill in the blank was often a feeling of being insignificant and marginalized.

"I know that, but when she called, I told her that was the first time I could remember her being excited about my work, and she cried. Before then, she'd never realized she hadn't told me how proud she was of me and my work. Then she told me about all the times she'd been proud of me over the years. I don't know what clicked, but I understood I could continue to be angry about what my ex had done to me, or I could let it go. I had a family who cared about me. They were proud of me. They love me. I had more to be happy about than to be angry about. My relationship with my mom and siblings wasn't bad, but I also didn't open myself up to them. I was the middle kid and I accepted I wouldn't get attention, but after I opened up to my family more, they opened to me. We're much closer now."

She wasn't the middle child, but she understood his feelings of not being seen. Of accepting your invisibility instead of asking for attention. Of not wanting to show that you cared because it could only expose you to a pain with the potential to hurt worse than being overlooked.

"You're saying tell my grandad he hurt my feelings?"

"Tell him you understand, but wanted to be in the show. Let people see the emotions you're trying to hide."

"I'm not hiding my emotions with you."

She'd confessed more to Damien than she'd confessed to Shonda or Quinn. Her plan to keep him at a distance was slowly eroding. Staying closed off was so much harder with Damien. He paid attention to her. Listened to her. Saw things other people didn't bother to see. She appreciated him and wished he wasn't so observant. Hiding was easier.

Damien flipped her onto her back and blanketed her on the couch. She shrieked then laughed. He kept his weight off her with one hand propped on the back of the chair and his forearm next to her head. His dreads formed a thick curtain around them.

"Good, because I'm not hiding mine with you either."

Chapter 25

Nicola stared at the glass vials and bottles on the rack in her lab. She'd chosen to work in the main lab with Tia and the interns today. She'd hoped their intermittent questions on the scents they worked on might spark inspiration in her.

"Nicola, you were right," Tia said, catching Nicola's attention. "Synthesizing the juniper instead of using vanilla really brought out the undertones in this soap. I think we've got a good blend for this season."

Nicola took the *touche*, a white paper strip used to sample the scent Tia held out, and sniffed. Juniper blended perfectly with hints of apricot and musk. Nicola smiled and nodded. "Great job!"

"Thanks, but this was all you." Tia's curls bounced as she nodded quickly. "You are so good at what you do. I can't wait to see what you put together for Desiree. It's sure to be a hit."

The admiration in Tia's eyes made Nicola uncomfortable. Sure, she'd made a suggestion for a soap for one of their retail clients, but that was easy. Desiree wanted worldwide success. Another Triumph.

"I'm sure it will be," she said with a half-hearted thanks before leaving the lab and going to her office. She took the vials of the various combinations of fragrances she'd put together with her. All were perfectly fine on their own. Even she had to admit that any one would be a successful perfume, but would Desiree love it? One had to hit the mark. She only hoped Desiree's manager didn't bring bad news.

You haven't gotten bad news yet.

Nicola clung to that thought. All she had was her own self-doubt, and a celebrity who was harder to please than she'd expected. She was letting the fight with Quinn and the break with her grandfather shake the rocky foundation she'd built her reputation on.

The phone on her desk rang. When she saw the number on the screen she cringed then answered. "Hi, Desiree, I was just thinking about you," Nicola said with forced cheer.

"Fantastic, because I can't get you out of my mind." The sound of the ocean was a perfect backdrop to Desiree's rhythmic voice.

"Oh really?"

"Yes, I was thinking about the samples you sent the other week. Sorry it took me so long to get back to you on that."

"You're on tour, I didn't expect a quick reply." She asked the question that terrified her. "What did you think?"

Desiree laughed. "I think you're close, but not quite there. I was worried that maybe we wouldn't get what I want, but then a friend of mine wore Triumph and once again I remembered why you are the perfect person to help me jump into the perfume field. You created that, which means you have to be capable of doing something just as great again."

Clearing her throat and taking a deep breath, Nicola filled her voice with confidence. "I've already gotten a few more blends I've worked on in case you wanted something different. I can't wait for you to see what I've put together for you."

"I know it will be fantastic. If I didn't have to finish this tour, I would come back to the states now just to smell what you've put together."

Nicola's one saving grace. "But your fans would be disappointed."

"As much as I want to say my fans will be okay, I know you're right. I'll just wait and see. I'm so excited!"

"Me too," Nicola tried to match Desiree's tone. Ignore the sinking feeling that she was on the verge of ruining her career and the company's reputation.

"I'll be home in two and a half weeks. I'm coming straight to Atlanta. Be ready."

"I will be." If she had to ignore everything and spend all her time trying every type of combination and creating a thousand samples for Desiree to try.

"Good. Bye, Nicola. Enjoy!"

"I will." She hung up the phone. Then dropped her head onto the desk.

Two and a half weeks. She could do this. She could think of something. She just had to get out of her head. That was all; she'd figure it out.

The sound of high heels clicking on the floor preceded her sister's voice. "What's wrong with you?" Quinn's voice.

Nicola sat up straight and pushed her hair out of her face. "Nothing. Just a headache."

The worry on Quinn's face disappeared. "Oh, good. Look, I came to talk to you about the trip next weekend."

"Next weekend?" Nicola frowned and looked at her calendar.

"Yes. Don't act like you forgot because I know you didn't. Not when you've got television crews ready to follow us down there."

The trip she'd agreed to because she'd assumed she would have Desiree's scent in the bag. That she wouldn't be struggling to think of something just as perfect as Triumph. By the time Cancun came up, she was supposed to be smooth sailing into pre-production and putting the finishing touches on the product debut.

"No, I didn't forget. I just . . . got busy."

"Well, you can't cancel now." Quinn said, crossing her arms. Her sister looked fabulous in a red jumpsuit with her hair falling into a smooth, sienna sheet to the middle of her back. Extensions. Quinn always looked good when she put long, light extensions in her hair. "I've confirmed the hotel and the flight, plus, *Your Morning Wake-Up Call* is already confirmed with me and Shonda."

Quinn walked over to Nicola's workstation and studied the various samples Nicola had put together for Desiree. She picked up a few and sniffed. Each one of her frowns only made Nicola's heart sink further.

"I wish they weren't coming."

"Why not? This is great. The publicity from this story combined with the debut of Desiree's perfume is everything Mom ever wanted. You'll have beaten out one of the largest perfumers out there for one of the most sought-after celebrities and be crowned top perfumer after delivering another perfect scent the world will adore."

She should tell Quinn the truth. That Desiree wasn't in love with the samples. That she was stuck and didn't know how to fix this. She kept her mouth shut. She'd gotten this far, no way could she backtrack and make everyone question all her decisions going forward.

"I just don't need the distraction right now," she said. "I need to make sure I get everything right for Desiree."

"Geez, Nicola, you overthink things. I'm sure you've already made something great and are just borrowing trouble." She had another vial in her hand. She brought it to her nose. Sniffed, considered, then sniffed again. "I like this one."

The knot in Nicola's shoulders eased. That was the one she hated the least.

"But it's missing something," Quinn said. She sniffed again. "Have you considered adding—"

Nicola jumped up from the chair. "I'm good with what I've put together. I just got off the phone with Desiree and she can't wait to come back and finalize the product." She didn't want to keep pushing Quinn away, but if Nicola didn't do this on her own then she didn't deserve the praise her family threw on her.

Quinn's face became a mask. She put the vial down carefully and stepped back. "Sorry. I know you have it all figured out."

"I do." She couldn't ask Quinn to bail her out. Not without revealing everything.

The shuttering of Quinn's emotions twisted the perpetual guilt in Nicola's stomach. They'd gotten past the argument over the bottle design in the same way they always did. Ignoring the problem and pretending as if it never happened. Shonda had helped with that in her usual let's all be friends fashion.

"I'll let you get back to work. I just stopped by to talk about Cancun. We can worry about that later."

She shouldn't go to Cancun, but a few days in the sun might be what she needed. She could always figure out scents while she was on vacation. Genius could strike while she relaxed with her sister and best friend.

"This trip will be just what I need."

Chapter 26

Your Morning Wake-Up Call asked if they could film the pottery class at Damien's studio to show how she was nurturing her creative side. She wasn't ready to broadcast their relationship, so she'd tried to get out of it by saying Damien wouldn't want cameras in his class. To her surprise, Damien was a good sport about it and hadn't complained when she'd told him about their request.

Darcy and her cameraman walked around the studio taking shots of the various artwork and talking to the other students. They asked everyone why they'd chosen a pottery class, what they'd hoped to learn, and how the experience impacted their lives. So far, everyone seemed excited to have Darcy there and to be appearing in a clip on *Your Morning Wake-Up Call.*

"You know I would have worn a better shirt if I'd known we were going to have a television crew here tonight." Mr. Goldberg tugged on the green and blue bowtie around his neck before running a hand down the front of his pale-yellow button up shirt.

Nicola raised a brow. "Seriously, Mr. Goldberg? You typically come in jeans and a t-shirt but tonight you're wearing a bowtie. I don't believe you didn't get the email Damien sent out before the class."

"Well, I wasn't sure if he was serious. My wife picked out this outfit. I would have worn something different."

Nicola bumped his arm with her elbow. Her hands were splattered with the aquamarine stain she was using to paint her last piece of artwork. A lopsided vase she couldn't wait to see once it came out of the kiln. She already pictured it sitting on her coffee table with a colorful arrangement of flowers.

"You look fine, Mr. Goldberg. Don't sweat it. They're just getting some background images. If you don't want to appear on camera, they won't even show your face."

Mr. Goldberg ran a hand over his neatly trimmed mustache. "Oh, I don't mind appearing on television. You know, only to help you out." He said the last in a solemn voice, as if he were doing her the biggest of favors.

Nicola suppressed a smile. "You don't know how much I appreciate your help with this."

"You're welcome. You know you're my tenth dearest friend."

Her smile couldn't be suppressed and she raised a brow. "Tenth?"

"I know a lot of people," he said shrugging.

Nicola laughed and bumped him again. "You know what, Mr. Goldberg, I'll happily be your tenth dearest friend."

Damien walked over to the two of them. There was a spark of interest in his dark eyes as he watched her laugh with Mr. Goldberg. A spark that made her breath catch in her lungs. They hadn't revealed to the class that they were an item. Nicola didn't want anyone to know. She liked having Damien to herself. No intrusions and no outside expectations of what they should be doing. Though Nicola suspected Mr.

Goldberg had an idea of what was going on. He always watched them with a raised brow and a sly smile.

Today she wanted discretion even more. After the cameras had caught her disastrous date with Bobby, she didn't want them to use her relationship with Damien as part of a comeback story. Sure, she and Damien agreed they were in a relationship, but that didn't mean the relationship was serious or long term. Another reason to keep what they had a little closer to the vest for a while longer. Moving on later when things fell apart, because, honestly, they were so different, things probably would fall apart, would be easier if everyone didn't know what was going on between them.

"What are my two troublemakers over here cooking up?" Damien asked.

He stood next to her and rested his hand on her lower back. She shifted from one foot to the next. Damien's hand fell away. He gave her a weird look which she returned with a bright smile.

"Mr. Goldberg was just telling me I'm his tenth dearest friend."

Damien scratched his chin and grinned. "Well at least he's honest."

Mr. Goldberg leaned toward the two of them and nodded. "Always honest."

"He was also worried he didn't look camera ready," Nicola said.

Damien leaned his forearms on the waist high table and studied Mr. Goldberg. "I don't know. You look pretty clean to me."

"Just to help out Nicola," he said again in the same solemn tone he'd used before.

"Of course." Damien winked at her when Mr. Goldberg went back to gently applying stain to his bowl.

Darcy and her camera guy came over. "Nicola, Damien,

thank you both for letting us come tonight. I think we've got some great shots to go with the segment."

"It was all Damien," Nicola said. "He was nice enough to agree to open himself up to the craziness that is my life right now."

Damien ran a hand up her back. "Anything for Nicola."

Heat flooded her face. Darcy's eyes practically glowed with interest. Nicola shifted again until Damien's hand fell away. This time she kept her eyes focused on her vase instead of the what's going on look she knew he was throwing her way. She hadn't actually told Damien about her plan to keep their relationship a secret.

Nicola focused on Darcy. "He's just being helpful. He's a great teacher."

"More than that," Darcy said. "The way he rescued you from the river. That footage you sent over from your portable camera. I can only tell you, he made every woman in the studio swoon."

Nicola's chest tightened. She'd turned the camera on and off during the canoe trip to try and make it appear less like a date. There wasn't much she could do to make Damien appear less heroic. "It wasn't that big of a deal. Damien mentioned he liked kayaking and when I mentioned I'd never been, he offered to take me. I never should have gone through the rapids."

Damien straightened. Nicola didn't look at him. Darcy raised a brow. "I thought it was a date."

Nicola tilted her head and met Darcy's eyes. "So the video came through alright? I'm glad. I was worried the water had damaged the camera."

A beat passed before Darcy spoke again, but she took the hint. "Yes, it came through okay. I'm glad you were okay."

Mr. Goldberg watched her with wide eyes. "You fell in the river?"

"I was trying to not appear afraid when I should have stayed behind on the banks. Damien did get to play the hero." She finally looked at Damien and grinned.

His lips raised in a closed mouth smile that didn't reach his eyes. "That's me. Playing hero."

He did not sound happy, but she'd deal with that later. For now, she needed to get Darcy to focus on something other than her and Damien. "But you know, Darcy, you'll get some really good shots next weekend in Cancun."

Darcy's enthusiasm picked up. "Yes. You're finally taking the spring break trip you always wanted. I'm excited to go."

"So am I."

Damien crossed his arms and leaned back on his heels. "You're going out of town?" His voice was calm. His eyes were cool.

Yeah, she'd forgotten to tell him about that, too. "Yes. We scheduled it weeks ago. Something exciting for the camera."

"Have fun." Damien said, not sounding the least bit sincere before he walked off. He pushed open the door to his office and disappeared within without a backwards glance.

Darcy cringed slightly. "Well, I think I've got all that I need for tonight. Thanks again, Nicola." She got out of there quick.

Mr. Goldberg leaned in. "Way to go."

"Thanks. I think the interviews tonight went well."

His browns drew together. "Nicola, unless you want to be my fifteenth dearest friend, you'll go tell Damien why you pretended as if you two aren't together."

"We aren—"

"Young lady, please." He held up a hand. "Me and nearly everyone in this class has run into you two kissing in the hallways last week as if no one would notice. You don't have to explain yourself to me, but that guy likes you. So explain it to him."

* * *

Nicola knocked on the door to Damien's office. Fran and the rest of her classmates had all looked at her with varying degrees of disappointment as they'd walked out. Mr. Goldberg may have a point, and everyone there did know she and Damien had something going on.

"What?" Damien's terse answer to her knock.

She was going to take that as an invitation. She opened the door and slid inside. Damien sat at his desk. The light from the lamp on his desk and the screen of his laptop, the only illumination in the room, cast long shadows across his face.

She leaned back against the door. "Hey."

He took a deep breath, flicked a glance her way, then focused back on his laptop. "Yes?"

Guess that meant he wasn't going to make this easy. She crossed the room. "Look, about that with Darcy."

"No need to explain. If you're ashamed of me that's all I need to know." The hard clicks of his mouse echoed in the room. He didn't take his gaze off the screen.

"Ashamed of you? Is that what you think?"

He shoved the mouse aside and leaned back in his chair. "What am I supposed to think? You were trying to hide that we're together from them. Crazy when it's pretty obvious to everyone in this building we are together."

He didn't yell. That's what made it worse. If he'd yelled, then she could have gotten angry and yelled back. Instead he sounded calm, resolute. Hurt.

"The cameras were there when I had the disastrous date with Bobby. I didn't want them to make the story about my turning a dating tragedy into triumph, now that I'm dating my very sexy pottery instructor. Enough of my uncomfortable adjustments are going to be the focus of the story. I didn't want this one to be another."

"I'm an uncomfortable adjustment?" He crossed his arms. Shut her off. Damien had opened up so much with her since they started dating. Having him shut her off was like losing a lifeline.

"You know you are," she shot back honestly. "I'm not used to this."

His arms relaxed marginally. "You've been in relationships before."

"Not ones I've wanted to protect before."

Confusion in his eyes, a slight release of tension in his shoulders. "Protect from what?"

Nicola licked her lips. She hadn't backed down from telling him what was in her heart before. She couldn't now, not without risking bringing back the pain she'd put in his expression. "From anything that could mess things up. I want to keep this ours for a while. Is there anything wrong with that? Can I savor this before we let other people in?"

He watched her for several long seconds. Finally, he uncrossed his arms and stood. He strolled around the desk and came to her.

"You want to savor us?" His voice was like melted chocolate. He ran a hand up and down her arms.

She released the breath she'd been holding and leaned into him, pressing her palms against his chest. "Can you blame me? You're kind of decadent."

His chuckle soothed the worry that had etched itself into her heart. She had the power to hurt him. The opposite had been true in all her other relationships. Typically, guys hurt her. Telling her she wasn't exactly what they wanted forever. She didn't want to hurt Damien, but there was also something a little satisfying in knowing he was just as invested in this relationship as she was.

"That doesn't change you keeping your Cancun trip next week from me." He sat back on the desk. Nicola settled between his thighs.

"I'm sorry. I agreed, but honestly haven't been thinking about it. If I could cancel I would, but not only are Quinn and Shonda looking forward to going, it'll be the only really fun thing I've done for the show."

"Then why would you cancel?"

"I've got work to do."

"You haven't figured out the scent for Desiree?"

Her stomach sank. She'd convinced herself beach sands and sunshine would prove to be the perfect inspiration, and she'd come back with just the right idea before her meeting with Desiree. So no, she hadn't figured it out, but yes, she would by the end of the vacation.

She didn't want Damien to worry about her. "Yes. I'm right on track."

"You sure? You seemed pretty upset the other day."

She blew air through her lips and waved a hand. "All in the past. I was being silly about my grandad and blew things out of proportion. Of course, I'm going to figure it out. I'm Nicola King."

Damien chuckled and wrapped her in his arms. "Yes, you are."

The confidence and pride in his voice made her want to bask in his admiration and also cry and admit she was a fake. But nobody liked a crybaby. She had plenty of time. Everything would work out.

She stood on her toes and kissed his neck. Breathed in the earthy scent of him. "Yes I am."

Chapter 27

Nicola only felt a mild sense of regret for taking a trip instead of staying home when she entered their beautiful hotel suite in Cancun. Really, with views like this she shouldn't be the least bit worried. How could she not be inspired by this view?

They were on the top floor. Brightly colored tile floors opened up to a balcony with a hot tub that overlooked white sand beaches and crystal blue waters. The air smelled of salt, sunshine and lush green vegetation.

"This place is amazing!" Shonda exclaimed. Her friend's flowing white skirt blew in the breeze. The off-shoulder yellow top exposed smooth brown skin.

"Didn't I tell you this was going to be great?" Quinn said leaning a hand on the balcony; Quinn looked twenty-two instead of thirty-two in her cutoff jean shorts and dark orange halter. Her long extensions were swept to the side in a loose braid. Aviator sunglasses hid the top half of her face.

Nicola felt plain standing next to her friend and sister. She'd traveled for comfort in white Bermuda shorts and a light blue v-neck shirt. Damien had said she was sexy when he'd seen her before she left. Either he didn't know what sexy was, or he really liked her and wanted to flatter her.

She would believe in the latter.

"It's inspiring," Nicola said.

That's what she was there for. Inspiration. She would figure out a scent for Desiree. She would rise to the challenge.

"Yes," Quinn said, clapping her hands. "This should inspire both if you to let loose and have a great time."

"I've already let loose," Shonda said.

Quinn lowered her shades to give Shonda the side eye. "No, you've revenge dated. You haven't let loose. I want you to hook up with someone sexy on this weekend." Quinn pointed at Nicola. "You too."

Nicola raised her hands to ward off the verbal attack. "No hooking up for me."

Shonda wiggled her eyebrows. "Oh yeah. Nicola already has a man at home."

Quinn rubbed her hands together and grinned at Nicola. "That's right. You are breaking off a little something for Damien Hawkins."

Nicola tried to suppress the I'm smitten smile fighting to take over her face. "Look, can we not make a big deal about me and Damien. We are just seeing how things go, and please let's not mention anything about what I am or am not breaking off with Damien after Darcy arrives with the camera."

Darcy's flight the day before had been cancelled due to a computer glitch at the airport. She was arriving later today. Good thing too, because the delay gave Nicola the chance to warn Shonda and Quinn about what was off limits.

Quinn pulled off her shades. Her arched brows drew together. "Why are you hiding this?"

"I'm not hiding. I just don't want to make a big deal out of me and him just yet."

"I don't understand," Quinn said. "After the Bobby Blowup, why not shine in the afterglow of a romantic liaison with Damien?"

"No. It's bad enough my list of regrets is all over the news. Let's not add another."

This time Shonda gave Nicola a skeptical look. "You regret being with Damien?"

"No. I'll regret answering questions about what it was like to date him after everything is over." Saying that out loud didn't sound much better.

Quinn waved a hand. "There you go thinking about the end before things have really begun. Just relax, have fun, and maybe things will turn out for the best."

"Is that how things worked out with you and Omar?" Nicola shot back.

She hadn't meant for the words to sound so harsh, but Quinn's *Nicola's-being-stuffy-again* tone of voice had pushed a button. She had every right to be cautious about her relationship with Damien. They didn't have much in common. They hadn't started out as friends. Now she was supposed to believe in fairytale endings, bask in the glow of a relationship, and tell everyone about her and Damien?

Quinn's mouth tightened a second before she shrugged and laughed. "You know what, do you. We'll keep whatever it is you're doing with Damien secret from the cameras." Quinn slid her shades back on and propped her straw hat on her head. "I think I'll go check out the pool." She was out the door without another word.

Shonda followed Nicola back into the suite. "Are you mad at her about something?"

"No, why would you think that?"

"Because, that Omar remark came out kinda nasty. You know the two of them are having problems."

Thing was, Nicola hadn't known that. Not for sure anyway. She got a sour feeling in her midsection.

"How do you know that?" Other than the offhand remark about thinking about leaving, which was quickly followed by an explanation of a not that serious disagreement before their trip to Los Angeles, Quinn hadn't given any hint of possible trouble with her husband.

Shonda sat on the arm of one of the bright orange lounge chairs in the shared living area. "We talked about it. That's all she talks about. You know that."

She didn't. She and Quinn hadn't really talked since the L.A. trip. Nicola wished she didn't feel jealous about Quinn telling Shonda and not her. They'd always had a good relationship even if it wasn't super close, now she felt as if they were slipping further apart.

"I didn't mean to hit a sore spot," Nicola said. "I'm just still a little sensitive about everything. The cameras coming, having to report back on how I'm living my best life for a live studio audience, Desiree's expectations. I'll apologize to Quinn later."

Shonda took a deep breath before nodding. Relief washed over her features. "Please do. I understand things are hectic for you, but we are here to have a good time. Let's not spoil it with a cat fight, okay?"

Nicola snorted. "When have Quinn and I ever fought."

"That's the problem. There are years of tension built up from you two not fighting. Let's not make this be the weekend you both decide to change your minds."

Nicola went in search of Quinn an hour after she'd left their suite. She'd figured her sister would need a little time to relax if she'd gotten as upset about Nicola's comment as Shonda seemed to think she was. Despite her claims to be ready to party, Shonda had fallen asleep on her bed shortly after their talk and was still knocked out. Nicola was tired from the day of travel along with staying up late the night before trying to force a solution to Desiree's perfume to magically appear in her brain.

She'd hoped to rest up and be refreshed before Darcy arrived with the cameras, but like the night before, her mind wouldn't shut down. On top of the worry about making the perfect perfume, she worried if wanting to keep her relationship with Damien a secret was foolish. They were an open secret at his studio, but she hadn't planned to admit to anything between them if asked. Was that a mistake or a smart move?

She hit her temple with the heel of her hand, hoping the act would push worrisome thoughts out of her head. This is why she rarely had relationships. They were so emotionally draining, especially in the beginning. Relationship worries easily diverted focus away from what needed to be done. Which was why she needed to find her sister, make sure they were cool before the cameras started rolling, then pray something on this getaway sparked a fire strong enough to inspire the perfect blend for Desiree's perfume.

She found Quinn where she thought she would. Outside at the pool bar. She sat alone with a bright fruity drink in front of her. A guy two barstools down from Quinn kept glancing her way, probably hoping to catch her eye, but Quinn was focused intently on her phone.

The urge to silently approach and glance over Quinn's shoulder to see what captured her attention was strong. Especially since Quinn laughed quietly before her fingers flew over the screen to respond to whatever she'd read. Instead, Nicola cleared her throat as she approached.

"Hey, what are you looking at?" she kept her voice light.

Quinn quickly darkened her phone and turned it face down on the bar. "Nothing. Just videos. Where's Shonda?" She looked in the direction Nicola had come from.

"Taking a nap."

"Ah, should have known. She's a lightweight when it comes to traveling."

"Well, she does have two kids. I don't know how she does it now that she's divorced. I'm tired most afternoons when I get off work, and I don't have to prepare dinner, go over homework, and help two other people get ready for the next day." Nicola slid into the barstool next to Quinn.

"I know, she has a lot on her plate. I didn't mean anything when I called her a lightweight."

"I know you didn't." Nicola kept her voice calm against Quinn's irritation. Maybe she should have given her sister two hours to chill.

"Why aren't you sleeping? I'd thought you would want to rest before having to be on for the cameras." Quinn took a sip of her drink.

The bartender came over and Nicola ordered a strawberry daquiri. She didn't really want anything to drink, but if she had ordered a soda, Quinn would have just given her crap about coming down here and not having any fun.

"I did for a little bit, then decided to come check out the rest of the resort. What have you found?"

"So far, the bar. Yusef, that's the bartender, did tell me about all the activities happening today and tomorrow. There's a lip sync battle in the nightclub later tonight. I think we should go to that."

"I don't know about that."

Yusef placed her drink on the tiled bar. With a grin and a wink, he left them to tend to the group of friends at the other end who wanted a round of shots.

"Come on, Nicola, don't come all this way to make up for not having fun only to spend the entire time still not having fun. What is it going to take to get you to cut loose?"

"I am going to have fun. I'm already having fun." She lifted her drink as exhibit A. "I'm here with my sister and best friend. The view is beautiful. What else do we need? Besides, you know fun for me is a book, a beach chair, and endless uninterrupted hours."

Quinn rolled her eyes but smiled. "Fine. You can lounge during the day with no complaints from me, but the nights are mine. We're going to have a good time every night here and you're not going to complain. And you have to because if you don't, Darcy and the rest of the *Your Morning Wake-Up Call* crew are going to question why you even chose to do this item on your list of regrets."

Quinn made a good point. She couldn't have them follow her down here just to spend hours filming Nicola lounge on the beach. If anyone would ensure she got out of her comfort zone and did something exciting for the cameras, it was Quinn.

"Okay, I'll give you the nights." Nicola held up a finger. "But on one condition."

"What condition? If it's that I don't bring up you hooking up with someone while we're here then the answer to that is no. If Damien isn't serious enough for you to consider letting people know about, then he's not serious enough for you to claim to have a boyfriend when you're on an island with a variety of single men."

Quinn sucked from her straw. Her knowing glance dared Nicola to argue with her. Nicola wanted to argue. To claim all other men need not apply for a seat at her table because she was with a man who could fill every need. To do that would be to admit in front of the cameras how much she was into Damien. They'd want to know why she wouldn't flirt. If things ended...when they ended...she'd be right back where she didn't want to be. Her personal life fodder for a rabid studio audience.

She wouldn't fight Quinn's condition, even if she wasn't happy about it. "Geez, that wasn't my condition, but now you're making me reconsider."

"Then what's the condition?" Quinn said triumphantly.

Nicola played with the straw in her drink before taking a deep breath and looking at Quinn. "Tell me you're okay. I mean with your marriage and everything. I'm sorry about what I said up there. I know you and Omar are having troubles, and I was out of line. But I do want to know if things are bad, and if there's anything I can do to help."

Quinn's smile tightened. Defeat flashed quickly in her sister's dark eyes. She looked away and took another long sip of her drink before she waved off Nicola's words. "Omar and I are just fine. I know I mentioned leaving a few weeks ago, but that was just me being extra. You know how I can get. It's like I told you. He'd made me mad, and I spoke too soon. There's no way I'd leave Omar."

She would typically have let the conversation drop. Not probe too deep into her sister's relationship. Keep things light for the weekend. And she would have, if that sense of helplessness hadn't crept back in Quinn's voice.

"Why not? I mean, if you aren't happy? Why stay?"

"Why not. What else am I going to do?" Doubt twisted and contoured the sound of Quinn's voice. The look in her eye was of someone who was lost.

Nicola placed her hand over Quinn's. "Quinn, you can go anywhere. You can do anything you want. You don't have to be tied to Omar if you don't want to be."

"That's easy for you to say, Nicola. You've always been the smart one. The one who had her life together. I know you like to be strong and noble and don't need anybody for anything, but I'm not like that. I'm the screw up. I couldn't even put together a perfume blend the one time Mom asked us to help. I know she hadn't expected much from us, but you made Triumph, and I got drunk and ruined my samples. Do you really think someone is going to hire me for anything other than hype girl?"

"Where is this coming from? Of course someone would

hire you." Guilt churned inside Nicola's gut. "You aren't a screw up. You're creative and smart."

"Nicola, stop." Quinn held up a hand. "I don't need your pity or your lies, okay. I came down here to have fun and that's what I'm going to do. Not let you try and pretend I'm good for anything other than being fun and pretty. Mom and Dad always said it, and I've accepted it."

"Then don't accept it. Try to step out and do something else. Prove to yourself you can be more than just a trophy wife."

Quinn's head jerked back as if slapped. "Wow. Just a trophy wife."

Nicola cringed. That hadn't come out right. "That's not how I meant it."

Quinn slid her hand out of Nicola's grasp. "You know what, it doesn't matter. You've just proven exactly what I was saying."

Nicola reached for Quinn's hand, but her sister avoided the touch by picking up her phone. "Quinn, stop. Look, I'm sorry if I offended you."

"You're hilarious, Nicola, seriously," Quinn said, her voice hard.

"I'm messing everything up. That's not why I came looking for you. I'd hoped we could clear the air before—"

"Before the cameras showed up. I know. Don't worry. I won't embarrass you in front of the cameras. When they're around I'll be your loving sister. That's what you like isn't it. The image of perfection for the world to see."

Quinn stood with her phone in her hand. Nicola jumped up too. She never could figure out what to say to make Quinn feel better.

Liar, you know what you have to say. What you've kept to yourself for years.

The truth about that night Triumph was made. The proof that Quinn wasn't the screw up she'd accepted. The proof that Nicola, savior of Queen Couture, was a fake and a phony.

"There you two are. We just knocked on your door." Darcy's voice prevented any further discussion. "Are we ready for a fun-filled weekend?"

Nicola shook her head. Now wasn't the time. She had to clear the air with Quinn. Quinn grinned so brightly she would have put Ms. America to shame, then linked her arm through Nicola's. "Yes, we are."

Chapter 28

Nicola did everything Quinn and Shonda wanted to do. She went parasailing, clubbing, and shopping, all without uttering one objection. Now she was spending the last night at a beach bonfire picnic party.

All with the hope inspiration would eventually hit.

As the weekend went by with no new ideas of how to put together something Desiree may like that she hadn't already considered, panic became a constant squeeze around her throat. She was going to fail. She was about to be ruined and proven a fraud in front of everyone. There was only one way to avoid the panic attack hovering in the periphery.

"Let's do shots!" she called out and slapped both hands on the bar.

A round of cheers went up from the crowd. Many of whom they'd seen and spoken with daily at the resort. Vacation friends is what Shonda called them. People they laughed and drank with during resort events and excursions. People they could let loose with because they'd never see them again.

"Shots? What's gotten into you?" Shonda's eyes were wide with disbelief, but she didn't sound at all like she objected to the idea.

Good, because Nicola needed to get her mind off what she was going to do when she met with Desiree. How she was about to disappoint everyone. How the idea that going on vacation would lead to a clear mind and some amazing epiphany was straight bull.

"It's our last night on the island," she said. She waved the bartender over. "Why not?"

The camera filmed her every move. Darcy and her small crew hadn't been intrusive during the trip. Mostly they got a few shots of her having fun doing whatever activity she was engaged in then they packed up and left her alone. She appreciated that they didn't hover or expect her to be entertaining for the entire trip. The camera crew and Darcy perked up at Nicola's request for shots, but she wouldn't give them too much of a show. She wanted to get distracted. Not drunk.

"You're right. Why not? Let's end the trip with a bang." Shonda looked around. "Where's Quinn?"

"Down on the beach on her phone again." Nicola tried to keep the annoyance out of her voice. Quinn had spent half of the trip on her phone ignoring them and the other half hanging out with their vacation friends at the bar and on excursions.

Nicola knew her sister. She was still upset with her. Nicola had decided to figure out how to get back in Quinn's good graces after the trip ended. *Your Morning Wake-Up Call* wasn't a reality show; therefore Nicola's heart to heart with Quinn didn't need to be filmed for their viewers.

Shonda rolled her eyes then shrugged. "She can catch up."

The first round of shots was passed out. Nicola downed the first one with a grimace as tequila fire blazed down her throat. Someone put on one of Desiree's club hits from the year before. Dread clawed back up Nicola's spine. She waved at the bartender for another round.

Three. She'd do three shots and that should be enough to loosen up her brain to keep Desiree and the upcoming deadline out of her head for this last night.

Quinn returned right after Nicola finished the third shot. "What's going on here? Looks like I'm missing a party." She put her cell phone on the bar.

Nicola's brain was fuzzy enough for her to not care that she and Quinn were kind of on the outs. She wrapped an arm around Quinn's shoulder and hugged her sister.

"Last night here. You've got to catch up. I'm on number three."

Quinn laughed and pried Nicola's arms from around her shoulder. "You might need to stop at number three."

Shonda snaked an arm through Quinn's other arm. "Oh, Quinn, don't you be a party pooper."

"I'm not doing that. At least let me get my three in before you two do more."

Instead of admitting three was going to be her limit, Nicola nodded when a group of their vacation friends called for her and Shonda to join them on the beach where a small group danced and played limbo next to the bonfire.

"I'm going dancing while you catch up." She hugged Quinn then whispered in her ear. "Hey, thanks for the trip."

The corner of Quinn's mouth lifted, and some of the frost in her eyes melted. Maybe it was the three shots. Pretty sure it was the three shots. But Nicola didn't want to end the night with Quinn passive aggressively ignoring her under the guise of having fun with everyone else.

"Go dance. I'll be there in a minute."

Nicola let her sister go and hurried over to dance with the group. She was clearing her mind. Relaxing and letting go. Hoping that when everything was free something brilliant would strike.

She danced until sweat poured down her face. When Quinn joined them, she danced some more. When Shonda brought her a fruity drink, she took it and drank it quickly. Eventually the worry slid off her and she was finally able to not think about fighting with Quinn, making Desiree's perfume, or that she shouldn't be dancing with the guy who'd flirted with her during the entire trip.

When her feet screamed for her to sit down, and her head said it couldn't take another drink, she pulled herself away from the crowd and trudged her way to the bar.

"Another shot?" the bartender asked.

Nicola shook her head. "Water, please."

He chuckled but nodded. "I've got you."

The ocean breeze did nothing to cool her off. She grabbed one of the laminated menus and fanned herself. Quinn staggered up next to her.

"I've got to pee." She put her phone on the bar. "Watch my stuff. I'll be right back. Order me another drink."

"I'm moving on to water," Nicola said.

"Make that two drinks." Quinn patted her on the head then pushed through the crowd toward the bathrooms on the side of the bar.

The bartender returned with her water. The cool, refreshing liquid was the best thing she ever drank. She downed half the contents before slamming down the bottle and sucking in air.

Quinn's phone vibrated on the bar. Nicola recognized the name. Joseph. That guy who was supposed to be helping Quinn go into television advertising and not just social media posts.

She shouldn't do it, but knowing her sister would be pissed didn't stop Nicola from picking up the phone to check out the notification. She darted a quick glance toward the bathroom. There was no sight of Quinn. The coast was clear.

She knew Quinn's phone password, but she'd never used it to go into Quinn's phone without her permission before.

She shouldn't look, but Quinn had spent so much time this weekend on her phone. Texting and giggling in corners when she thought no one was looking. What was going on? Was she texting and giggling with Joseph?

Quinn had something going on. Something she'd never tell Nicola because they could never get on the same page. Something she'd feel more comfortable telling Shonda than her. Something Shonda probably already knew.

Jealous anger spiked in Nicola's stomach. She was Quinn's sister. She should know what her sister was up to.

She quickly tapped in Quinn's pin, opened Joseph's text message, and was greeted with a dick pic. She lost her grip on the phone. Caught it before it fell and hit the floor. She lifted it back just to be sure she wasn't losing her mind.

Hurry back so I can give you more of this. *eggplant emoji* *squirt emoji*

Those words accompanied the picture. Nicola shook her head. What the hell! No way was her sister sleeping with Joseph? She couldn't be. Quinn hadn't mentioned his name in weeks. Quinn wouldn't do something like this. Not so sloppy that she was getting dick pics on her phone. Not when she knew she'd lose everything if Omar found out.

She scrolled up, not caring about privacy anymore. Read the texts between her sister and Joseph. Coughed on her own spit when she saw the nudes sent by Quinn over the past few days. She sputtered, too shocked to believe what she saw.

The phone was snatched out of her hand. Nicola looked up into Quinn's angry eyes. "What are you doing?"

Nicola pointed at the phone. Disbelief swirling with the alcohol she'd consumed to make her mind spin. "Quinn, tell me you're not sleeping with him."

"If you didn't want to know you shouldn't have looked." Quinn shoved the phone into the cup of her bikini top.

"But why? I thought you were staying with Omar."

"I am. This has nothing to do with Omar's tired ass. He doesn't even care enough to try and have sex with me anymore."

Nicola brought her hands to her temples. "That doesn't mean you should cheat on him." Quinn should leave him. Not send naked pictures and get caught sleeping with that guy. Omar obviously wasn't making her happy.

"Oh, go somewhere else with that judgmental attitude," Quinn said in an angry hiss. "This is why I couldn't tell you, Susie Straight and Narrow. You wouldn't understand."

"Then help me understand. Do you know what would happen if word got out about this? He'd take everything."

"You think I don't know that? You think I'm not aware that despite any work I may have done to help my husband secure clients and investors, that he'd say I had no impact on his business. That if I step out of line not only will it ruin the image we've created, but he will snatch everything away from me and not care."

"Then why do this? At least get lawyer. Leave him."

Quinn placed a hand on her hip and glared. "Leave him? Are you crazy? For who, Joseph?" she said with a humorless laugh. "Joseph is married and has his own family. I'm not breaking up what I've got just because I want to sleep with someone else."

"Obviously what you have isn't that special or worth it if you're doing this. He deserves better than that."

Quinn's eyes narrowed. "*He* deserves better? What about me? Don't I deserve some happiness? Don't I deserve better?"

"You're cheating on him!" Quinn was a lot of things, but not a cheater. She'd felt so guilty of accusing Quinn of sneaking out to see Nathaniel in L.A. Now she felt stupid for not seeing what was right in front of her. Angry that Quinn wouldn't tell her the truth and trust her to help her through this instead of hiding things from her.

"And he's been cheating on me since the day of our wedding when I caught him getting a blowjob from one of my bridesmaids," Quinn yelled back. Tears filled her eyes. "Why do you think I spend so much time trying to build my own brand? Because he controls everything. He cuts me off if I make him mad. He's even said everything I built is because he supports my lifestyle, and I wouldn't have a damn thing if it weren't for him bankrolling my lifestyle."

Nicola stepped back as if slapped. "What? Why didn't you tell me?"

"Because you wouldn't care." The utter sincerity in Quinn's words sliced through Nicola's anger.

"Of course I'd care. You don't need him. You can do more work for Queen Couture. I've always wanted you to spend more time there."

"Don't give me that bull, Nicola. We both know the little bit of work I do for the company is just for show. I won't take a job out of pity."

"But you'll stay with a man who doesn't respect you. A man you don't even want to be with anymore."

"I've got a decent life." Quinn's voice was firm. The look in her eyes said she was defeated. Somewhere along the way she'd believed this crap. That the work she did for the company wasn't important and that she needed Omar to be successful.

"You're unhappy." Nicola couldn't believe she'd never noticed before. All this time she'd looked at her sister's jet-setting lifestyle and thousands of followers and assumed Quinn was happy.

"I'm not good for anything else. I can't be the brilliant perfumer like you and make the scents everyone loves. All I've got is my looks. It's all I've ever had. I'm building what I can until I can leave Omar or he gets tired of me and trades me in for a younger wife."

Nicola's hands balled into fists. She wanted to shake Quinn. Punch Omar for stealing her sister's confidence. "Stop saying that. Quit doubting yourself. Jesus, Quinn, you're smarter than that."

"Don't patronize me—"

"I'm not patronizing you, it's the truth. It's the truth because you're the one who really saved the company. You're the one who came up with what was needed to fix Triumph. If it weren't for you, we never would have gotten where we are." The words she'd been holding onto for years rushed out. The knowledge that she was so inadequate brought tears to her eyes. She was the fake. The imposter.

"Don't lie to me," Quinn said quietly.

She couldn't hold back the truth anymore. "I'm not lying to you. It's true. You were drunk that night and angry. You came into the lab and tossed your samples, but I got there and stopped you. You were crying and talking nonsense about not being able to do it. I said I couldn't either. I was struggling and couldn't figure out how to make the blend work. Then you said offhand I was using the wrong lavender. That French lavender was more distinct that Californian. You knew what I missed when I didn't and fixed it in an instant. The next day you didn't remember, and when Mom loved it . . . I didn't say anything."

The disbelief in Quinn's face slowly morphed into a hard mask. "All these years. All these years you made me believe I didn't know what I was doing," her voice was a cold sheet of ice.

"Quinn, I'm sorry. I didn't know how to admit that everything was your idea."

"I said yes to Omar that day because I thought I'd never be as good as you." Anger filled Quinn's eyes. "You skank."

The slap turned Nicola's head to the side. Tears sprouted and her cheek burned. She brought a hand to the side of her face.

Rage boiled in her stomach. Rage, guilt, and drunken jealousy. She turned around and lunged at her sister. They hit the floor in a heap. Twisting and ineffectively trying to hit each other. Someone pulled the two of them apart.

"You lied to me," Quinn yelled. "All these years. I thought I was nothing and you knew it was me. Why couldn't you tell the truth? I wouldn't be here if it weren't for you." Her sister fought to get out of the hold of one of the patrons at the bar separating them.

"I didn't tell you to marry him. Don't blame me," Nicola shot back. Her own anger was fueled by Quinn's violence.

Quinn jerked out of the arms of the guy holding her. "Don't you ever speak to me again." She turned on wobbly legs and stormed off.

"What happened?" Shonda asked. She loosened her hold on Nicola's arms.

Nicola hadn't known her friend was the one holding her back. Her eyes scanned the crowd. The camera was trained directly on her. Her face stung in multiple places. Probably from scratches. Her knees, hips, and elbows hurt. Mortification swamped her. Followed by crushing guilt.

"I've got to get out of here."

Tears streamed down her face as she ran in the opposite direction of Quinn. She ignored the calls from Shonda and Darcy. Her life was pretty much ruined now.

Chapter 29

"What the hell happened down there?"

Nicola groaned and dropped her head in her hands. She never should have given her mom a key to her place. Quinn had gotten an earlier flight and left Cancun before Nicola and Shonda. Nicola had hidden in their suite and avoided all calls and knocks on her door. Especially the ones from Darcy. She could only imagine all the bad information they picked up.

She'd gotten home an hour ago, showered, and was ready to wallow in self-pity, righteous indignation, and the half a bottle of Merlot in her kitchen. How in the world did her mom know about the fight already?

By the time she lifted her head from her kitchen island her mom rushed in. Adele froze in place. Her eyes widened and she brought a hand to her chest. "What happened to your face?"

"Quinn has really long nails."

She'd seen the scratches. They'd heal and shouldn't leave scars. Shouldn't. She probably deserved scars.

"What the hell happened? Omar called me earlier saying

Quinn was ranting and losing her mind. Something about you ruining her life. I went over there and didn't get much more from her. She says she hates you and that you're responsible for her unhappiness."

"I'm not responsible. No one told her to marry Omar." Guilt and self-loathing laced her words.

"I said yes to Omar that day."

Adele put her purse on the island and stood next to Nicola. She rubbed a hand up and down her back. "What do you have to do with her marrying Omar?"

"She didn't tell you?" She'd figured Quinn had shouted Nicola's betrayal from the rooftop by now.

"No. I just got that she's angry. You know how your sister gets. She's always extra. I hoped you would tell me something. Otherwise, I think Omar is going to think she's lost her mind and kick her out of the house."

Which would be good for Quinn. "She deserves better than Omar."

"He's good to her," Adele said not quite convincingly.

"He treats her like she's an idiot and doesn't love her. He only wants her to be pretty and by his side." She shifted to stop her mom from rubbing her back. She didn't want comfort right now.

"Where is this coming from? Is that what you two are fighting about. Are you putting foolish ideas in her head? Making her think she can do better than Omar."

"She can do better than him. She can stand on her own. She should stop this part time mess and work full time at Queen Couture."

Adele gaped then laughed. "Don't be ridiculous. You two are always going at it for no good reason. Look, you don't have time to get twisted by your sister's shenanigans. You need to focus on the meeting with Desiree later this week. I can do your makeup and help cover up those scratches. They shouldn't leave any marks. Give Quinn a few days and she'll calm down."

Adele fussed with Nicola's hair and she brushed her mom's hands aside. "No, Mom, you don't understand. This isn't something for her to calm down over. She's really mad at me."

"I don't know why. You've never done anything to her. All of her decisions were decisions she made. We both know she's not the responsible one."

"If that's what we always tell her then that's what she'll believe. She can do more. She has done more."

"What do you mean?"

Nicola swallowed hard. Her eyes met her mother's. "She's the one who really fixed Triumph. My original scent was off, and I couldn't figure out what to do next. Quinn told me how to fix it. I never told her, or you. I should have."

Adele raised a brow. "So."

"What do you mean so?" Nicola said the words slowly. Hadn't her mom understood what she just said.

"People collaborate on projects all the time," Adele said with a shrug. "Just because she helped you out doesn't take away from what you created or the work you've done since then."

"But what if she could have come up with something better if she hadn't ruined her samples?" Nicola had never asked Quinn what had driven her to the lab, drunk and angry, that night. *I said yes to Omar that day!* Had something Omar said made her sister doubt her abilities?

Nicola locked gazes with her mom. "What if we never gave her the chance because we were too afraid to let her try?" Because Nicola had been too afraid to let go of the attention she'd always craved from her family.

"Look, we don't have the time to gamble on what ifs. Your sister might have had one brilliant idea, but at the end of the day, you're the one who got us where we are. Don't let your sister try to steal anything from you just because she's going through some type of crisis."

"But Mom."

"No buts." Adele's voice was firm. She placed her hand on Nicola's shoulders and forced her to sit up straight. "You get things right with Desiree and leave your sister's rants out of things. That's what's important."

"What if I can't do it?" Her voice was small. Full of the fear she'd tried to hide over the past few weeks.

Her mom waved off her concerns. "Of course, you can do it. You've always done it. And if you don't do it, Desiree will choose IHF and our reputation will be ruined. We can't afford to mess this up with Desiree. Everyone in the industry is waiting to see what we come up with. Now is not the time for you to start questioning your abilities. Forget the fight with Quinn. You didn't do anything wrong. Your sister will be okay. You've got things ready for the meeting, right?"

After that speech, Nicola couldn't form the words to say she didn't. That she wasn't sure if she'd be ready. That she had no idea what to do next. That she was about to plunge them into a potentially crushing situation. If she didn't come up with something, then her fears would be true. She wasn't the genius everyone took her to be. She was a fake and a phony. She had ruined her sister's life only to falter later. The worry in her mom's eyes made Nicola swallow all her fears.

"I'll be ready."

Chapter 30

Nicola's cell phone vibrated on her desk. She turned away from the three samples she'd been working with and checked the notification. A message from Damien.

I'll pick up dinner. What r u in the mood 4?

Nicola groaned and rubbed her temples. Last night when Damien asked about coming over, she'd put him off. Saying she was tired from the trip and promising to have dinner with him tonight. She wanted to have dinner with him. Wanted to wrap up in his arms and forget about everything.

That's exactly what she couldn't afford to do. Even though she still had no idea how to make anything better happen. Working constantly and trying out different things hadn't given her the answer. Going on vacation had been a disaster. Maybe spending time with Damien would help.

Pick up Tai. She texted back.

Seven work for you?

Perfect.

She smiled as she put her phone down. Damien was the

one thing going relatively well in her life. Even if she didn't want to let everyone in on what was happening between them. She wasn't used to having someone care about her at the end of the day. Or even look forward to seeing her. A part of her felt bad about keeping them a secret, but a bigger part of her loved that he was all hers.

She glanced at her phone again. Quinn still hadn't called. She didn't know what to say to her sister. What could she say? It wasn't her fault Quinn rushed into the decision to marry Omar. She might have been wrong for not telling her sister about how she'd helped with Triumph, but that didn't make Nicola responsible for every decision Quinn had made since. She'd deal with that once this crisis with Desiree was over.

There was a knock on her door before LeShawn came inside. Her eyes were wide and worried. "Um . . . Nicola, I tried to buzz you."

Nicola picked up one of the vials with her latest juice blend. "My ringer is off on my desk phone. I'm not to be disturbed."

"Yeah, about that. Desiree is here to see you."

Nicola's stomach fell to her feet. She clutched the vial in her hand and spun toward LeShawn. "She's what? I'm not meeting her until Thursday."

Desiree walked up behind LeShawn and pushed her way into the door. "I got back in the states early and decided to come by. I'm so excited to check out what you've put together. I couldn't wait to get here and check on things."

Nicola tried to control her breathing. *No!* She wasn't ready. She didn't feel confident that she'd done anything to make the perfume what Desiree wanted. "Oh . . . things have been great."

Desiree clapped as she rushed to Nicola's side. "Good. I was worried after the last few samples you sent. Then your assistant told me you'd gone on vacation. I was worried you wouldn't be ready for our meeting on Thursday."

The vacation had nothing to do with it. "I promise I'll be ready. I'm always ready."

"Good. Then you wouldn't mind letting me preview what you've put together before we get in front of the entire creative team." Desiree studied the various vials on Nicola's workstation with interest.

Nicola almost swallowed her tongue. "I don't have the final product here."

Desiree picked up one of the vials and read the label. "These have my name on them." She screwed open the top. "Is this the latest version?"

As much as Nicola wanted to snatch the vial away from Desiree and tell her it wasn't ready, she didn't. Nicola pressed her hand into her stomach. There was no need to stop her now. Knowing what Desiree thought was the only way for her to get to a resolution. "Something like that."

Desiree raised a brow. "Is it okay if I smell them. I'm sure this is better than what you gave me last time."

Before Nicola could reassure her that it was, Desiree brought the first vial to her nose and breathed in. She grunted, frowned, then carefully put the vial back down. The process was repeated with each of the three. When she turned back to Nicola disappointment was heavy in her gaze.

"You said these are prototypes. That you don't have the final product here?"

Those were her final products. She had nothing else. If she were honest with herself, she wouldn't come up with anything else before Thursday. She was good and screwed. But she'd still hope for a miracle.

"No. The final isn't here."

Desiree didn't look convinced. "Where is it? I want to try it."

"At my house," she said quickly. "I took it with me on vacation because I have to let a scent sit with me for a while. I test it in various settings to see what I like."

"And that's what you'll bring me on Thursday?" Desiree crossed her arms delicately and raised a brow.

The truth was wedged in her throat. She couldn't give up now. Not when she could use a few more days and possibly do better. Be better. "Yes. I'm sure you'll love it."

"I really hope so." Desiree glanced at the three vials on Nicola's desk. "Look, Nicola, if you can't come up with what I want then just let me know. There are other perfumers who can help me."

There was no way in hell she was going to lose this project. "I've got you, Desiree. Don't worry. You'll be pleased."

"I'd like to think so, but honestly, you haven't delivered so far. Between that and the rumors surrounding your family."

Nicola blinked several times. "Rumors? What rumors?"

Desiree's eyes widened. "You don't know?"

"Know what? Our company is above reproach. We have worked hard to meet the expectations of our clients and deliver quality perfumes."

"Maybe so, but your sister also works here. I'm not one to judge other people. I think women and men can and should do whatever they want. But after seeing the video of you and your sister fighting in Cancun, followed by the leaked tape of her affair with that advertising guy, it makes me wonder if you can focus on what I need right now."

Video of their fight? Leaked tape of Quinn's affair? What the hell happened in the past forty-eight hours? Why hadn't anyone called or said anything to her?

Desiree continued talking. Nicola couldn't follow along. Their fight had been recorded. She shouldn't be surprised. Camera phones were everywhere. The problem was, how much of their fight was publicized? Had Desiree heard Nicola confess about the making of Triumph?

The words *find someone else* came out of Desiree's mouth and snatched Nicola's thoughts away from what was recorded and back to the problem at hand.

"Desiree, please, don't look for anyone else. I haven't seen any of the gossip you're referring to. My sister and I did have a disagreement, but we're okay. We'd been drinking and got annoyed." She really hoped there wasn't video proof of her admitting to feeling like an imposter when it came to making scents. "As for my sister's alleged affair, that has nothing to do with me. We want your business and I'll do whatever it takes to prove you've made the right choice."

"I don't know."

"Please. You understand how the media blows things out of proportion. I'm not distracted. You are my number one priority. I will make a perfume that you and your fans will love and wear for years."

She held out her hand. Her heart pounded in her chest. Her head hurt and she held her breath. Desiree watched her for a second before taking her hand.

"Okay, we'll see how things go on Thursday."

Nicola was going through her books on chemistry, fragrances, and the art of making perfume, when her doorbell chimed. Cursing because she couldn't afford an interruption right now, she slammed the book closed and hurried to the door. If this was her mom coming to talk to her again about fixing things, then she didn't want to be bothered.

She'd looked up what was in the media with Quinn. There was grainy cell phone video of Quinn and Joseph out on a date. They'd been caught kissing at a party as well. There was also cell phone video of Nicola lunging at Quinn after getting slapped in Cancun. She hadn't found any video of their actual argument, though the sites that obtained the cell phone video alluded to the fight being about Quinn's affair.

If she hadn't looked at Quinn's phone, the fight wouldn't have started. She'd have to find a way to fix things with her sister, she just couldn't fix it now. Not when Queen Couture's reputation depended on what happened this Thursday. She'd call Quinn on Friday. She'd fix this on Friday.

When she looked through the peephole she cringed and cursed again. She opened the door and tried to smile. "Damien, hey."

His bright smile dimmed, and he lowered the bags of food he'd held up when she answered. "That doesn't sound like you're happy to see me."

"No, it's not that. Actually, I am happy to see you. It's just not a good time."

"What's going on?"

She stepped back and motioned for him to enter. "Work, family, you name it."

He leaned in to kiss her and she gave him her cheek. The briefest of hesitations before his lips brushed her cheek. When he pulled back there was confusion in his eyes.

"Want to talk about it?"

She shut the door and avoided eye contact. If she looked into his eyes, she'd get lost. She'd break down. Now wasn't the time for breakdowns.

"Not really. I won't be good company tonight. Why don't you take the food back to your place and enjoy? I'll give you a call at the end of the week."

Damien's body stilled. "The end of the week?"

"Yes. I've got the presentation with Desiree on Thursday and it's really got me stressed."

"I know about the presentation on Thursday. That's why I thought I'd be helpful and bring you dinner." He walked into the kitchen.

Nicola followed and tried to suppress her annoyance. He put the food on the island then walked over to her.

He placed his hands on her hips and pulled her close. "Tell me what you need, and I'll get it for you."

How easy would it be to lean into him? Wrap her arms around him, breathe in his scent, and let him hold her. Forget everything she needed to fix and let Damien take care of her instead. The idea was so tempting she leaned toward him. Except, when he let her go all her problems would still be there, and she'd be even further behind because she avoided doing what needed to be done to steal a few moments with him.

His brows pulled together and he placed a finger under her chin. "How did you scratch your face?"

Nicola pushed his hand away and pulled out of his reach. "It's nothing. I need to get back to work." She walked away from him and went back to the books she had spread out on the kitchen table.

Damien followed her. He picked up one the books and read the cover. "What's the problem? You said you had things under control with the scent for Desiree."

She pulled the book out of his hand. The accusation in his voice ramping up her irritation. "Well I lied."

"Why?"

Nicola hugged the book to her chest and met his eye. "Because I thought going to Cancun would help me figure things out. Now I know it won't."

"You didn't have to lie to me. If you're having a problem, we can talk about it. Maybe I can help?"

She didn't need help. She had to do this on her own. She had to prove to herself that she deserved all the accolades she'd gotten since Triumph. She had to know she belonged here. That she hadn't hurt her sister by keeping the secret only to ruin everything later.

She turned away from Damien and dropped the book on the table. "If I need help making a bowl for Desiree I'll come to you. I don't need your help when it comes to making perfume."

"Hold up." He took her elbow in his hand and stopped her from walking away. "Just because you're having a rough day doesn't mean you can talk to me any kind of way."

"I told you it wasn't a good time. It'll be better for you to just take the food and go."

His hand dropped from her arm and he took a step back. "Are you really coming at me like this right now?"

She put a hand to her head. "Look, I'm sorry. I just really can't focus on anything else right now."

"You don't have to. Let me help out. I've got dinner. After we eat, I can run you a bath and then give you a shoulder rub."

Her heart melted at the prospect. The tension in her shoulders was begging her to say yes. She could feel his fingers massaging her back and shoulders. Taking away the stress and agony of the past few days. His wonderful lips would follow the trail of his hands. They'd make love and he'd make sure her mind was completely clear of everything except what it meant to be in his arms.

Maybe he saw the longing in her face because the tightness around his eyes lessened. He stepped forward and reached for her. If he touched her, she'd say to hell with working tonight.

Nicola held up her hands and jumped back. "Just stop, okay. I'm not giving you any if that's what you're here for."

Damien stopped short. He'd only look more stunned if she'd slapped him. "Who said anything about getting any?"

"Let's be real, Damien. We both know you ultimately

want us to end up in bed tonight. I don't have time to play around. I'm too busy."

"I don't know what you think we've got going here, but out of the two of us, you're the only one whose sought out the other just for sex. I thought we were in a relationship."

"We are." She rubbed her temples. She just wanted this entire conversation to be over.

He pressed a hand to his chest. "Then why are you acting like I'm your friend with benefits? I didn't come here for sex. I came here because I haven't seen you in a week and I'd like to spend time with you."

Nicola dropped her hand and met his eyes. "And I said I'd call you in a week. The company's reputation is on the line. I'm fighting with Quinn. Desiree hates everything I've put in front of her. And I have three days to come up with something brilliant. I can't get distracted with romantic dinners and back rubs. Why can't you understand that!"

His face closed up. The door to his emotions slammed shut as he looked at her as if she were a stranger. "You know what, I'm going to go." He turned and stalked toward the door.

"Damien..."

He spun around and held up a hand. "Nah, and when you're done with your meeting, don't bother to call. I've been overinvested in a relationship one time before. I'm glad to find out now before I got too in over my head."

"Damien, wait!" Nicola hurried after him, but he was slamming the door. By the time she opened it he was in his car. He didn't bother to look up as he backed out of her driveway.

Worry flooded her system. She'd hurt him. Deeply. She'd seen it right before he'd walked out. She hurried back into her house and searched for her car keys. She'd follow him and apologize. Let him know she didn't want them to end. Tell him that he wasn't overinvested and that she cared about him just as much as he cared for her.

She found her keys next to the pile of books on the table. *Follow him. Get no work done. Find no solution.* The weight of what she needed to do pressed down on her. Her fingers unclenched and the keys fell back on the table. She'd call him at the end of the week. She'd fix everything just as soon as she got through this week.

Chapter 31

Guilt got the better of Nicola and she went to Quinn's house the next afternoon. She was no closer to finding a solution, but after getting three phone calls from clients asking if she knew about Quinn's affair, the only thing Nicola cared about was making sure her sister was okay.

She was reaching for the doorbell when the door swung open. Omar looked as startled to find her there as she was at having the door opened so suddenly. His normally congenial face was a mask of disgust.

"I suppose you're here to try and tell me why I shouldn't leave your sister out in the cold."

The contempt in his tone snapped her out of things. "Actually, I think Quinn should leave you."

He scoffed. "Quinn leave me? You do realize she's nothing without me?"

She never wanted to hit another person in her life as much as she wanted to hit Omar. "She doesn't need you for anything."

"Oh really? You're suddenly her advocate," he said with a raised brow. "We all know Quinn is nothing but a pretty face."

"I can't believe you would talk about her like this. I thought you loved her."

Omar sneered. "And I thought she knew her place."

Nicola once believed he was handsome and nice, if slightly arrogant. The guy made millions managing a hedge fund, so of course he would be arrogant. She'd tried to like him because Quinn was married to him. Now she wished she'd let herself see him for the asshole he was and had urged Quinn to leave him. "Her place isn't with you."

Quinn appeared behind Omar. "Nicola, what are you doing here? Stop talking about things you don't understand."

Omar glanced over his shoulder. "Check your sister." He turned back to Nicola, smirked, then pushed past her to stroll out the door and toward his car.

Not believing what had just happened, Nicola went inside and faced her sister. "Check me? Is he serious? Please tell me that you're leaving him."

Quinn sighed and rubbed her brow. She was dressed in an off-white jump suit. Her makeup was perfect, her hair in a loose braid down her back. "What are you doing here, Nicola?"

Nicola closed the door behind her. "I came to check on you."

Quinn's hand dropped. "Why?" She sounded as if she'd expect aliens to invade before Nicola would come to check on her.

If she hadn't heard the malicious curiosity in the voices of people calling her to get more of Quinn's business, aliens probably would have invaded before she would have come over to face her sister.

"Why?" Nicola said. "How can you even ask that? I've seen what they're saying online about you and Omar. Our fight is all over the web, too. I came here to make sure you were okay. To see if you needed anything."

Quinn crossed her arms. "Oh, now you care?"

"I've always cared. Can't we move past what happened in Cancun? I'm sorry about checking your phone. I never should have invaded your privacy."

"What about I'm sorry for stealing your idea and not telling you." Quinn rolled her eyes and walked away.

Nicola hurried to follow. "I didn't steal your idea."

Quinn went into her home office which was set up more like a photography studio. Natural light streamed in from the windows that overlooked the outside lanai. It's where Quinn took many of the pictures she posted onto her social media. A rack filled with clothes people sent her to try and a bookshelf covered in various makeup, creams, and other items Quinn reviewed took up much of the space.

Quinn sat on the edge of her desk and glared at Nicola. "You said that I came up with the way to fix the juice that became Triumph. Instead of telling me, you took credit for it. You stole my idea."

"You made a suggestion," Nicola explained. "It worked out, but that doesn't mean I stole your idea."

Quinn raised a brow. "Now your story is changing."

That is what happened. A change Quinn suggested when she'd been drunk and angry. A change that had led to perfection. A change that had Nicola questioning her abilities ever since. Something so simple that made such a huge difference. Why hadn't she been able to see that? How could she really be good when she'd missed something so small?

When Triumph became a hit, she'd chosen to keep Quinn's suggestion to herself instead of admitting she hadn't bottled perfection by herself. If she'd known that decision would have led them here, she would go back and admit the truth.

"My story remains the same," Nicola said evenly. She

didn't want this to turn into another fight. No matter what happened with Desiree's scent, Nicola couldn't let the rest of the week go by with Quinn believing she didn't care what people said or that Nicola didn't want what was best for her. "I'm sorry I didn't admit your part, but that doesn't mean I'm responsible for the decisions you made after. There's still time to make things right. There's still time for you to leave Omar."

"Why? To come work full time for Queen Couture? To be the pretty face of the company instead? What if I don't want to leave Omar? What if I like my life the way it is?"

Nicola didn't believe her. Quinn was unhappy with Omar. She'd seen enough to know. Especially if she'd stepped out on him with another man. She'd only consider staying if Omar made concessions. Concessions Nicola doubted would be in Quinn's best interest. "Are you saying he wants you to stay?"

"I'm saying that we're stronger together than we are apart. He's realizing it won't be so easy to leave me with everything as he thought. We can get through this and be stronger for it."

"But you're not happy."

Quinn's arms uncrossed, but her hands clenched the edge of her desk tight enough to lighten her knuckles. "I'm comfortable. We've built a brand that benefits my online presence and his client list. I'm good."

"Quinn—"

"Stop." Quinn jumped up and waved a hand. "You're going to wow everyone in a few days with your latest creation and then your life will go back to being perfect. You don't have to come check up on me. I can figure out what's best for me."

The sureness in her sister's voice was like a kick to the gut. Despite discovering how Triumph was made, and being mad, her sister still believed in her. "But that's just it. I won't wow everyone in a few days. I don't—"

Quinn's cell phone rang. She pulled it from her pocket and glanced at the screen. "Look, I've got work to do. You don't have to check on me. Our fight was a finger snap of the attention span of the internet. In a few days everyone will have moved on."

She didn't care about what the public thought. She wanted to make sure she and Quinn would be okay. "But I don't want to leave things unsaid."

Quinn met her gaze with bold determination. "We both said everything we need to say. You do what's best for you and I'll do what's best for me." She answered her phone and turned her back to Nicola.

Chapter 32

Nicola had her epiphany. Brilliance struck her at two in the morning. Waking her immediately from her sleep. As her grandmother would have said, if the answer was a snake it would have bitten her it had been so close.

Now, as she sat in the conference room of the Queen Couture offices with the rest of the creative team and Desiree's entourage, anticipation buzzed through her like a million agitated bees. She was going to nail this debut.

Conversation hummed around the conference room table. The bottle designers, marketers, sales team, and lawyers were all having individual conversations. Conversations that all relied on her creation. She crossed her fingers beneath the table. *Please, please, please let this mixture work.* She needed a win after the week she'd just had. She could fix everything once this was done. Damien, Quinn, her own self confidence. All of it would be perfect once this was done.

Finally, her mom knocked on the table and got everyone's attention. Adele sat up straight and cleared her throat.

"Thank you all for coming," Adele said with a big smile. "As everyone here knows, we are very excited about the launch of Desiree's first perfume. Love by Desiree will be one of the biggest hits of the spring perfume season. Desiree, thank you for trusting us at Queen Couture with your vision. After today, I hope we can look forward to future strong partnerships with you and your brand."

Everyone around the table clapped. Desiree pressed a hand to her chest and grinned graciously as she was applauded. "Thank you, Adele. I cannot wait to see what your team has come up with. A lot of larger houses approached me when I considered stepping into the realm of fragrances. Many of them with bigger clients and a larger reach, but from the start I knew I wanted to support a business with people who would understand me and where I was coming from. That's why I chose Queen Couture."

Adele beamed. "Then let's get to it. Nicola has brought the juice and we're ready for your final approval."

Her mom looked at her with an expectant smile. Nicola's hands sweated, and she ran them over her skirt before standing with the vial in her hand.

"I have a small sample of the juice I created for Desiree." Her voice was steady and strong. Not a hint of her inner nervousness. "When you came to me you asked for a fragrance that was as sexy as red lace panties, but as comfortable flannel pajamas. You wanted something that exuded sex appeal, everyday life, and contentment. The 'essence of perfection' I believe was how your briefing started. What I have here is a mixture that will give you all of those things."

Praying her hands didn't shake, Nicola put a few drops on the square of linen paper in front of her. She walked over and placed the paper in Desiree's outstretched hands. She then went back and put drops on other small pieces of paper for the rest of the creative team.

She didn't need to smell it. She'd spent the early morning hours putting this together. Knowing she was missing something but never being able to put her finger on what was missing. What had slapped her in the face in the middle of the night was cumin. The spice that also gave off the heady musk of sweat. Just the hint of sex and life the rose based scent needed.

The creative team sniffed. Several people nodded. The gleam of pride brightened in her mom's eyes. Murmurs of appreciation went around the table. Her heart rate picked up. Had she done it? Her late-night epiphany had been right.

She wasn't a fake or a phony. She really did know how to create a lasting and timeless fragrance. She was going to continue to elevate Queen Couture. Once Love by Desiree hit store shelves, Desiree's millions of fans would flock to it. They'd wear this perfume for years even if Desiree never published another album, because it was timeless.

She glanced at Desiree. Her lips pulled between her teeth to try and stop her smile of excitement. She would not gloat or bask in the sunshine until she got the final approval.

Desiree had the paper to her nose. Her brows were drawn together. When she pulled the paper away, her shoulders stooped. The eyes that met Nicola's weren't excited, happy, or pleasantly surprised. Instead, the disappointment that had first sprung in Desiree's eyes on Monday deepened.

Nicola sank slowly back into her chair. "You don't like it?" The question was spoken softly, but it was heard over the buzz of enthusiasm in the room.

Desiree slowly placed the paper on the conference room table. "I wish I did. It's just . . . not what I wanted."

Silence fell like an executioner's blade over the room. Swift and heavy. Nicola barely stopped herself from rubbing a hand across her neck.

"We've still got plenty of time before the launch," Adele

chimed in quickly. Leave it to her mom to not leave empty space for disaster to fall. "Nicola and our other perfumers can go back to the drawing board."

Desiree shook her head. "I don't think so. I had reservations after the first sample Nicola created."

"What? I had no idea?" Adele's eyes darted to Nicola.

"I didn't make a fuss. She promised she understood what I was getting at. Then earlier this week, I was still unimpressed. I'm sorry, but I think I'll need to go somewhere else."

Nicola wanted a hole to open up in the floor and swallow her whole. She'd been sure she'd finally gotten it right. Instead, she'd been right all along. She wasn't the best perfumer in the business. She was a fake.

Her mother ranted for at least an hour after Desiree's team left. Gaston Demacy, a perfumer at IFH in New York, had apparently sent Desiree new samples she'd liked. Even Adele's clever negotiation skills couldn't convince Desiree to let them try again.

Nicola wanted to crawl under the nearest rock and stay there for an eternity. She considered calling Quinn and asking her for advice, but after their talk earlier in the week she knew Quinn still didn't want to see her. She thought about Shonda, but her friend had her kids for the week, and Nicola did not want to dump her problems on top of her friend's other responsibilities.

She found herself at Damien's home. He hadn't called her since she'd sent him away. She hadn't called because she didn't want to confirm that he didn't want to give them a chance anymore. Popping up at your man, who might not be your man's home, wasn't the best idea, but she needed to see him. She needed to talk to someone about what was going on.

He answered after she rang the bell. He wore sweatpants and a white t-shirt. His dreads hung loose around his shoulders. His chocolate brown eyes were aloof.

"Hey," she said with a hesitant smile.

"What's up?" he asked. No hint of warmth in his voice.

"Can I come in?"

He watched her for a second, then stepped back. She crossed the threshold and leaned in to hug him. Her efforts were thwarted when he turned to close the door.

"What are you doing here, Nicola?" He walked further into the house.

Not a good sign at all. She swallowed hard instead of backing down. "I told you I'd come by at the end of the week."

"Yeah, when you were ready to make time for me." There was no bitterness in his voice. Just cold resignation. That hurt worse.

"I'm sorry about earlier. I was really stressed out. I don't know how to accept, you know, help from people when I get like that."

He folded his arms and leaned against the wall. "Mmmhmm."

"Anyway, we had the meeting today."

"And let me guess. It didn't go so well."

She rubbed a hand over her face. How had he known? Did even he sense that she was a fake? "It went terrible. Desiree hated the scent. Some fancy perfumer at a large New York house is going to make her scent now."

"I'm sorry to hear that." He actually did sound sorry. That was promising.

"I don't know what to do next."

"Did you ask anyone for help?"

That left her momentarily speechless. "No, why would I?"

He shook his head. The corner of his mouth raised. "Did you ever stop to think that maybe collaborating with someone, asking for help instead of trying to do everything yourself might have made this work."

"My job isn't to ask other people to do my work for me," she said defensively.

"Asking for help doesn't mean you don't have what it takes to be successful. It just means you're open to hearing new ideas."

She'd confessed to him that day at the farmers market about her insecurities. At the time, she hadn't thought he'd end up in a position to call her out on her insecurities. Her cheeks burned. "I didn't tell you that so you could throw it back in my face."

"I'm not throwing this back in your face to be mean. I'm trying to point out that you're so busy trying to prove you don't need anyone that you're screwing up everything you've built. Maybe letting people in, seeking their advice or assistance when you're stuck isn't such a bad idea."

"I can take care of myself." She'd taken care of herself for this long. Handled her own hurt emotions and feelings of inadequacy. She didn't need validation or support from others. Not when she'd been younger and not now.

He shook his head. "Unbelievable."

"What?"

"You sound just like my ex-wife. I don't need help. I can do all things on my own. You know it doesn't hurt to be vulnerable. To open yourself up and let people in."

"I'm not that person."

"Only because you don't want to be. You'd rather pretend to be strong for everyone else and push away people who love you in the process."

Love? Did he mean . . .

No, she was reading too much into this. They may have agreed they would do the relationship thing, but he was adamant against marriage again. Which meant nothing serious would come from what they were doing.

"Pushing people away is easier than hoping they'll want to get close and being disappointed when they don't," she said with all the knowledge and disappointment she'd felt over the years when the people she cared about most hadn't bothered to give her a second thought. All the times she'd heard *"Nicola can take care of herself"* or *"We don't have to worry about Nicola, she's not going to cause any problems."* Her life had been nothing but being ignored until she'd done something great, and even that hadn't been done on her own.

"I don't wait around for validation or special attention," she said. "I don't because it's not coming."

"Maybe it would come if you didn't act like you didn't care. I know you care."

"I don't. I'll figure something out. Maybe I can even change Desiree's mind again." She crossed the room and put her hands on his still crossed arms. "But that's not why I came here. I'm sorry about the other day. Can I get a do over from Monday night?"

He stepped to the side. Away from her touch. "No."

"No? So, you're serious about breaking up with me?" Her chest contracted. She'd known one day things would end with her and Damien. She'd thought she'd be ready for that. But this was too soon and hurt a lot more than she'd expected. Her attachment to him was more than she'd realized.

Damien met her gaze. "I'm serious about not signing up for what I had before. You're either all in this or you're not. I'm not signing up to be a distraction when you're mad or stressed out. I won't wait around for you to be ready only to realize you never will be."

"We just had a fight. That's all. Isn't that part of a relationship?"

Couldn't he see that she was trying? She wasn't good at this, but she wanted to be with him. She'd never begged for anything in her life, but for a split second the idea of pleading with him to give her another chance popped into her mind. Until he spoke.

"Relationships are more than making up after a fight. If you weren't so intent on pretending as if you don't need anyone in your life, maybe you'd realize that."

Chapter 33

Nicola was buried under the covers in her bed. She was settled in for a day of watching movies on *Lifetime* and wallowing in self-pity. When her grandfather called and interrupted her Saturday plans, she groaned and considered sending him to voice mail. Yet another person who didn't need her.

She'd been doing that all morning. Going over the people who'd pushed her aside. Her mom. Her sister. Damien.

She'd lost a new boyfriend and an important client all in one week. This was why she didn't open herself up to other people. She just needed a day. One day to feel sorry for herself and then she'd get back up and tackle the world.

No one needed to know how much her feelings hurt. They didn't want to see or hear about her hurt feelings. One day, and then she'd be better and could face the world.

She didn't send her grandad to voice mail and answered. "Hey Grandpa."

"Nicola, good, you're coming tonight right? I need you to come."

"Tonight?" Her brain took a millisecond to catch up. The talent show at the senior center. She'd completely forgotten about that with everything else going on. Her mom and Quinn hadn't mentioned it either which meant the show had probably slipped their minds as well.

"You can't tell me you forgot about the show?" Jeremiah asked, sounding stricken.

"No, of course not. I've just had a really rough week at work." She didn't want to see her grandad and his wonderful assistant who'd replaced her. She put on a brave front, but she doubted she would be able to be that brave.

"I know. Your mom told me. Bombed the perfume presentation. That sucks." The closest she'd get to words of comfort from her grandfather.

"It does suck."

"Yeah, well, figure out how to fix it. I know you. You'll bounce back. But that doesn't mean you can't come. I need you."

"You don't need me, Grandpa. You've got Valeria, and I think Uncle Carl is still coming. I'm sure you'll be great. Send me pictures or get one of your friends to record it and send me the video."

"Valeria has shingles. Probably from the stress of working with those damn kids all day," he grumbled as if the kids had gotten Valeria sick just to interfere with him. "I need you to come and help me."

Nicola sat up in bed and pushed the covers aside. "Are you serious? Grandpa, I can't help. I don't know the routine. I don't have a costume."

"None of that matters. I need my granddaughter here to help me. You're part of the reason I'm doing this in the first place. Don't leave me hanging."

She looked at her clock. "But . . . I haven't even showered."

"Please, Nicola."

The words squeezed her heart. She'd never heard her grandfather say please when asking for anything in her life. He always demanded. Always expected. Never showed he needed anyone.

"I'm leaving in twenty minutes."

Nicola arrived in just enough time for her grandfather to rush out the door, sparkling purple bundle in hand, and rush to her car.

"You're late," he said after tossing his bag and the purple sequins in the back seat.

"I told you I had to shower."

He got in the passenger seat and slammed the door. "Did you have to make your own soap, too?"

"You know I could just go home."

"You won't. Hurry, it'll take us twenty minutes to get to the senior center."

On the way there her grandfather gave her the gist of his routine. Starting with a simple card trick and ending with his big flourish of making her disappear. Whenever she expressed her skepticism about being able to help him pull it off, he assured her that practice wasn't necessary.

They arrived at the center, and after that there wasn't much time to talk. They were hurried into one of the classrooms converted into a dressing area. Other seniors practiced singing, tossing a baton, and there was even a ventriloquist. Her grandad was the only magician.

She put on the costume designed for Valeria. The purple sequin was a size too big for Nicola, but she grabbed spare safety pins from one of the other participants and made the outfit work. The show was taking place in the large ballroom of the facility. She and her grandad huddled up backstage where he tried to instill several weeks of practice he'd had with Valeria into a few minutes with her. Just as Nicola prayed they would be the last act, the host called their name.

Her grandfather gave her a shoulder squeeze and a nervous smile. Seeing the mixture of nerves and excitement in his eye made her give him a quick hug. They might bomb, and she wasn't sure about exactly where she needed to go during the disappearing act, but she was glad she'd come.

"You've got this, Grandpa," she said and kissed his cheek.

The tension around his mouth melted away. He nodded and they went onstage. Nicola scanned the crowd. Her eyes widened after seeing her mom and dad there, along with Uncle Carl and Aunt Kim. Her cousins hadn't shown, but Quinn was in the audience, too. When her grandfather spotted them, his chest puffed out.

To say the show went off without a hitch would be an exaggeration, but they made it through. She, as his lovely assistant, guiding the audience's attention where it needed to be. Her grandad was great at playing to the crowd. He drew laughs, applause, and even a few amazed gasps. At the end, just as he promised, he made her "disappear," thanks to mirrors and a trap door in the closet.

There was a standing ovation when their bit was complete. Their family cheered and called out their names. Nicola's cheeks hurt she smiled so hard. She was so proud of her grandfather, and so happy for him.

Backstage, they were greeted with claps and hugs. At the end of the show they won second place. The ventriloquist beat them out, but considering she was a stand-in, she wasn't going to complain. She laughed right along with everyone else, and beamed as she watched her grandfather soak up the praise. Their family all came back to congratulate them after the show. Hugs and kisses were passed around.

Her dad gave her the tightest hug. "You did a great job."

When her mom kissed her cheek and said, "Thank you

for making him smile again." They both wiped away tears. Nicola may have messed up the Desiree account, but her mom still loved her.

Quinn didn't come backstage. According to Adele, Quinn had to get back for another engagement. Nicola recognized an excuse when she heard one. Quinn was still avoiding being around her.

On the ride home all her grandfather talked about was how he still had it. Ways he could get even better with his next show. Ideas for more dazzling tricks.

She followed him inside and sat at his kitchen table while he made coffee. The rest of the family had headed back to Atlanta. "It's good to see you like this, Grandad. Grandma would be proud."

His smile softened as he scooped coffee grounds into a filter. No fancy coffee maker for him, even though she knew her mom had given him a Nespresso last Christmas. "No, she wouldn't be. She'd say I was being a damn fool for wanting to do magic again." He chuckled. "Then she'd roll her eyes and shake her head the way she used to before kissing my forehead and telling me she doesn't know why she loves my fool ass."

"Grandma didn't curse at you like that. Did she?"

He laughed. "All the time. Just never in front of the kids." He sighed, put the filter in the machine and pressed the button. "I miss her."

It was the first time he'd said as much. Nicola's heart twisted. "I know you do."

"She thought magic was silly, but she also understood. I liked doing magic because it was a way I could test theories. To see if I could do something people said was impossible. I just couldn't make a living out of it."

He came and sat at the table while the coffee brewed. "Your grandmother was always pushing me to do better. Be realistic. Get my head out of the clouds."

Nicola leaned back and raised a brow. "Your head? I don't believe it. You're the most pragmatic person I know."

"I am. Because I had to be. I was the oldest of six children. When my mom died and my dad was left alone, I had to help raise my brothers and sisters. I had to be the strong one. It was hard, but I did it, and I'd do it again, but I gave up being young and having fun. So, I found other ways to express myself. I started simple magic tricks just to entertain my brothers and sisters. When I figured out an illusion, I wanted to know more. It became my one hobby. My one creative outlet."

Nicola had heard her grandfather's story before, but she'd never heard him talk about using magic as his outlet. He'd talked about stepping up and helping his dad, doing what was right, and carrying his weight. She'd never imagined he'd felt burdened by the responsibility.

Nicola ran her fingertips over the smooth, wooden table. "Kind of like me and the perfume?"

"I wouldn't say that. I enjoy magic. You, I don't think you enjoy making perfume."

"I do. It's what's made me successful." The response was automatic. Defensive. Perfume had given her everything she'd wanted.

"Your creation made your mom's company successful. You and Quinn agreed to help out, but neither you or your mom thought anything you made would be what it became. You made something great, and then you were burdened with the responsibility of doing it again and again. Not because you love it, but because it was expected."

Nicola couldn't meet her grandfather's eyes. She watched her fingertips run across the tabletop as the rich scent of coffee filled the kitchen. She'd just been playing around. She'd been trying to fit into her mom's world and use some of her knowledge of chemistry in her mom's world of beauty. She wasn't supposed to be Queen Couture's top perfumer, but she was. And she loved it.

"I wouldn't change anything," she admitted.

Jeremiah placed his hand over hers, getting her attention. "I'm not saying you would, but I saw the same look on your face when you gave up going to graduate school and doing that medical research you always talked to your grandmother about to make perfume for your mom. I had that same look when I dropped out of high school to help my dad raise five other kids. You wouldn't change a thing, but the pressure to live up to expectations is hard."

Very true. For so long she'd felt bad for not living the dream she'd imagined for herself. Not applying her education to some noble cause. Her mom was right, there were no guarantees she would have made a breakthrough that would have saved her grandmother's life. She'd found her way in an industry she'd known nothing about. The loss of Desiree's account sucked, but it also made Nicola want to try harder. It made her want to prove the last few years hadn't been a fluke.

"I didn't want anyone to see that. I'm supposed to be the strong one."

"Being strong means also knowing your weakness." He reached over and placed a hand over hers. "I don't know what happened with that perfume for that singer, but we both know if you really wanted this you could do it."

"I do really want this. I wanted Desiree to love what I created. I just couldn't figure out what she wants. What the hell is sexy as a red thong but as comfortable as flannel pajamas?"

He shook his head. "The hell if I know. But that doesn't mean you can't ask for help. Ask her what it means. You've got a bunch of other perfumers working under you. Ask them too. Don't think just because you were asked the question that you have to find the answer alone."

"That's the only way I know how to work. The only way I've ever worked." She never wanted to appear unsure. She could offer advice, but asking for advice always felt like admitting some sort of failing.

"That doesn't mean it's right. You'll burn yourself out if you never open yourself up and accept help when you need it. And when you're burned out and good for no one else, you know what happens?"

"What?"

"The world keeps spinning and everyone else's lives keep going on. Don't ever forget the Earth has been here a million years and will be here a million more. Your life is a finger snap in that time. Make room for others so you can enjoy every second."

Nicola went to Quinn's house the next morning. There was something she needed to do that was long overdue. After her talk with her grandfather she knew she couldn't put things off much longer.

Quinn answered the door this time. Her eyes widened and one brow rose when she saw Nicola.

"Good, you can help me pack." Quinn turned and went back into the house.

Nicola hurried inside and closed the door behind her. "Pack? Where are you going?"

She looked into the rooms downstairs and listened for signs of Omar somewhere in the house. After seeing him the last time she was there she wasn't in the mood to put up with his smug attitude again. If Quinn chose to stay with him, that was her business, but Nicola wasn't going to pretend as if she liked him.

"I don't know," Quinn said over her shoulder. She headed up the staircase to the second floor.

Nicola waited until they were in Quinn's bedroom to respond. Quinn's luggage was open on the bed and the floor. Clothes, toiletries, and shoes were strewn across the room.

"How do you not know where you're going when half of your closet is out here?"

Quinn chuckled and folded a shirt that she put in one of the suitcases. "This is far from half of my closet."

"Quinn, seriously, what's going on?"

Quinn stopped folding clothes on her bed and crossed her arms. "I'm leaving Omar."

Nicola crossed the room and sat on the bed. "Seriously?"

One of Quinn's shoulders lifted. "At least for a little while. I need to figure out what to do with my life. My life without him in it."

"What changed your mind?" Nicola asked. Inside she jumped for joy, but she knew if she displayed any sort of *I knew it* attitude her sister would clam up.

"Okay, don't laugh or anything, but it was you and Grandpa on stage last night." Quinn darted a glance at Nicola. Her body was stiff, as if she were waiting for Nicola to laugh. Nicola just nodded. Quinn released a breath and kept going. "You weren't afraid to be up there in that god-awful suit. Then Grandpa was up there so excited and . . . alive. I've never seen him like that."

"Me neither. It's why I couldn't say no when he asked me to help."

"Well, it made me realize I'm not happy. I haven't been happy for a while. It's time for me to find out what makes me happy."

Nicola bumped Quinn's leg with her knee to get Quinn to look at her. "I think that's a good idea. If that's what you want to do, then know that I'm here to support you." She looked around the room. "Where's Omar?"

"He stormed out last night when I told him I was leaving. He said he'd give me time to come to my senses. I'm pretty sure he's with his mistress." Quinn said the words without any bitterness. "I want to be gone by the time he comes back. I just have to figure out where to go."

"There is no figuring it out. You're coming to my place." Nicola didn't have to think about it. If Quinn wanted to step out on her own, then she was going to help her.

"What? No. You do realize we'll kill each other after a few days."

Nicola shook her head. "No, we won't. Okay, maybe we'll attempt murder, but we'll work through it. Besides, I need your help."

"My help? With what?"

"I don't know what I'm doing with Desiree's perfume. I don't think I ever knew what I was doing. Your suggestion is the reason Triumph worked out. Take a look at Desiree's briefing document and help me put together a blend. We can still try to see if she'll go with Queen Couture."

Quinn held up a hand. "Wait, you can't be serious. Look, I know I was drunk and pissed and said things I shouldn't have said in Cancun, but let's be real. Triumph was a fluke. How can I possibly make it better?"

"Because you actually live the kind of life Desiree wants to inspire. I don't. Just look at my list, the things I don't do. Let's face it, I'm not the person in the family that people are drawn to for my sparkling personality. I couldn't figure it out, which means maybe you can, like you did before."

Quinn pushed the suitcase aside and sat next to Nicola. She turned to her side so she faced her fully. "You're not a fake and your work isn't a fluke. I may have helped with Triumph, but you're the one who made every other successful perfume since then. You're brilliant and you always have been. I rely on you to keep me straight, Mom knows you're the one who keeps the company in balance, even Grandad knew if he needed help, that he could rely on you. Stop thinking you're not supposed to be where you are and accept that you got yourself there."

Nicola put her hand over Quinn's. "If you'll do the same. Quinn, you know scents just as well as I do even without the formal training. You can just sense things. I'll work out the science, you figure out the..." Nicola looked at the ceiling and searched for a word. "You figure out the essence."

Quinn cocked a brow and flipped her hair. "The essence? Have you been drinking?"

Nicola rolled her eyes then bumped her sister's shoulder. "You know what I mean. I'm analytical, you're more abstract. You sense things I can't figure out." She took Quinn's hand in hers and squeezed. "Help me. I don't think I can do this on my own. This time let's work together. We accidentally made something great before, imagine what we can do now if we try?"

Chapter 34

Thanks to Quinn's connections, they were able to verify Desiree would be in Miami attending a party that Nathaniel was also attending. The fact that Quinn still had contact with Nathaniel through their ongoing direct message conversation via social media was something Nicola decided to stay out of. Her sister had enough drama in her life without Nicola's commentary.

They'd spent weeks working together. Just the two of them in her lab at home. No help from Tia or the other perfumers at the company. Not a word to their mother about what they were doing. They'd argued, laughed, collaborated, stayed up late, and taken a few shots of tequila when things got tense, but in the end, they'd done it. They'd crafted a scent Nicola was sure Desiree would love.

She hoped.

"Are you nervous?" Quinn asked as they took the elevator up to the penthouse suite of the luxury condos in South Beach.

Nicola had meant to ask her sister for the details on the

party, who was throwing it and why, but she'd forgotten. She didn't know if she was more nervous about crashing a party or trying to convince Desiree to smell what they'd come up with. Quinn, however, appeared to harbor no concerns about either.

"What if she hates it?" Nicola replied.

"If she hates it then obviously she's hard to please. We can still put this scent out on our own and see what happens. I think it's great."

Her sister's confidence soothed Nicola's nerves just a little. "Thank you, Quinn. For helping me with this. Getting us here. Everything."

"You're my sister. I wouldn't leave you out here hanging."

"Really? After everything that I did?"

"You also apologized. Plus, it's not your fault Omar found out about me and Joseph."

They were good, but they hadn't talked about Quinn's marriage or her affair with Joseph. Omar hadn't called once. Nicola figured that was for the best. That didn't change the fact that Nicola's snooping is how they got in this mess in the first place.

"It kind of is."

Quinn shrugged. "A part of me wanted him to find out. I wondered what he'd do if he realized I was really unhappy. I guess I got my answer."

"Whatever you decide, we'll figure it out."

Quinn smiled and shrugged. "I guess we will. Now come on. Let's go convince Desiree she's made a terrible mistake."

Nicola let her sister lead the way. They'd made the scent, but Quinn didn't talk much about what her plans were. She'd poured herself into helping Nicola make the perfume. Nicola got the feeling, even though Quinn had packed her bags and moved out, she was still wrestling with the idea of leaving her husband permanently. She hoped Quinn's decision was final, but was also preparing herself to accept her sister's decision if she chose to stay.

She didn't have long to contemplate Quinn's jumbled love life, because the elevator opened right into the party. Three dozen or more people milled about the space. Nathaniel immediately came over and kissed Quinn's cheek. "Yes, the party can start now. I'm glad you made it."

Quinn batted her lashes and smiled prettily. "Thank you for inviting me. You know I wouldn't miss your birthday." She turned to Nicola. "You remember my sister."

Nathaniel smiled widely and kissed Nicola's cheek. "Of course, I do. Welcome, Nicola. Come in, get comfortable, and have fun."

The elevator doors opened again, and Nathaniel excused himself to greet the next guests. "You were invited but you let me worry?" Nicola asked after Nathaniel walked away.

Quinn shrugged. "You would have worried regardless, and this was the fastest way to see Desiree. So, you're welcome. Now let's go find her."

Nicola shook her head but smiled. Every day was a new surprise with Quinn. Nicola found out the penthouse belonged to one of the editors of *Clef Magazine*, a magazine that focused on the trends in music and fashion, and the party was in honor of Nathaniel's birthday. They mixed and mingled with the people in attendance. All the while, Nicola scanned the crowd for Desiree. The vial in her pocket feeling heavier with each passing minute she didn't see her. Desiree wasn't by the pool, in the den, kitchen, or mingling around the pool table.

Maybe Quinn was wrong. Maybe Desiree was supposed to be there but hadn't shown up. After circling downstairs twice, Nicola was sure Quinn's connections hadn't worked in their favor this time.

The sound of music drifted down the stairs to where

Nicola stood trying not to look like a kid whose bike had just been stolen. Her ears perked up when Desiree's distinctive husky voice accompanied the music. Her heart jackhammering, Nicola hurried up the stairs and down the hall.

Desiree was in the music room with a few other musicians. The music came from the speakers, a beat Nicola wasn't familiar with. Desiree sang along with a big bright smile on her face. When she finished the people in the room clapped.

"Thank you," Desiree said. "That's off my new album. You think people will like it?"

"They'll love it," one of the women replied.

Nicola came into the room. "I agree. It's hot."

Desiree turned to face Nicola. The grin on her face remained. It appeared genuine, even if wariness entered her eyes. "Hey, Nicola, I didn't know you were coming by."

"Quinn was invited. I decided to tag along with her."

Desiree nodded and stood up from the piano. "Cool. I'm actually about to head out. I only wanted to pop in for a few minutes."

"Do you mind if I talk to you for a second?" Nicola asked, as Desiree and the rest of the small group moved to exit the room. "I promise, it won't take that much time."

Desiree glanced at her bodyguard, who raised his brow in an I-don't-know fashion. Desiree shrugged then turned to Nicola and nodded. "Sure."

"Thank you." Nicola stepped away from the door and watched as everyone filed out. Desiree's bodyguard didn't go far. His large shape hovered right outside the door.

"Look, Desiree, I know you were disappointed with what I came up with for your perfume and that you think Gaston will make a better perfume for you."

"I wanted to support your house, but I know Gaston. I can only hope he'll do better."

Nicola straightened her shoulders. "I can do better."

Desiree shook her head. "Come on, Nicola, we've already been down this road. I'd like for us to remain cool."

"We will, regardless of what decision you make, but I would like you to give me another chance."

"What will have changed?"

"This time I asked for help."

"Excuse me?"

"Triumph, the perfume that brought you to Queen Couture in the first place, I didn't make that on my own. My sister gave some input. I asked for her help again with yours."

Desiree shifted and placed one hand on her hip. "Why didn't you do that from the start?"

"Because, I'm not used to asking for help. The truth is, when we work together, we do a pretty good job. I think we've done a good job for you now."

"I'm meeting Gaston next week."

Nicola reached into her pocket and pulled out the vial along with testing strips. "No need for you to wait until next week."

"You brought it with you," she sounded surprised and impressed.

Nicola shrugged. "You're the one who said to never do anything by halves. I believe we did it right this time. I didn't want to sit on it."

Desiree raised a brow, but she reached out a hand. "I admire you spirit. Let me see what you put together."

Nicola put a drop of the perfume on the strip and handed it over to Desiree. She held her breath and clenched her teeth. If this one failed, then she'd be disappointed, but Quinn was right. She loved this scent. Queen Couture could still launch it. She was good at her job. Desiree's rejection didn't diminish all the hard work she'd put in so far.

Desiree brought the strip to her nose. She took a deep

breath. Her brows drew together, and her head tilted to the side. She sniffed again. Her face cleared, and she grinned at Nicola.

"That's it."

Nicola let out a breath and pressed a hand to her chest. "You like it?"

"I love it! Oh my God, Nicola, this is fantastic."

Clapping came from the door followed by a yelp. "Yes! We did it!"

Nicola laughed and turned to her sister. Quinn rushed into the room and wrapped her arms around Nicola. Nicola squeezed her sister tight and laughed.

They both faced Desiree who beamed. "I don't know what magic trick you two pulled over the week, or why you haven't collaborated before, but this is perfect. It's sexy without being overpowering. Just light enough to wear every day, and it's so bright and earthy. My fans are going to buy this stuff by the gallon."

"Does that mean you're going to keep working with us?" Nicola asked.

"Hell yes, I'm going to keep working with you. Ladies, thank you. I've always wanted my own perfume and now I have it."

"Desiree," her bodyguard said from the door. "We have to leave now if we're going to catch your flight."

Desiree waved at him. "I'm coming now. Ladies, tell your mom to assemble the entire production team. Let's plan a launch everyone will remember."

She left the room with one last smile. Nicola and Quinn stared after her. Nicola couldn't believe that just happened.

"Did she take that vial with her?" Quinn asked.

"It's okay. I have two more back home." She turned to Quinn. "You did it."

Quinn shook her head. "No, we did it."

"I can never repay you for helping me get through this," Nicola said sincerely. "If she had walked, our reputation would have been ruined."

Quinn's eyes glistened and she blinked quickly. She straightened her shoulders. "I know one way you can help me."

"Name it."

"Consider letting me collaborate with you on a few other projects in the future. I know you prefer to work alone, but I had fun this past week. We don't have to work on everything together. I know I'm not the best person for big projects, but I'd like to still work on more scents."

"I'll do you one better," Nicola said. "How about we collaborate on everything? Quinn, our best products have come when we worked together. I like working with you, too. I'd like it if we could be partners in this."

"Are you sure? My life is a mess right now."

"So is mine. We can be single and strong together."

Quinn shook her head. "About that. You and Damien. I think you should try to fix that. You were really happy with him and from the way you described him, he seems pretty decent."

She missed Damien so much her heart hurt. Nicola wanted to pick up the phone and call him too many times. She'd put her emotions out there already with reconciling with Quinn, if she did the same with Damien and he turned her away, she'd be crushed. "I really hurt him."

Quinn placed a hand on Nicola's shoulder and gave it a light shake. "Take it from someone who's been with a man who didn't love her for years, when you find someone who makes you happy, it's worth apologizing to keep them in your life. Especially when you know you were in the wrong."

The rejection in Damien's eyes had broken her heart. How could she subject herself to seeing that again? "What if he says no?"

Quinn shrugged in that all-will-be-well way of hers. "Well then, his loss. Now let's go downstairs and drink champagne because we just made the perfume that Desiree will have everyone buying by the gallon."

Nicola laughed. She put the thoughts of Damien aside for now. "I'll drink to that!"

Chapter 35

After celebrating and later reveling in telling their mom the great news, Nicola found herself home alone on Saturday night. Quinn had decided to stay in Miami. Nicola didn't ask for details on why. She figured her sister needed some space to work through her own stuff.

She wasn't typically upset about being home on a Saturday. She used to enjoy the solitude. Tonight, she couldn't find a thing on television to watch—including all streaming apps—she tried relaxing with a book, but had read everything on her shelf, she wasn't in the mood for a reread, and couldn't decide on a new book to purchase. She tried listening to music, but since she didn't buy albums, but instead subscribed to music streaming services, none of the songs that played soothed her. All her playlists were created to motivate her when she worked or worked out.

Why couldn't she get comfortable in her own home? She would not accept she'd gotten used to having first Damien then Quinn around. That she knew if Damien were there, he would have planned something special to celebrate her success with the perfume. That on other Saturday nights, he would mention some movie he loved which she'd never seen, and they would curl up on the couch to watch. That if she was jittery and stopped by his studio, he'd welcome her in without a word, drop a slab of clay on the wheel and let her work out her worries by losing her mind in another form of creation. That even if what she created looked atrocious, he would smile, say it was perfect because she made it, and then put it on the shelf for firing next to his own perfectly symmetrical pieces.

Tightness spread through her chest. She looked around her home. She wasn't supposed to feel like this. She was strong. Independent. Didn't need a man to feel complete. Yet, still she couldn't ignore the hole left in her life.

She thought about their last conversation. His accusation that she pushed away the people who loved her. She didn't push people away. She'd shielded herself. That was different.

Her gaze landed on her first creation in his class. The disproportional gingerbread man. Her self-portrait, except she wasn't that person anymore.

Frustrated anger simmered as she paced her living room. She knew how to let people in. This past week proved just that. She should tell him just how wrong he'd been. She had grown and wasn't as closed off as he accused her of being.

Nicola searched for her keys. She didn't care that she was dressed in leggings covered in chemical bond symbols and a thin, long, grey shirt. Damien was probably at his studio and no one would see her.

Except he wasn't at his studio. Fran was the only one there. Working late on a piece. Her eyes frosty when she opened the door to Nicola on the other end.

"I need to talk to Damien," Nicola said.

"He's not here," Fran said stiffly.

"Fine. I'll go by his place." Nicola turned to go back to her car.

"He's not there either."

Nicola swung around. "Where is he?"

"Why should I tell you? Damien was doing fine until you came into his life. Do you know I watched him slowly try to rebuild his trust after his wife left him? He was devastated and angry and had finally found a way to be happy again. Then you go and break his heart all over again."

The accusation in Fran's voice made Nicola's defenses rise. "I didn't mean to break his heart," Nicola snapped.

"It doesn't matter if you meant to or not. You did. He's hurting. Oh, he's trying not to show it, but I see it."

The anger that fueled Nicola's rush to the studio cooled. She'd seen the pain in his eyes when he'd talked about his divorce. She'd never wanted to be the cause of more pain. She owed him an apology for the way she'd acted. "Then let me make it right. Tell me where he is so I can talk to him."

"If he wants to talk to you then he'd answer the phone if you called."

The stubborn set of Fran's jaw, and fierce protectiveness in her eyes said one thing. "I get it. You love him, too."

"He's my closest friend. I'll stand up and do what's best for my friend." Fran lifted her chin, but didn't deny it.

Nicola recognized stubbornness when she saw it. No amount of pleading would work. Her only option was to be honest with herself and Fran. "He's also the guy I'm in love with. You can try to do what's best for him, but at the end of the day, I'm going to let him know how I feel. Apologize for hurting him when he only wanted to help me. Hope he's willing to give me a second chance. If he does, I'll remember you cared enough to try and protect him."

Fran's face twisted. "Why, so you can try and turn him against me?"

"No, but I would hope you'll respect his decision, whatever it is. And that one day you'll believe I'll never hurt him like this again and be just as good of a friend to me as you are to him."

Fran crossed her arms over her chest. She looked skyward and shook her head. "He's at Sienna Sun Gallery and Lounge. One of his friends is performing."

Nicola let out a breath of relief as excitement rushed through her. "Thank you."

"Don't thank me just yet. He's the one who said he never wants to see you again." Fran went inside and shut the door.

Nicola didn't let Fran's words sidetrack her. She loved Damien. The realization had come as soon as she saw the protectiveness in Fran's eyes. The idea that Fran believed Nicola would hurt him again sparked a determination to never give a reason for someone to defend him against her. She loved him. Even though those three words may not be enough to make him accept her apology or give her another chance, she was damn sure going to try. She'd just convinced Desiree to give her a second chance, maybe luck would be with her.

The second she walked through the doors of the gallery and lounge Nicola realized she should have thought this through a little better. At night, the art gallery side was illuminated with dim spotlights on the artwork. Jazz music accompanied by singing drifted through from the connected lounge. The entire place had a warm welcoming vibe.

Warm, welcoming, and appropriate wardrobe required.

The men and women were dressed in cocktail dresses, sleek shirts and slacks, heels, makeup, and expensive cologne. She, on the other hand, was in leggings, a thin t-shirt and her hair...she didn't want to think about what her hair must look like.

At least you left the bonnet at home.

The woman who'd greeted her weeks ago when she'd

first come in walked over to Nicola, stopping her before she could make her way to the lounge.

"Excuse me, ma'am, but you have to purchase a ticket to enjoy the music."

"How much?" she didn't have her purse, but she'd taken the time to slide her credit card and license in her bra.

Nicola reached toward the collar of her shirt to retrieve the money. The woman raised a hand. "Umm...the cover is twenty-five, but we also have a strict dress code. If you'd like to go home and change, we'd love to have you back."

Nicola dropped her hand. "Look, I don't want to stay long. I just need to pop in there and look for someone."

"I'm sorry, but I can't let you interrupt the show." The woman placed a hand on Nicola's arm and gently tried to turn her away from the door.

Nicola dug her heels into the ground. "No, I really need to get in there. Please, it'll only take a second. Or you can go in and ask him to come out. I'm looking for Damien Hawkins."

"Damien is here with a private party. I don't think he'd like to be disturbed." The woman's gentle pressure on Nicola's arm increased. "If you'd like to leave a note and wait outside."

"No, I would not like to wait outside. Damien knows me. You met me before. A few months ago. I came in and he greeted me."

"I remember you."

Relief made her shoulders relax. Finally, some headway. "Then you understand he knows me. I need to tell him something."

"Ma'am, you're making a scene." The lady glanced around at other patrons who were looking at Nicola. "If you could save your drama for somewhere else I'd appreciate it."

So much for being recognized. "It's not drama. I messed up. I broke his heart. I need to apologize. I need to tell him that I love him. That he was right and that I want to try and do better."

The woman's eyes softened. Nicola released a breath. Maybe pouring her heart out to people would always make things easier.

"That's really sweet," she said. Then her fingers tightened on Nicola's arm and she forcibly pulled her toward the door. "But you'll have to confess on another night."

"What? Wait? Let me go. Please. Just one second. Let me tell him I love him."

"Nicola?" Damien's deep voice cracked through the melee. "What are you doing?"

The woman let Nicola go. She swung around toward him. He stood in the door separating the lounge from the gallery. His dreads were pulled back in an intricate style. He wore a loose white shirt, silver chains peeked through the open neckline, dark slacks loosely hugged his long legs. His beautiful eyes were wary, confused as they focused on her.

In that second, she felt like the single most ridiculous woman in the world. "I . . . I wanted to apologize."

He took a few steps forward. "You could have done that without interrupting my boy's set."

Heat flamed up her face. All eyes in the room were on her. "I know. I'm sorry. I would have called, but you aren't really accepting my calls."

"I told you we weren't doing this anymore."

Her anger from earlier came back. She'd come down here, revealed her heart to two people, embarrassed herself completely, and now he didn't even want to hear her out. "Why? Because it wasn't easy and perfect?"

"You're the one who wants perfection."

"And you want things not to be messy. You want someone who won't do you like your ex-wife. Fair enough. But you can't take every fight we have as another sign I'm going to hurt you the way she hurt you."

"We tried. It didn't work out."

"We tried. I did what I usually do and tried to handle everything on my own. You bailed instead of calling me on my BS. We both messed up."

"Look—"

"No, you look." She pointed a finger. "I love you, okay. That's the other thing on my list. Tell someone I love them. I never did it, even though I thought I'd been in love before. I know now I wasn't because I never said it. I just internalized it. Kept it to myself and hoped one day they'd see the love in me and realize they loved me, too. That isn't how life works. That isn't how relationships work. I should have told you. I should have let you try and help me when I didn't know how to accept help. I shouldn't have pushed you away, but it was easier to do that than to admit that someone I loved didn't love me back. If you don't want to try again, fine. I'll accept that, but I couldn't go another day without saying it."

The silence that fell after the declaration was thick and huge. Wide eyes of the other people in the gallery swept from her to Damien. His face was a mask. His eyes impenetrable. Humiliation made her face flame, but she wouldn't take the words back. She'd done it. She'd admitted her feelings, and while it was awkward as hell, she didn't regret letting Damien Hawkins know that he'd worked his way into her heart.

"What do you want me to do with that?" he asked, his voice thick.

She swallowed and shrugged. "Do what you want with it. I just had to say it." She glanced at the woman who'd tried to usher her out. "I'm sorry for causing a disturbance."

She turned and hurried out the door. The night air held the chill of autumn and cooled her flaming face. Her eyes burned with tears threatening to spill. The exhilaration of declaring her emotions warred with the pain of knowing her declaration had been met with rejection. This hurt like hell, but she'd survive.

Tears spilled and she jogged toward her car. She had to get away from here. Screw it, maybe she'd go back to Miami. Or Shonda's. Shonda made more sense. Who could cry when faced with the excited faces of Shonda's kids?

"Nicola, wait!" Damien's voice called.

She ran harder. No way was he seeing her tears. She'd opened her heart to him. Whatever he had to say could wait until tomorrow.

She got to her car and struggled to press the button to unlock it. Damien's footsteps closed in. His hand slapped the roof of the car with his sudden stop.

"Didn't you hear me calling you?"

Nicola pressed a hand to her face. She quickly scrubbed away the tears and turned. "I was trying to leave."

"Why?"

"So you wouldn't see this." She pointed to her wet face. "I think I've embarrassed myself enough."

"You didn't let me finish," he said breathless from his sprint.

"What else is there to say?"

He straightened and stared her in the eye. "I love you, too."

She sucked in a breath. Everything went still for an endless moment. Words she longed to hear didn't register. "But you asked what to do with what I said."

"I've never had a woman declare her love for me in front of a crowd. It was . . . life altering."

He came closer. The earthy smell of him enveloped her as he placed his hands on her hips. "I shouldn't have compared you to her. You're nothing like her."

Nicola stared up into his deep dark eyes. The reality of the situation finally bursting through her. Disbelief and happiness scattered and sank into every cell of her body until joy clouded her senses. Still, she tried to focus. She had to get this right. "I can't promise to never close up. I've done that for thirty years, but I promise I'll try to let you in when I want to retreat. You have to promise to remember that when I get like that it's not because I don't love you."

His hands tightened on her hips. "I promise to try. You've got to talk to me, okay." She nodded. "And I'm sorry for shutting down. I won't do that again. I said I'd be there for you, and that's what I'm going to do. If you're ready to give me another chance?"

"That depends," she said. Her breath hitching at the nearness of him. The longing deep in her midsection.

"On what?" his forehead dropped to hers.

"On how well you kiss me."

His grin hung the moon in her sky. "Challenge accepted." He kissed her, and thoughts of not giving Damien another chance flew right out of her head.

Chapter 36

"Nicola, thank you for agreeing to the follow up on our Living Your Dreams series."

Audience applause accompanied Cassandra Duncan's enthusiastic greeting. The bright lights shining on Nicola in the studio for *Your Morning Wake-Up Call*'s show were just as hot as they'd been the last time. Cassandra and Tom's bright smiles almost as blinding.

"Thank you for having me back."

"Were you surprised so many people asked for a follow up to your story?" Tom asked.

Nicola thought back to how hard she'd tried to pretend people would lose interest and smiled. "I did. I didn't believe your viewers wanted to hear more about my plans."

"Well," Cassandra said. "You have quite an update. You've done a lot in the nine months since we last spoke to you. Do you mind if we take a look?"

"Go ahead."

Nicola had prepared herself for this. The video flashback of all her antics over the past few months. There it was, the disastrous date with Bobby. Her awkward dancing at an L.A. night club with Quinn. The videos of her feeding the tiger cub and doing magic with her grandfather. There were also the interviews with her pottery classmates, and their not so great artwork. The plunge in the river and Damien's swift rescue of her. The video ended with her laughing with Quinn and Shonda in Cancun before segueing into the massive launch party for Desiree's perfume. Not one second of the fight with Quinn.

"Wow!" Cassandra clapped with the audience after the clip ended. "You really did pack a lot into a few months."

"When I view it like that, it's hard to believe I did all of that." Nicola was surprised to see how amazing they made the last several months of her life look. She remembered every single moment of pain, insecurity, and joy. To see it all together made her appreciate getting through.

"And your work didn't suffer," Tom said. "I mean, Desiree's perfume was the hottest debut of the season. It sold out immediately and is already on back order. I think you clearly made the case that you can be dedicated to your work and also be successful."

"You could say that, but I'll admit it wasn't always easy. I don't think I'll cram as much in so few months in the future."

Cassandra crossed her legs and leaned forward. "What did you learn from this experience? What would you tell our viewers who may still be afraid to step out and do the things they're afraid to try?"

Nicola took a moment to consider the question. She thought back to that speech she'd given at the luncheon when she'd met Damien. The practiced speech that didn't have any of her truth in it. "I'd tell them that it's hard. I opened myself up to things I always believed would distract me from my goals or topple me from the pedestal I'd set myself on. Instead, I gained so much more. I grew closer with my family, I fell in love, I found success, but I could have just as easily not had those things. I won't paint a false picture that doing everything you want to do will magically make your life better."

Tom's head tilted to the side. "What will it do?"

"It will teach you more about yourself. What you can handle. What you want to handle. What you don't want to handle. You may lose, I almost had some losses. I would have lost a lot more if I hadn't been honest with myself and chosen to do things that were uncomfortable."

"Would you do it all again?" Tom asked.

"Maybe not all of that," Nicola said laughing. "But I will continue to make time for the people and things that matter in my life. That's what I really learned. To open up and let other people help you, love you, and support you. That's the greatest gift of all."

A READING GROUP GUIDE

THE ESSENCE OF PERFECTION

ABOUT THIS GUIDE

The suggested questions are included to enhance your group's reading of Nita Brooks's *The Essence of Perfection*!

Discussion Questions

1. What was your first impression of Nicola and her position at Queen Couture?
2. Did you think Nicola's family put pressure on her to be perfect, or was she the only source?
3. What is something from your past you would go back and change if given the chance?
4. Do you agree with Nicola's decision to go along with filming her tackling the items on her list?
5. What were your thoughts on Nicola's relationship with Quinn?
6. Nicola was upset about Quinn's growing friendship with Shonda. Do you agree with her being upset? Why or why not?
7. How did you feel about Nicola's romance with Damien? Do you think they'll last? Why or why not?
8. Nicola never thought she belonged in the world of fashion and cosmetics, despite proof of her abilities. Have you ever dealt with feelings of not being as good as people say you are?
9. What did you think when Nicola checked Quinn's phone during their vacation? Was Quinn's reaction too strong?
10. Nicola and Quinn eventually had to work together. What were your thoughts on their collaboration at the end?

DON'T MISS

Redesigning Happiness

Witty, sharply-observed, and warmly wise, Nita Brooks's debut novel tells the heartfelt story of a suddenly successful single mother who finds her perfectly-designed, fame-bound life upended by a surprise from the past . . .

Chapter 1

The Power of Perfection.

Yvonne Cable stared at the headline and grinned. The glowing feature on her latest design made her want to do cartwheels down the hall in her office. If only she'd mastered the art of a cartwheel.

The picture below the headline was of the completed home office for her latest client. Muted blue-grey colors created a cozy and restful feel. The natural light from the picture window overlooking the home's intricate landscape brightened the room. A mixture of textures—cotton, leather, and wood—added depth and visual interest.

After clawing her way through Atlanta's cutthroat interior design community, the article in *Atlanta Life Magazine* was the coveted crown after a hard-fought battle. She created perfection for her clients. Gave them the spaces they needed to be comfortable and content, a haven in their hectic lives. Money, family, status . . . she didn't care. Whatever her clients needed, she was going to give them.

She put the magazine on her desk and walked over to the perfectly organized whiteboard in her downtown Atlanta office. Nine sections partitioned off. The title of her projects in blue at the top of each section. Tasks associated with each project in green. Due dates written in purple. Red checkmarks for completed tasks. The board served as a quick reference guide to where she was and what she needed to do next.

Her grin widened as she a grabbed the green dry erase marker to add the title for a new project to the ninth box. Sandra Covington Project. Or, as her assistant Bree liked to call it, the super enviable commission of every designer in Atlanta. The people who'd vied for Sandra's new home project were many, but Yvonne was the one to land it.

Sandra Covington, self-help author turned radio personality, had just announced that her radio program was going into nationwide syndication. Yvonne was familiar with Sandra's radio show. The woman's advice was quoted everywhere. Known for going deep into her readers' and clients' pasts to help them unlock the "key to their potential," her famously quoted words, Sandra kept her own personal life out of the spotlight. Yvonne didn't care about Sandra's past, all she cared about was that she'd gotten the project. Designing Sandra's house, and possibly getting a shout-out on her show, combined with the notoriety she'd gotten from her appearance on *Celebrity Housewives,* would go a long way toward increasing the demand for an original Yvonne Cable Design when someone needed decorating for their home or business.

She'd arrived. Shed the mistakes of the past and become a household name. Her mom still couldn't believe it. On most days, Yvonne couldn't believe it either.

"Yvonne, I got the fabric swatches you needed for the Tyson project, and don't forget that you've got a call with the editor of *Lady Entrepreneur* magazine in fifteen minutes."

Bree Foster, Yvonne's administrative assistant, swept into

Yvonne's office with an arm full of fabric. She laid the material on the drafting table in the creative corner of Yvonne's office. Vision boards for projects adorned the walls in that corner. Sketch pads, colored pencils, and drawing notebooks littered the drafting table where Yvonne created her designs. Bree continually purchased organizers to keep Yvonne's samples in order, but when Yvonne was in the middle of the creative process, materials scattered the desk. As usual, Bree picked up the strewn color charts, pencils, post-its, and papers and put them back into their correct spots.

"Crap, I completely forgot about that call." Yvonne hurried over to her desk, in the working corner of her office. *Lady Entrepreneur* magazine wanted to start a lifestyle section which would include design tips. Yvonne wanted to be the person who supplied the articles.

Lady Entrepreneur had a wide circulation. Women all over the country subscribed to the magazine, which provided everything from tips for running a business to interviews with successful women on its pages. Of course, she wanted those same women to think of her when they thought of interior design.

"That's why I'm here," Bree said. A recent graduate of design school, they'd met when Yvonne hired Bree as an intern the summer before. After graduation, Yvonne had snatched up the brilliant designer immediately. "Besides, you've got a good excuse. I can imagine your head is elsewhere." Bree grinned and squeezed her hands together in front of her chest. Bree's curly hair was worn in a cute pixie cut and her brown eyes sparkled with excitement behind a pair of black framed glasses.

"I know. I've been busy thinking about what I need for my first meeting with Sandra Covington."

"I'm not talking about that. I mean your proposal over the weekend. The way Nathan surprised you! That was so romantic!"

Yes. The proposal. You'd think saying yes to the man she loved after he proposed via the jumbotron at the Atlanta Braves game wouldn't slip her mind. Honestly, she was still getting used to the idea of being engaged. For the past six years, she'd been a single mom and business owner. Now she was part of a team. Of course, she would have a hard time believing it.

Nathan Lange, home improvement television star, boy-next-door sex symbol, and all-around good guy, was *her* fiancé. She couldn't be happier. And if she happened to notice that saying yes to Nathan had gotten her more congratulations and well wishes than starting her own business, being named business woman of the year twice, or working for a star on *Celebrity Housewives,* she didn't let it bother her. Not too much.

Marriage was a big deal. Her son, Jacob, would have a father. She would have a man who loved and supported her. That was worth congratulating.

She glanced at the three-carat diamond on her left hand. "I can't wait to marry Nathan, but no, that's not what distracted me. Now that I've got Sandra's account, I want to make sure I don't let any other projects slip through the crack."

"That's what you have me for," Bree said. "As your administrative assistant, I'm determined to keep you on track. But once you and Nathan get the television show, I may need an assistant for all of the work that's going to come your way."

Yvonne knocked three times on the oak surface of her desk, then crossed her fingers. "I hope so. The television show is still up in the air."

She'd met Nathan on the set of *Celebrity Housewives,* where he'd worked as the contractor. The disagreements and attraction between them had sparked almost instantly. So much so, they'd stolen every scene they were in. Their chemistry had given Nathan's publicist the idea they could be the new helm of a home improvement show. While Yvonne had never thought about television, she wasn't one to turn down the opportunity to grow her business even further. She'd once been forced to accept whatever scraps she could get from the person who claimed to love her. Not anymore. Neither she, nor her son, would ever be in that position again.

"You guys will get it."

"Maybe, but until then I can't forget what got me here in the first place. No matter what happens with me and Nathan, Yvonne Cable Designs is and always will be my priority. I fought too hard to build my brand to this point to let it go just because I'm getting married."

"But you will be making time to plan your wedding."

"You know it!"

"I'd expect nothing less." Bree looked at her cell phone. "Five minutes until the call. I'll leave you alone so you can get ready."

Yvonne went through the notes she'd jotted down for why she should be their go-to person for the lifestyle section. When she'd spoken with Lashon, the editor of the magazine, she'd still been considering a few other designers. This call would, hopefully, convince Lashon to go with her.

Lashon called right on time. They went through the normal pleasantries: quick stories about their kids, Lashon had two girls, and the latest good news from the magazine staffers. Then Lashon got to business.

"Look, Yvonne, I know you've gotten really busy lately."

"Not too busy to supply design tips for the readers of your magazine. I was thinking of a focus on commercial spaces. Restaurants, offices, things like that."

"Actually, I was thinking we could go in a different direction," Lashon said before Yvonne could go into the reasons why she was the right choice.

"You're no longer looking to include interior design tips?"

"No, silly. I'm surprised you haven't already figured that out," Lashon said laughing. "I want the feature to be with you *and* Nathan."

"Really?" That idea had not crossed her mind.

"It's genius, right?"

"I'm not sure I'm following along."

"*Lady Entrepreneur* is still going to focus on women business owners, but I'm thinking of expanding the lifestyle section to also tackle relationships. Doesn't that make sense?"

Not entirely, considering the magazine was supposed to be a business resource, but Yvonne never claimed to be an expert in magazine editing. "I'm intrigued by this new direction. Tell me more."

"We did a survey of our subscribers. Many of them are single women who are also struggling to find a balance between work and family. You, my friend, are now the epitome of what so many single women want. You made a successful career despite having a child."

"Despite?" A child wasn't an automatic liability.

"And even though you are a single mother, you still happened to land a great guy like Nathan Lange. We think a quarterly feature on how you balance being a wife, mother, and business owner would go a long way to giving our readers hope."

Giving the readers hope? Landing a great guy like Nathan hadn't been part of her life goals. If anything, after the disaster that was her relationship with Jacob's father, she'd never believed she would trust a man again. But she had, and yes, Nathan was great, and she was happy things worked out, but she wouldn't say her life was now defined by her engagement. Was it?

"So, what do you say?"

"Can I think about it? I really wanted to focus on Yvonne Cable Designs."

"Yes, of course, you can still mention that, but just include more information about your happy ending. You two are perfect together. Don't underestimate how much more your brand is worth now that you have him tied to it."

How much more her brand is worth? She'd thought her brand was fine as it was. Sure, people called more after she and Nathan's relationship developed on *Celebrity Housewives*. They'd done a few interviews promoting the idea of doing a show that focused on blending their styles to achieve southern sophistication, but she was more than the *Vonne* in their tentatively titled show, *Nate and Vonne.*

Or was she? She wasn't a stranger to being in this situation. Not being enough. She glanced at the *Power of Perfection* article that had given her such joy just a few minutes ago. Even that interview request had come after she and Nathan appeared on the show.

"I'll let you know about the feature with Nathan. I need to talk it over with him first."

"Great! Just think about it some more. We love what you've done and would like to work with you. Let's find a way to make that happen."

Yvonne turned over the magazine and drummed her fingers on the desk. "Sure. I'll talk to you later."

Yvonne got off the phone and leaned back in her chair. She looked around her office. The awards on the wall. The layouts for projects. Everything she'd built. Maybe Lashon had a point. Maybe people would be more drawn to her business now that she was getting married. Ignoring an angle that allowed her to expand would be ludicrous. Power couples were a big deal. Maybe that was her brand now. One half of a whole.

She took a deep breath and sat up straight. She'd come

too far to backtrack. No matter what happened, she wouldn't lose the Yvonne Cable who had overcome adversity and built a small empire. She wasn't just a master at creating fabulous interior designs. She'd spent the past six years carefully crafting her own image. Maybe it was time for another personal redesign.